ON THE PINEAPPLE EXPRESS

H. L. Wegley

ON THE PINEAPPLE EXPRESS

Contact Information: titleadmin@pelicanbookgroup.com

Scripture quotations, unless otherwise indicated are taken from the King James translation, public domain.

Cover Art by Nicola Martinez

Harbourlight Books, a division of Pelican Ventures, LLC
www.pelicanbookgroup.com PO Box 1738 *Aztec, NM * 87410

Harbourlight Books sail and mast logo is a trademark of Pelican Ventures, LLC

Publishing History
First Harbourlight Edition, 2013
Paperback Edition ISBN 978-1-61116-297-4
Electronic Edition ISBN 978-1-61116-296-7
Published in the United States of America

Dedication

This book is dedicated to my four beautiful granddaughters, Valerie, Taylor, Andi and Charlie. I pray this book will both inform you of a danger that exists in our society and help keep you safe from it.

Here's a heartfelt thanks to all who helped bring this project to publication. I especially want to thank the Pelican Book Group team, including my editor, Jamie West, for working patiently with me through a major rewrite, and EIC, Nicola Martinez, who designed the cover. Thanks to my critique group members, Dawn Lilly and Gayla Hiss, for helping me navigate the opening of this story. Thanks to my test readers, Duke Gibson and my wife, Babe, for patiently reading the manuscript multiple times and providing feedback. Finally, thanks to the Author of the greatest romantic suspense story of all, our Lord and Savior, who taught us the true value of stories.

Praise

Hide And Seek

"Wow, Mr. Wegley definitely keeps you on the run and out of breath through this whole story." ~ Donna B. Snow, Author

"The author has done a great job of weaving a very exciting, well written story together that I could not put down until I finished it in one reading. I had to find out what happened." ~ Thomas H. Hinke, IT/Computing Security

"Mr. Wegley—let's see more of Jennifer & Lee. Either write faster, or get your publisher to publish faster. I'm waiting!" ~ Kate Hinke, Writer & Editor

"...the story really comes alive and pulls you along for a heart-stopping ride. *Hide and Seek* by H.L. Wegley is a definite keeper if you love suspense with a touch of romance. " ~ Ginger Solomon

1

Olympic Peninsula, Saturday, November 2, 11:00 AM

Jennifer Akihara's SUV slid sideways on Highway 101 when she turned in at the Lake Quinault store. She jerked the wheel left, tapped the brakes, and coaxed the vehicle into a parking spot. Huge raindrops assaulted the windshield like bullets trying to blow holes in the safety glass. The wipers slapped out their liveliest rhythm, but her heart thumped even faster as she hit Special Agent Peterson's speed dial number on her cell.

Lee Brandt, her fiancé, sat silently in the passenger seat, but his foot tapped out a tempo somewhere between *andante* and *presto*.

She pushed the speakerphone.

Lee needed to take his fair share of the coming abuse.

"Peterson, this is Jennifer Akihara."

"How is my favorite NSA sleuth on this miserable day?"

"I stumbled across something near my research site on the peninsula…something you should know about."

"Is there a little smuggling going on along the coast?"

"You could say that. Drugs smuggled in, young girls smuggled out."

1

Peterson's end went silent.

"This morning I analyzed the data downloaded from my wireless scanner near Forks. Nearly thirteen days ago, it recorded an encrypted cell-phone conversation."

"Cell-phone conversation? You chose that location for your testing because there's no cell service. But you need to—"

"You mean no *legal* cell service. When I had a colleague from Fort Meade decrypt the call, I heard traffickers selling girls."

Silence again.

"Can you get the unencrypted conversation to me today?" His usual booming voice of authority had softened.

"I'll e-mail it from my cell when we're finished talking. But, Petersen, the next exchange of girls is set for tomorrow night. Can you move quickly enough to stop it?"

"You intercepted a private call. That raises some legal issues we—"

"Legal issues? There's nothing legal about that call, and what they're doing is worse than illegal."

"You're not thinking like a defense attorney. First, I need to analyze the conversation. If we have enough to go on, I can form a team by late tonight or tomorrow. But without specific information, no, I can't guarantee we can stop the exchange. If we botch things, we might never get a conviction."

"Lee is forecasting the Pineapple Express rainstorm to transition to a strong windstorm by tomorrow. The message indicated they don't do exchanges if there's even a small craft advisory. So the storm may delay the exchange and buy us a little more time, but we can't count on that. We do know they're holding the girls at an abandoned mill site on the peninsula."

"Where's the mill?"

"We haven't located it yet." She had lit the fuse on her bomb.

Lee plugged his ears.

She waited for the FBI agent to explode.

"We? Yet? Where *are* you, Jennifer?"

"At Lake Quinault. Lee's with me, and we have five possible sites to check out."

"Far enough so I can't stop you." Peterson mumbled. "So...you don't know where the girls are, but you're driving around to abandoned mill sites?"

"Something like that."

"Jennifer, you need to back off. If you're right, these people will kill anyone who is a perceived threat. You could get the girls killed by charging in."

"Look, Petersen, Lee and I have collected some information. We've planned well, and we won't do anything stupid. But there's no way I'm going to stand by and let a group of girls be sold into a living hell. So you get your team out here as fast as you can. We'll call you when we find the girls. But for now, Lee and I are proceeding."

"You can't do that! It's too dangerous. At least wait until we can get out there."

"There's not enough time. I'm going to terminate the call now so I can send you the intercepted message. And, Peterson, ten days ago one of the girls hanged herself with her own shoelaces rather than let these guys sell her. Lee and I are going forward. I suggest you do the same. Good-bye."

Before she terminated the call, one loud, rare

expletive blasted through the speakerphone, "...that girl is stubborn!"

Jennifer held her thumb back for another second.

A barely audible mumble came across before he hung up, "...but I hope my daughter's just like her."

She smiled and pushed the red icon on her phone.

"Well, you stirred up a hornet's nest at the field office," Lee said.

"Then maybe they'll get out here by tomorrow. But if we find the mill, drive to the nearest cell reception, and call them, they'll come."

"If the storm doesn't prevent them from coming. On Sunday, they won't be able to fly here in either planes or choppers. Too much wind. Trees will be falling like bowling pins, and who knows about the roads—probably all blocked by a million board feet of timber."

Her meteorologist fiancé had raised some legitimate issues.

"Are you saying I made a miscalculation?"

"No. I'm as proud of you as Peterson." Lee chuckled. "He thinks of you as a daughter. Has since the terrorist incident last March." Lee paused. "Unless we get FBI support, we could be on our own."

"Been there before. We're not stupid, Lee. God and right are on our side. And He says nearly four hundred times, don't be afraid. So we go for it, right?"

"No other options. We can't let...what was the trafficker's name?"

"Trader."

"We can't let Trader sell any more kids. But promise me this...if we find the mill site, at the next opportunity you'll call Peterson and give him all the details. If something should go wrong—if something happens to us—help can still come for those girls."

"Nothing is going to happen to us. Well, only what God allows."

"So where did all the newfound confidence come from? You were pretty gloomy when you called this morning to tell me what was going on."

Gloomy hardly described what she felt. The voice of a young girl crying for help ripped at her heart. Only the scriptures she remembered had pulled her out of the pit. "I started thinking about my Bible study yesterday and a song on the CD you gave me—especially the part that says everything's for His glory and we shouldn't be afraid. We forget things—important things—so quickly, it's a wonder God doesn't lose patience with us all."

"If there's a wonder, it's you." He could always find a way to make her smile.

She squeezed his hand. Feeling its warmth and strength calmed her, gave her confidence. She pressed the accelerator and the SUV skidded. She steered out of the slide, clenched her jaw, and slowed. "This incessant rain! I can't go over forty-five without hydroplaning. How far to the first mill site?"

"Less than nine miles."

"That's about fifteen minutes. How should we approach this one?"

"According to the satellite pictures you printed out, three or four hundred yards before the road to the mill there's a BIA road."

"Bureau of Indian Affairs road?"

"Yeah. We can park on it and walk to the mill through the trees." He looked up at her. "I hope your raincoat has a hood."

"Well, it doesn't. So what?"

"So at the end of the day you'll look like a drowned…"

"Finish it, Lee."

"No. It isn't the truth. I've seen you with wet hair, and you're still beautiful."

"What are you buttering me up for?"

"I brought a waterproof cap. It's in my pack in the back seat. You need to wear it."

"You know I don't like that baseball-cap look."

"But you love baseball, Jenn."

"Baseball's a wonderful game. It's like an athletic chess match. But no way am I going to let my hair hang out through the back of a baseball cap like a horse's tail."

"This isn't about fashion. We need to stay warm and dry, because there's no telling—"

"Just hand me the cap, Lee. I might as well put it on now. What color is the stupid thing?"

He reached for the pack in the backseat. "Women. No matter how bright they are, they're still…women." His remark didn't deserve a reply.

She gave him a pair of rolling eyes instead. Lee was a man, a good man. But no matter how bright he was, he was still a man.

In a few minutes, she spotted the BIA road, drove down a short distance, and then veered off among some trees to park. "Show me on the map how we're going to approach this site."

He traced a path with his finger. "See…it's pretty much straight ahead through the trees. In about two hundred yards, we should come to the mill near the only building suitable for—" He stopped. His expression told her his thoughts.

"It's hard to say it, isn't it?" She pursed her lips,

quelling her own horror at the unspeakable future the girls faced if she and Lee didn't find them.

He nodded.

"Can we pray first?"

"Yes, but would you please do it?"

"Having second thoughts?"

"No. Only a lot of first-time thoughts. You do have your .38 with you, don't you?"

"Of course. But I'll pray. God's better than bullets." She kept it simple, asking God to protect them and help them find the girls.

After five minutes of slogging through the rain and being soaked by dripping branches, they approached an opening in the trees.

"Wait here for a second. I'm going to move closer. That big bush will provide enough cover," Lee whispered.

"But I'm the one with the gun."

"We don't need any guns yet. Let me take a look."

****

After reaching the bush, Lee pushed his head through the dripping boughs. Their target lay less than fifty yards ahead. His pulse quickened as he studied the building. Something drew his gaze upward. He exhaled slowly, backed out, and walked back to Jennifer.

"Well, what did you see?"

"The satellite picture was outdated. This isn't the place, Jenn. The roof's falling in."

It took several more drenching minutes to get back to the car.

He picked up the map and ran his finger along

Highway 101. "Only five miles to the next stop." He looked up. The back of her neck was wet. "Jenn…"

She turned her head, and her large, almond-shaped, brown eyes peered warmly into his.

"You're getting wet. Are you cold?"

"Not really. It's amazingly warm out there." She turned on the ignition. "Sixty-five degrees according to the thermometer in my car."

"That's the Pineapple Express—straight from Hawaii. Warm and wet."

"We still have four sites to check and the interview with that retired logger near Forks. We need to hurry, Lee. The rain is slowing us down more than we thought, so show me how we approach the next mill."

"First there's something we need to nail down. When we interview this logger-turned-chainsaw-sculptor, or talk to anyone else out here, what're we going to tell them? We can't divulge our real reasons for being here or we might reveal something to Trader or that other guy…Boatman. Something that would get us killed, maybe get the girls killed, too. For all we know, the traffickers live and work out here."

"How about this for a cover story? I look pretty young, so—"

"Pretty, young. That's an understatement on both counts." He scanned her face and his heart shifted to a higher gear. Jennifer's Japanese-Hawaiian heritage gave her a permanently perfect tan. Like many Asian women, she looked young. She was also a stunning beauty, like none he had ever seen. "It's hard to think about a cover story when I'm looking at a cover girl."

"Without a good cover story, we could get ourselves into trouble." As usual, she ignored his comment about her looks. "Let's see…we can say we're researching the history of the timber industry on the Olympic Peninsula, and that I'm currently focusing on Grays Harbor, Jefferson, and Clallam counties." Hearing Jennifer say anything that hinted of deception was out of character.

It deserved his smirk.

"Don't look at me that way. It's the truth, Lee. It's just not the *whole* truth...which could get us killed." She shot him a frown. "Look, we may not be policemen, but we're working undercover and to keep us safe we need a cover story."

"OK. We're doing timber history research. We just won't tell people why. Back to your question about the next site. If we drive a quarter mile beyond the road to the mill, an old timber access road goes a short way into the trees. But this is all privately managed forest land, so we might find a locked gate across the road."

"Then you'd better watch for alternate parking spots as we go by."

"I will."

Jennifer braked and turned the vehicle onto the BIA road, heading back towards Highway 101.

"You know something? The cap looks kind of cute on you. But you need to make a ponytail, so you can let it stick out of the opening *above* the hatband and—"

"I already told you. No ponytails. In this rain it would hang like an old mare's tail."

"Old mare...I wonder what we'll look like when we're both old. I'll bet—"

"Keep studying that map, or someone might not get the chance to know."

Ouch!

Maybe she didn't always ignore his comments about her appearance.

They found a place to park the car, got wet, struck out at the second mill, and got even wetter on the walk back.

When they climbed back into Jennifer's SUV, he wondered how they were doing for time. Nearly 1:00 PM. He shook his head. Approaching the mills in a cautious manner took more time than he'd planned.

When Jennifer pulled out onto Highway 101, his stomach grumbled. *A foot-long BLT smothered in jalapenos.* The image, the spicy smell, and the delightful tingle on his tongue had leased a chunk of his gray matter. "You know, I don't remember actually planning to fast today."

"When we left I wasn't thinking about lunch." She glanced his way. "If you're hungry, we could go to Kalaloch before mill number three. We'd only have to backtrack three or four miles."

"Sounds good to me. Let's hit the deli in the convenience store. We can probably find a sandwich. If not, there's always the junk food."

****

Jennifer drove as fast as she dared—forty-five miles-per-hour in the heavy downpour. When the road turned parallel to the shore, she turned on the defroster.

"It's on the outside, Jenn. Fog. The defroster won't help."

Soon the visibility dropped to less than fifty yards.

"And you say tomorrow the rain will be worse?"

"To start the day it will, and then the winds come." Lee pointed his thumb towards the mountains to the east. "The rivers down the lee side of the

Olympics will certainly flood. Some rivers out here could also. Don't worry. Highway 101 usually stays open except where it skirts Lake Crescent."

"If we have to drive this slow all the way back to Seattle and maybe even slower coming out again, that's twelve hours of driving. It doesn't make any sense to go home if we don't find the mill today."

"No, it doesn't. If we don't hit pay dirt before dark, we need to stay out here."

"Do you think that's a good idea?" Jennifer glanced at him again. "I mean you and me—"

"I know what you mean."

Their marriage counseling with Pastor Nelson had begun with a commitment to enter their marriage morally pure.

Not only had Lee made this promise to God, but also to Jennifer's granddad when he asked to court her.

Granddad held a sixth-degree black belt in karate and had promised to kick Lee's head into orbit if he dishonored or hurt Jennifer in any way. Knowing Granddad meant it, and knowing he could deliver on his promise provided yet another motivation to keep the commitment he'd made to God.

"We could get a two-bedroom suite at that inn on the edge of Forks. We'd have separate rooms, and they have Internet access. That is your laptop case on the back floorboard, isn't it?"

She nodded.

"Then we're all set. You can use the laptop to check out any other sites we locate, and I can get storm updates on the Internet."

Jennifer laid her hand over his. "But even with separate rooms...well, there are temptations we've been careful to avoid."

"Surely you can restrain yourself for one night." He grinned.

"Not funny. And it's not me who needs to be restrained."

"Can you think of a better option?"

"Better than what? Restraining you, or staying out here?"

"Considering what's at stake, Jenn, we've got to stay out here tonight if we haven't found them by this evening. Look at that stuff. I've never seen so much fog and rain at the same time." He nodded towards the low visibility outside.

Jennifer's eyes widened. "Was that the ranger's station?"

"I think so. Visibility's really bad. The ocean water here cools the air until it becomes pea soup, even with the heavy rain."

"Well, the Kalaloch store should be right—there it is." She steered hard left.

An air horn blasted. A logging truck swerved, inches from their rear fender.

"Sorry. No way I could see him coming."

"It wasn't your fault. We haven't seen another vehicle in the last hour, so it's pretty improbable he would pass us just as we turned in. Makes you think Someone's watching out for us and wanted to drive the point home."

Jennifer pulled into a parking spot by the store. "We need Him to keep watching out for us. We could encounter things a lot more dangerous than that truck."

2

Lee groaned at the deli stripped bare of everything. Tourist season at Kalaloch had ended. So much for his BLT. Instead it would be imperishable, semi-junk food, or hardcore junk food.

Jennifer stood at one end of the hardcore row.

Like her face, Jennifer's figure was something most girls would die for and most guys would—he needed to keep his thoughts in check.

God had blessed him with a soul mate, soon-to-be wife, with incredible beauty and an IQ that was off the scale. To him, she represented perfection, except for her temper, her difficulty forgiving people, and maybe—

"Lee Brandt, what do you think you're doing?"

In front of the rack, his hand was frozen onto a king-sized candy bar. His gaze had been following Jennifer as she walked up and down the aisles of the small store. He didn't have a clue how long he'd been staring at her, soaking her in.

"Wake up. Let's get going. We've got work to do."

All things considered, they hadn't done too badly. An assortment of protein bars, energy bars, juice, and one king-sized candy bar. They walked out of the store and rounded the corner.

Enveloped in pea-soup fog, there would be no prying eyes. How convenient, except for the deluge.

He tugged on Jennifer's arm and pulled her close.

She turned her head up and let him pull her nearer, obviously not opting out of his kiss.

It started out wonderfully, but she pulled away coughing. She put her cheek against his neck and whispered half-choked words. "Was that...for anything...special?"

"Not unless you consider me special."

"I do, but the water dripping off your hood kept running up my nose. You nearly drowned me and—" Jennifer put her arms around his neck and pushed his hood forward. Then she joined him under the hood's shelter, returning his kiss without the deluge.

If she was exercising a woman's prerogative, he wasn't going to complain about it.

When he opened the car door a few seconds later, his thoughts followed a familiar migration route...from Jennifer to food. "Let's get in. I'm hungry. Can't live on love, you know."

"How could you possibly know that, Lee Brandt?"

"Good question. Maybe someday soon we can test that hypothesis."

They devoured their lunch while Jennifer drove slowly up Highway 101 towards Forks. In a continuous roar, the rain peppered the vehicle with watery bullets, building up a thick blanket of water on the surface. Perfect for hydroplaning.

The brief interlude at Kalaloch seemed to restore something missing since Jennifer's discovery of the trafficking, a full realization of the depth of their love for each other. Lee sent a heartfelt thank You to the Lord.

As they passed Ruby Beach, he swallowed his last bite of a peanut butter and chocolate candy bar. He gathered up the paper and stuffed it in a trash bag.

"Great meal. Should we thank the chef?"

"If he sampled his own cooking very often, he's probably dead."

"Dead, but well preserved." He paused. "Uh...Jenn?"

"Just ask me, Lee. It'll save time."

"OK. Why are we driving to Forks when we were supposed to check the third mill site?"

Jennifer slammed a palm into her forehead. "How could I have forgotten what we—it was your fault, Mr. Brandt. You...you made me forget."

He couldn't let her mood slide into the abyss where it had been this morning. "You're right. It was my fault. I distracted you and I got...really distracted."

Jennifer drove in silence for a while, then reached across and took his hand. "It wasn't your fault, Lee. I wish we could've stayed at Kalaloch for a while. But we don't have any time to waste and—"

"Let's assume it was providential and choose our next target."

She gave him her squinting frown. "Providential? A kiss, providential?"

"Let's see what it provides. Right now it's providing us an opportunity to check out the mill north of Forks. We both thought it was one of the most promising sites."

"On to Forks, then. You know, it's looking awfully dark for the middle of the afternoon." Jennifer craned her neck to look up through the windshield.

"Yeah. The cloud depth is increasing as we approach the rainiest part of the storm. It'll get dark around 4:00 PM. That means we probably won't get to visit all the sites today, and we'll still be here tomorrow when the wind picks up. We don't want to be on this highway in the afternoon."

Water droplets still covered the back of Jennifer's neck. He wiped them off. "When we go through Forks, we need to stop at the supermarket and get you a proper raincoat—one with a hood."

"Aren't those usually bright yellow, orange, or florescent green? I thought you wanted to marry me, not make me a target."

"Some are camouflage-colored. After the store, and then checking the two sites near Forks, we need to stop and get a room."

"Rooms, Lee. A suite with *rooms*."

"That's what I meant, sorry. Provided we haven't found the girls." He smiled at her. "You know, it would be kind of nice to say goodnight, and then close a door instead of having to drive home alone."

"Mmmm…very nice."

They rolled through the timber land south of Forks in silence. Would the trees still be standing after tomorrow? Probably not all of them.

Soon they entered the south end of the town.

Jennifer pulled the SUV into the supermarket parking lot. "Look, the coffee shop in the store is open."

"I could use some caffeine."

They walked into the store, and then turned towards the coffee shop's entrance.

The barista popped out from behind a row of flavoring bottles. "Hey, it looks like two more vampire lovers—oops. You're not into those famous vampire books, are you? You're the gir…uh, lady doing research, right?"

"Yes, and we'd like two grande caramel macchiatos. Extra hot, please."

"Coming right up. By the way, who's your friend?"

Jennifer took his hand. "This is my fiancé. He's helping me with some of my research."

"Fiancé. Lucky girl." The barista smiled at Jennifer, and then let her gaze linger on Lee. "Oh, and lucky guy too."

Ten minutes later, Jennifer sipped the last of her coffee while they checked out with their accumulated goods—water, snacks, and one olive-green foul-weather coat. When they walked to the front entrance, they passed the coffee shop.

The barista waved to them. "Try to stay dry out there tonight."

Jennifer held up her new raincoat.

"Good choice," the barista responded with a smile and another lingering look at him.

Jennifer stopped under the covered area by the entrance. "You certainly seem to have gotten her attention."

He raised his cup, smiled, and took a sip. "She got my attention, too. She can make me a caramel macchiato any day. But, Jenn, only *you* can make my day."

Jennifer gave him a side hug. "And your evenings and your—"

"You'd better stop there...and we need to run for it unless you want more rain down your neck."

They sprinted towards the vehicle while the rain pelted the pavement, creating miniature explosions with each drop that pounded the water-blanketed parking lot. Both jumped into the car and buckled into their seats, shaking droplets off their clothes.

"Harder tomorrow?" Her dark eyebrows pinched

until they nearly touched. "Any harder and the atmosphere may as well turn to water."

"That's exactly how a sea captain described it when he sailed through the wall cloud of a Caribbean hurr—"

"Look. I'm glad you went back into meteorology last summer, but I've heard your story, and I don't want to hear about hurricanes." She squeezed the steering wheel until one of her white knuckles popped. "We're not having a hurricane on the peninsula. No way, Lee."

"Actually a hurricane did hit the peninsula in 1921. You're right though, it's technically not a hurricane. But if I had my choice, I'd pick a Florida hurricane over what's going to happen out here tomorrow afternoon."

Indeed, I would.

3

Lee took a sip of his coffee. The caramel syrup lay thick, salty, and sweet in the bottom of his cup, a delightful taste that filtered through the hot liquid. He looked at Jennifer's full lips. A good comparison, but he needed to get focused on the next mill and the potential danger there.

He pulled out the map and satellite photos for the two mills that lay a short distance to the north.

"We need to make the most of the time we have left today, so let's take the closest mill first, the one three miles north of Forks."

He scanned the area around them, and then found their location on the map.

"In another mile or so, we'll see a small road on our left. Then turn right onto the next dirt road and hide the car just off the highway. I think we should walk to the mill."

The driving rain still obscured visibility and Jennifer nearly missed the small road on their right. She drove beyond the trees lining Highway 101 and parked between two large bushes.

After they slid out, he checked her new raincoat and adjusted the hood. "How does that feel?"

"Dry. Much better."

"We need to walk about two or three hundred yards parallel to the highway. We'll be close to the mill at that point. From there, we wing it."

"You were the point man at the last mill." Jennifer stepped in front of him. "It's my turn."

The thought of Jennifer walking into danger brought a nauseating cramp that tightened deep in the pit of his stomach. She was fully capable of protecting herself, something she'd proven time and again. But still...

"OK. But be careful and keep out of sight of the building. Use your camouflage to—"

"I can handle it." She gave him an exasperated look. "Let's use the long line of bushes for cover."

"I don't think we have to go any closer." He grabbed her shoulder and pulled her to a stop. "This isn't the place."

"How do you know that?"

"I'm taller than you. I can see all that's left of the buildings. There's nothing there with four walls still standing. We couldn't see that from the satellite pictures."

She stepped beside him as they walked back. "You knew this wasn't Trader's mill, didn't you?"

"I was fairly certain."

"Is that why you let me lead?"

"Yes." He knew better than to deny it.

Jennifer stepped in front of him, and then placed her arms around his waist. "I understand, sweetheart. I feel the same way whenever you take the lead. No matter what precautions we take, what we're doing isn't safe."

"You got that right. With each site we visit the probability of danger increases."

"I know. I'm a mathematician, remember?" She paused. "You take the next mill, and we'll alternate."

"OK. That's how we'll proceed. But you'd better

be careful when you lead, or I'll..."

"Or you'll what? Kill me if I misbehave?"

"No, I'll probably do this." He kissed her and for a few seconds became oblivious to everything except the sweetness of Jennifer. The caramel in the bottom of his cup wasn't even a close second.

She leaned into his chest. "You'll do that if I misbehave. Are you trying to get me to throw caution to the wind?"

"No." He gave her his warmest smile. "I wanted to remind you of what you'll miss out on if you're not careful."

"I think about that a lot more than you realize. It would drive me crazy if I thought the God who brought us together in such a wild and wonderful way wouldn't allow us to spend our lives together. And Lee..." Her warmest smile finished her sentence. No more words were needed.

Her smiling face also broke the remaining tension...as well as his ability to concentrate. He took a deep breath to focus. "Let's head for the next site. It's not far from here."

They walked hand-in-hand through the downpour back to the SUV.

"When we hit the highway, go north for two miles. Maybe we'll find them there."

"I hope so."

The map and the satellite photo painted a troubling picture.

"This site could be tricky to reach on a day like this."

"It's on the other side of a bridge, isn't it?"

He nodded. "But the river under the bridge is the problem. I should've checked for flood warnings on the Sol Duc River while we passed through Forks. I guess we can check it for ourselves in a few minutes."

"Lee…" Alarm spread across her face. "We can't chance getting the car stuck on the wrong side of the river."

"No, we can't. If it looks that dicey, we'll cross on foot."

Jennifer turned right onto Highway 101. "Where should I hide the car?"

"We'll have to look for a parking spot this side of the bridge. That leaves us about three-eighths of a mile to walk in the rain." He pointed ahead. "There's the road."

Jennifer parked in a spot surrounded on three sides by a mixture of bushes, berry vines, and scrubby trees. "I don't think anyone will spot us here."

"This is fine. Let me show you our approach." He traced the path to the mill on the satellite picture. "If we cross the bridge, and then cut between the river and the mill, we can approach from the south. That's a direction they won't be expecting anyone. There's nothing but forest for several miles. What do you think?"

Jennifer thumped the map with her finger. "Let's go with it."

"But, Jenn, it's predicated upon us being able to cross the bridge and also upon the land east of the river not being flooded."

"So what do you recommend for a backup plan?"

"What would you do if you saw the river overflowing its eastern banks?"

"I'd go down this road beyond the mill. Then I'd head south and come in from the higher land to the southeast." She was sharp, intuitive.

"I like your idea. Now let's go have a look at that bridge and the river."

They slid out into the rain.

He offered his hand.

She took it and the warmth of her hand filled him with such a sense of her presence that—he really needed to concentrate on approaching the bridge or he could get them both killed.

"What is it, Lee? What's—" She looked into his eyes. "Oh." The exposed parts of her cheeks were a rosy color, vivid enough to see even through the rain and the gloom.

She used to get mad at him for what she called his gaga-eyes episodes, like the one he had the first time he saw her.

"Lee, the coach says if you don't get your head in the game he...uh...she is going to pull you." She squeezed his hand. "So what's it going to be?"

"Tell the coach I'm good to go now." He smiled at her. "We've got some girls to find. I can lead."

"You'd better be right about that, or I'll—"

"Kill me?" He felt his smile fading. "If I'm wrong, you may not have to."

When they reached the west end of the bridge, Lee scrambled up the bank. His first glance felt like a punch in his solar plexus.

On the far side, the swollen river overflowed its banks. The bridge and the road beyond weren't under water...yet. He motioned for Jennifer to climb up beside him.

Jennifer had conquered her acrophobia, but he was bringing her face-to-face with her one remaining phobia, raging water. If they were going to check out this mill site, she would have to win at least one battle with fear.

Jennifer struggled for traction on the muddy bank, slipping backwards with each step.

He reached down and grabbed her hand, pulling her onto the bridge. "Take a look and tell me what you think."

Jennifer gasped. "I think this bridge isn't long for this world—at least not in one piece."

"Can you feel the bridge shaking?"

"Honestly, I can't tell if it's me or the bridge."

"It's mostly the bridge. That big cedar tree lodged against the middle could eventually take it out. But if another tree was to shoot down the river like a big battering ram, the whole bridge would go."

"The coach left you in the game. What play are you going to call?"

He stared at the river. "I'm calling timeout. We need to do some risk assessment."

"You'd better factor in the risk to the girls if we don't cross this bridge."

"I was afraid you'd say something like that. OK, we cross it. I think we can run across. Even if it starts to give way, we can sprint to safety. But, Jenn, what if the bridge goes while we're on the other side?"

In the semi-darkness under her hood, the whites of her eyes flashed at him. "Whether we find the girls or not, we need to get back to the car as soon as possible."

He pointed up river. "Isn't there another bridge upstream?"

"Yes. I remember looking at it when we planned the approach to this mill."

"OK. Worst case, we can get back to your car by making a three- or four-mile walk in the rain."

"There aren't any chunks of that bridge lodged

against this one. So let's assume the other bridge is still standing."

"Then I say we run across now and pray we can get back. The flooding's only going to get worse."

"Let's go, Lee."

He grabbed her hand and they sprinted across the bridge.

At the eastern side of the bridge, Jennifer stepped ahead of him.

He pulled her to a stop. "Remember, it's my turn to lead."

"Can't blame a girl for trying." She grinned.

He was torn between wanting to wring her neck or kiss her, but there was no time for either.

Ten minutes of trudging through mud, around bushes, and walking between dripping trees on a sodden forest floor, had brought them even with the mill.

He crept towards the road, stopping behind a row of scrubby trees and motioning for Jennifer to follow.

"There's the mill," he said when Jennifer reached their secluded vantage point. "Since we're worried about the bridge, we need to short-circuit our southeastern approach. I'll go straight in from here and check for signs of recent traffic in the mill yard. If I don't see any, we can scratch this place."

"I don't want you to do that. Too risky."

"I can use the vegetation over there for cover and slip in close without being seen."

"I'll let you do that on one condition."

"What do you mean, you'll let—"

"You're forgetting who the coach is, Lee."

"OK, coach, what's the condition?" Coach. It was a reasonable concession. Jennifer's reactions in times of danger were incredible. She had saved his life on several occasions.

"Once you're on the other side of the road, give me a signal, and then wait for me. You're not going near that place unless I'm there watching your back."

"You've got it, coach. And, by the way, you're a pretty wise coach. Prettiest one I've ever seen."

"Get over there wise guy." Jennifer poked him in the ribs. "And…please be careful."

Within five minutes, they were crouched behind blackberry bushes beside the mill entrance.

The building they'd marked on the satellite picture still looked like a candidate, but so far he hadn't seen any signs of traffic. "I need to get in closer."

"In that case, you'll be close enough to use this." Jennifer handed him her Smith & Wesson .38.

"I'm not sure I'll need it. You're a better shot than I am, anyway."

"But you're the one who's going to be close enough to hit a target near the building."

"OK, I'll take it. But you better stay hidden, or I'll kill you." Lee smiled.

Jennifer did not.

He found a long opening behind the blackberry bushes and crept along until he drew even with the back of the buildings.

From here he could reach the back wall without being seen. Going down the backside of the buildings was the safest approach. But it would take longer than he'd planned.

Jennifer was probably getting worried about him being out of sight.

As he crept towards the target building, something drew his attention. It was a dark area on the back of the target building, a hole. Lee moved towards the hole. It still appeared dark—no lights of any kind.

The roar of the rain would drown out his footsteps, but if a head popped out of the hole…he pulled the .38 out of his coat pocket.

He moved to the edge of the opening, but he didn't look through it, fearing his head would become a target silhouetted against the light from outside. He picked up a rock, readied the .38, and tossed the rock into the hole.

No response.

But what if they'd gagged and tied up the girls inside?

He walked around to the front of the building and strode up to the door.

Jennifer jumped up from her hiding place. "No, Lee! Get back!"

It was too late to back out now. He needed to be sure. He readied the gun and kicked in the door. Light from outside flooded the room. Only a rotting wooden floor with a few boards scattered across it. This wasn't the holding site.

But now he had to face Jennifer.

Where was she? He ran towards the bush where Jennifer stood a few seconds before.

Jennifer was down on one knee, sobbing.

In one thoughtless moment, he had caused this.

He knelt and wrapped an arm around her. "Jenn, I'm so sorry. I didn't realize what it looked like to you. I didn't think about that until—"

"No matter what excuse or baloney you're about to tell me, promise me you'll never do that to me again."

This wasn't the Jennifer he met last March. That

Jennifer might have shot him, with her eyes, if not with bullets. But seven months of God's grace in her heart—what a difference.

Her arms circled his neck. "I'm OK, Lee. But do you promise?"

He took a deep breath, exhaled, and looked down into her teary, brown eyes. "I promise. But it wasn't what it looked like. I was certain the building was empty, but—"

"No more buts and no more Rambo, got it?"

"None. I promise. I never meant to hurt you." He realized his cheeks were wet and not entirely from the rain.

Jennifer wiped his cheeks. "I understand."

"I don't deserve you, Jenn."

"Right now, I'm inclined to agree." She smiled.

He covered her smile with his lips, but their inclined heads created a waterfall of raindrops cascading from their hoods onto their faces. It was wet, wonderful, and—Jennifer broke it off.

She coughed, trying to catch her breath. "Lee, we can't do that in the rain."

"Says who?"

She coughed again. "Me. I'm shorter than you. That miniature Niagara Falls from your hood goes right up my nose."

"If you start to drown, I can give you mouth-to-mouth."

"Very funny, Mr. Brandt."

"Jenn?"

"Just tell me, Lee."

"We need to get across that bridge before a big tree takes it out."

"What are we waiting for?"

4

When they jogged a few yards down the road, an alarm sounded in Lee's mind. He took Jennifer's hand and pulled her to a stop. "It's been barely thirty minutes since we passed here. Look at the water."

Jennifer scanned the ground. "It's about six inches deeper."

"I've got a bad feeling about this. Come on, let's hurry to the bridge."

"I don't think we're going to like what we find."

Water flowed across the lowest point on the road.

"Jenn, your eyesight's better than mine. What do you see along the bridge?"

"Not sure. Let's move closer."

After they moved onto the edge of the bridge, Jennifer grabbed his coat and yanked him backwards.

"What is it?"

"Another tree is lodged against the supporting structure."

"I don't think we should chance it." He sighted down the edge of the bridge. "Look how the bridge's midsection is bowing, slipping downstream. The whole bridge is ready to go."

Jennifer pointed up river. "Lee! Two more trees!"

"We need to get off. Now!"

He clasped her hand. They broke into a run. "Don't stop until we're on higher ground."

A deep groan sent vibrations up their legs. It

changed to a loud staccato of cracking sounds.

Lee looked back.

The bridge was gone. Its entire midsection floated downstream, bobbing on its edge.

"Faster. If that bridge section catches, it will dam up the river."

"The water!" Jennifer's voice pierced the roaring of the water. "It's rising!"

The bridge caught, forming a dam. A wave of water six feet high curled and broke like an ocean wave, surging towards them.

Jennifer stepped in a pothole and stumbled forward.

He yanked on her arm, pulling her upright.

Another wave caught the previous one, adding to its amplitude, sending an even higher wall of water towards them. If the wave swept them away, the turbulent water, filled with its eddies and undertows, would have its way with their bodies.

"My ankle! I think it's—"

He scooped her up in his arms and ran. Water splashed over his hiking boots.

The wall of water broke and sloshed towards him.

He stumbled thigh-deep in muddy water. The surge of water propelled him forward. Lee gained his footing and sprinted up a small hill.

Breathing hard, he set Jennifer down at the top of the hill.

They looked back. A large lake had formed. The mill was now an island.

"How's your ankle?"

"Ankle? Didn't you see that water? I was worried about the rest of me."

She put her weight on the ankle and shuffled her

feet around. "I think it's OK. I just tweaked it when I slipped." Jennifer put her arms around him. "Lee, do you think the car's all right?"

"I don't know, sweetheart. I honestly don't know."

She leaned against him and put her ear against his chest for a moment, and then looked up at him with wide eyes. "I guess we head up river now."

"Yeah. And we pray the west bank is high enough to protect your car. Don't worry, Jenn. We'll get across, and it'll be fine."

"But you saw the river. How can you know that?"

"Remember, we've got God and right on our side. Like you said, 'Don't be afraid. Nothing will happen to us unless He allows it.'"

"Lee, please don't mock me."

"Mock you? I was only reminding you of what you told me you believe. Nothing has changed that, has it?"

"You're doing it again."

Lee took her hand. "What am I doing?"

"Trying to make me feel better about things."

"Did it work?"

"Yes...like it always does."

"Jenn, we're not going to make Kalaloch before dark. The other site will have to wait. That means the girls ..."

"I know what it means." Her eyes held a haunted look. "Let's hurry and get back to Forks. We've got to get up early." Her head tilted towards the ground.

After his reminder and that look in her eyes, she was probably through talking. But was some voice talking to her?

For the next half hour, he led Jennifer northward, parallel to the river. They caught glimpses of the swollen stream from time to time.

When they reached the top of a knoll, Jennifer pulled him to a stop. "Do you see it?" She met his gaze. No traces of the eerie look. That was a good sign.

"I'm not sure. Your eyesight's better than mine—too many days in front of computer screens."

"I started working with computers at age four. My eyesight is fine. What were you doing at age nine, Lee?"

"Point taken, Einstein."

"I see the bridge. Enough to know it's still standing."

"That's encouraging, but let's not waste any time. Point the way."

"It looks like we can make a beeline straight to the bridge without any floodwater interfering."

It took five minutes of brisk walking down the gradual slope towards the river to reach the east end of the bridge.

"Besides being saved from that backwash, we've got something else to be thankful for. This is a modern bridge, much higher than the one that washed away. The trees that took out the other bridge must have come from farther upstream, on the mountain. Evidently they passed under this bridge without hanging up."

"Still, I think we should run across it." Jennifer stared at the churning water below them.

"You really don't like water do you?"

"You know I like water, when it's warm, calm, and I can swim in it. But see the boiling, angry look of this water. It's menacing, evil."

"We'll run then. Race you to the other side."

She took off.

He had to break into an all-out sprint to keep up with her.

At the west end of the bridge, he headed downriver, but Jennifer stopped him. She looked at the gray shroud above them. "Something's different. A few seconds ago the rain blew into my face, but not now."

"Rapid cyclogenesis is starting, maybe explosive."

"English, please."

"The windstorm that's coming—the low pressure system driving it is deepening. This storm didn't just move in on us. It's forming right now, and we're in the outer part of its circulation. The wind is nearly calm at the moment, but in a few minutes it will shift to the north. Then it will slowly increase in speed over the next twelve hours. The direction will shift towards the east, then to the southeast, and to the south. The speed will—"

"That's enough. Let's get the girls before the wind shifts to the southwest."

"Amen to that, because then...it might be too late."

5

Lee glanced at his watch. Three fifty PM. It was beginning to get dark.

Jennifer's SUV sat in front of them, unscathed by the surging water.

He studied the ground around it. No signs of flooding. Another reason to be thankful. They hadn't found the mill site, and yet their lives had been threatened and spared at least twice. If he believed in luck, his would have been all used up by now. But a good and gracious God transcended that thing called luck.

"Lee, if we hurry we could make the first mill before—"

He shook his head. "It'll be completely dark. They could see our headlights."

"I know. But I feel panicky, and I can't control it. It's like a child, my child, crying out to me for help."

"It's frustration. I feel it, too."

"No, Lee. It's a whole lot more than that."

He stopped her, placing hands on her shoulders. "Tomorrow, we'll help those girls. Nothing's going to happen now before late Sunday or early Monday. Trader can't continue his ugly business until the storm passes. By then, he'll be toast."

"I'll try to hang on to that thought."

He wrapped his arms around her and kissed her forehead. "Let's get out of this rain. After two days, the

Pineapple Express is wearing on us."

She unlocked the doors, sat down on the seat, and slipped off her boots.

The maps and satellite pictures of the eliminated mill sites weren't a total waste. He pulled them out and spread them on the floorboard, setting both pairs of muddy boots on the papers. Besides being muddy, his were saturated.

"Turn on your heater and blow it at our feet." He scooted both pairs of boots near the heater's floorboard exhaust. "You know, we should be thankful the ground is still in good shape and that the river didn't come over the bank on this side."

"I am. Your feet are wet, Lee. They got wet when you carried me, didn't they?"

He nodded. "We both nearly got submerged...permanently."

"I'm trying not to think about that. Raging water terrifies me." She paused. "I have some dry socks in my workout bag in the back. We'll get you some dry socks at the store." Jennifer steered the car back to the gravel road. "I wonder how close it came when the bridge dammed up the river."

"We probably don't want to know."

They were alive and safe. On to the next item of business.

He propped his elbow on the back of the seat and put his hand on her shoulder. "Now...where did you say that logger-turned-sculptor lives, John what's-his-name?"

"John Braithwaite." Jennifer turned on her headlights and pulled out onto Highway 101. "His house and shop are about eight miles south of town, along the highway."

The clock on the dash displayed 4:05 PM. "Good. You can interview him in about fifteen or twenty minutes."

"OK." Jennifer rubbed her forehead. "But the cover story we came up with needs to be changed."

"Why is that?"

"Think about it. Who is going to be out here doing research in a storm like this?"

"You're right. But we don't need to change the story much. Let's say you have a deadline to meet for your research. It's the truth."

"What if he gets suspicious? What if—"

"Don't worry. If he's not Trader, he'll cooperate, and—"

"And if he is?" Jennifer countered.

"Trader, an artist?" Lee shook his head. "I don't think so."

"You're right. It doesn't fit."

"So, after you talk to Braithwaite, we'll get a two-bedroom suite at the inn, and tomorrow morning we'll check out the last site, plus whatever comes out of the interview. You'll be on the phone to Peterson with the girls' location before the wind peaks tomorrow."

"You can stop trying to make me feel good about everything. You've already bagged your woman."

"What are you talking about now? If that kiss in the rain made you this loony, I'll have to swear off kissing."

"And how long would that last? Do you even know what I'm talking about? From day one, when the terrorists were chasing us, you kept trying to make me feel better about things, even when the things were my fault. Like when I got us trapped on the freeway, and they started shooting. When I let them see our brake lights in the dark, and they found us again. When I—"

"Enough, Jennifer. I don't want to relive all that running for our lives. Don't you like it that I try to make you feel better when things get you down?"

"Lee, I didn't say I didn't like it. I only asked why you do it."

"But you...never mind. I can't believe we're even having this conversation."

"We're having it because I need it."

She was testing his patience, and he was about to flunk the test. He took a deep breath and blasted it out. "OK, tell me why you need it."

"Driving in these conditions is tiring. I can't even see fifty yards ahead. And I'm tired. I need some help staying awake."

"I would have thought that backwash at the river would be enough to...you could have asked, Jenn. I would've helped."

"But you did help. You got louder and louder. We had this invigorating discussion, and it kept me awake."

Lee opened his mouth to speak.

"Lee?"

"Yes."

"We haven't set the date yet, but we're getting married soon, and there are things I still don't know about you like...all of your hot buttons."

"Jennifer, do you need me to help you stay awake, or are you just randomly pushing my buttons?"

"It isn't exactly an either-or situation."

"What has gotten into you? By—"

Her eyes were welling. The one nearest to him overflowed.

Oh brother. She's crying.

Whatever battle they were fighting, he had lost. Now what was he going to...wrong question. "I'm sorry, Jenn. I love you. What do you need me to do right now?"

"I told you before we left Seattle that I probably wouldn't be good company today, wouldn't feel normal until we found those girls."

He remembered her words. *Until the voice that keeps crying out to me for help stops.*

"Tell me again that everything's going to turn out all right."

"We're going to talk to this Braithwaite fellow in a few minutes, then we'll have all the information we need to find the mill. Tomorrow morning we'll find it. After that, everything's going to be fine. At some point, we'll probably get to meet those girls. Then it will be wonderful. That's what I believe. I wouldn't be here with you now if I didn't. Somewhere deep inside, I know you believe it, too. Right?"

Jennifer grabbed his hand. "Please, remember that speech, Lee. I may need you to give it again soon."

"Are you up to talking to this logger?"

"Yes. I am now."

Jennifer caressed his hand until they reached the Bogachiel River, where Highway 101 inscribed its squiggly line on highway maps of the Olympic Peninsula. She used both hands to navigate the winding stretch of road.

Lee glanced at the odometer. "I think we're approaching Braithwaite's house."

Jennifer slowed.

They had driven through forest land for the last five miles, but up ahead was an opening and possibly a driveway. "Slow down some more, Jenn. This may be it."

As she turned in, he glanced at her face.

"Are you ready with the cover story and your questions?"

"Ready as I'll ever be."

Lee scanned the buildings. Lights were on in both the mobile home and the shop.

"Wait here. Let me try the door to the shop first. The lights are on, so maybe he's still working."

Lee slipped on his wet boots and strode to the door. It wasn't locked. "Knock, knock. Anybody home?"

A tall, wiry, gray-haired man looked up from his desk. Sculpture work of all sizes and in various degrees of completion stood evenly spaced across the shop floor.

"I'm home," the man replied as he stood. "Who's the fool out on a day like this?"

"Are you John Braithwaite?"

"Yes, and who's the fool asking?"

"The fool is Lee Brandt. But it's my fiancée who needs to talk to you. May I—"

Braithwaite looked towards the door when Jennifer entered the shop. "My word, she's absolutely...By all means, come in. May I get you anything? A cup of coffee?" His words were directed at Jennifer.

Jennifer gave the man a warm smile. "Did you say coffee? I'd love some. My name is Jennifer and you, I hope, are John Braithwaite."

"In the flesh, Miss. Black or with cream and sugar?"

"Black please."

He poured Jennifer's cup, then looked at Lee.

"And what would you like, young man?"

"If you've got plenty, I'll have mine black, too."

"Glad for the company, any company this time of year." The old logger poured Lee's cup full and set the pot down. "Now, what can I do for you?"

Jennifer gave him their cover story and spread out her peninsula map on a workbench. "Now, here are the old mill sites we've located. See the black dots?"

Braithwaite studied the map for a few seconds. "Yes, but some have circles around them."

She pointed to one of the encircled dots. "Those are sites we want to visit. What I really need are locations of any mills we might have missed, whether they were cedar shake mills or lumber mills."

"Well, over the years I probably hauled logs into every mill that ran out here from 1950 to 2000. Let me see what you've got."

Braithwaite pored over the map, smiling as he placed his finger on some of the black dots. "You know there was a mill here, but I think they tore it down about twenty years ago."

Jennifer marked the spot with an X. "We found a lot of mills between Lake Quinault and Kalaloch, but not many between Kalaloch and Forks."

"That's about the size of it," Braithwaite mumbled, while his finger traced Highway 101. "But I think you missed one small mill about right...here." He pointed to a location a few miles south of Kalaloch on the south side of Highway 101. "I think the road's still there, maybe overgrown a bit. But I see it's not shown on your map."

Jennifer added a black spot to the map while Braithwaite continued to talk. "This was a small, family-owned mill. It operated as recently as twenty years ago, maybe less. So it's probably in pretty good shape. Don't know if they abandoned any equipment there. When the lumber industry took that nosedive, some owners just walked away and left behind rusting saws, forklifts, everything." He sighed and a droopy smile touched the corners of his mouth. "I guess they were just hoping...but you aren't interested in all of that."

Jennifer's hand trembled as she drew a red circle around the mill Braithwaite pointed out to them.

Obviously, she held the same suspicion he did.

"Let's see, you've got Johnson's and..." Braithwaite named most of the mills marked on the map, then announced, "I think you've got them all now. If I missed any, it's because they shut down before 1950. In that case, there wouldn't be anything left on the site. The forest would have reclaimed everything by now."

Jennifer set her coffee down. "Thank you so much, Mr. Braithwaite. You've been a big help to me in completing this research. If it turns out well, I'll give you an update when I'm out here sometime."

"I'll look forward to it, young lady."

Lee stretched out his hand. "Thanks a lot, sir. Sometime we'll stop in when we can look at your work. It's fantastic."

A sculpture of a Roman soldier stood at least twelve feet high near the center of the shop. Braithwaite had created the entire carving from a single large log. This man was an artist, creating art as God intended, art that captured the beauty of God's creation.

Unlike Trader, who only captured beauty and then destroyed it.

Once they were inside the car, Lee put an arm around Jennifer and gave her a side hug. "I think we struck gold. He knew every mill that could possibly be used, and he added the only one we didn't have on our map. If we visit the last two mill sites, we *will* find where they're holding the girls."

Once again a genuine smile graced Jennifer's face. "I believe you're right.

"And we don't have to worry about flooding rivers anymore. The last two sites are on high ground south of Kalaloch."

"Lee, it's the men that we need to worry about. That river only looked evil, the men *are* evil."

6

Lee sat with wet feet and thoughts of warm coffee when they turned in at the store.

Jenn stared at the floorboard. "It's my fault we didn't find them today."

"There were things beyond our control. It's not your fault. He pulled her head close and kissed her forehead. "Nothing was your fault. I'm the one who blew it. I'm sorry for not thinking about how you might feel at that last mill and—"

"Hush." Jennifer pressed her fingers over his lips. "It's OK." She kissed him softly. "We have better things to do than sit in a parking lot in the rain. We're wasting time here."

Lee watched as she walked towards the store entrance. He could never consider any time spent with her as wasted.

In a few minutes Jennifer trotted through the downpour, slid in, and tossed him a package. "Hurry up and get these on. There's a certain barista who can't wait to see you."

He slipped on a warm, dry sock. "The caramel macchiato lady?"

"You'd better be sure that's your only interest in her." She gave him her mock frown.

The thought of Jennifer being jealous brought a grin. "Do I detect a subtle threat?"

"It's not a threat. I promised to marry you, but

only if you survive the courtship."

"Jenn, you've never acted like the jealous type." He slipped on his second sock.

"And you don't want to see me act that way. Believe me."

"I'm engaged to the brightest, most beautiful woman on the planet, who seems to have been custom-made for me by God." He pushed his feet into his boots. "I'd have to be a complete fool to even look at another woman."

"Then everything's fine, because I would never promise myself to a fool. Now let's get some coffee."

Lee jumped out, ran to the driver's side and took her hand. "Come on, I want to lay the issue of macchiato maiden to rest." He stepped towards the coffee shop's side entrance.

"Don't be silly. I was only joking...like we always do."

"I'm not convinced." He opened the shop door. "I think you need some proof."

At the sound of the doorbell, the barista looked up.

Lee drew Jennifer close and gave her the most convincing kiss he could muster, a kiss she seemed to become totally lost in. As they began their deep look into each other's eyes, Jennifer looked away. Her cheeks were flushed.

"I rest my case," he whispered in her ear.

She clung to his arm, but looked at the floor.

Macchiato maiden stood behind the counter, smiling while she stared at them. "Hey. What type of research are you doing out here, anyway?"

He looked up at the smiling barista. "Compatibility testing."

"Was that the final exam?" Macchiato maiden fired her question across the shop, continuing to smile at him.

Jennifer leaned close and whispered. "She'd better not ask if I passed the exam, or I'll kill you."

He put his mouth next to her ear. "Wouldn't you at least wait for my answer?" Before Jennifer could respond, he replied to the barista. "Yeah. That was the final."

"Well, don't keep me in suspense." Macchiato maiden raised a palms-up hand. "Did she pass?"

The frown lines deepened on Jennifer's forehead.

"You need to ask *her* that question. I'm only the student."

Jennifer leaned her head onto Lee's shoulder. "You weasel," she whispered as she slipped her arm around his waist. "You always find a hole to slip through. Tell her you passed."

Lee put an arm around Jennifer's shoulders and leaned his head on hers.

The barista looked at the couple and smirked. "It's pretty obvious. You aced the exam." She paused. "Same order as before?"

"Yes, please," Jennifer spoke softly.

"Two extra-hot, grande, caramel macchiatos coming right up."

When they entered the supermarket sipping their coffee, Lee grabbed a hand basket from the stack. Jennifer also reached for one.

"I can carry everything. We're not getting much."

Jennifer took a hand basket, disregarding his offer.

"We're not getting anything heavy. It'll all fit in my basket." He reached for her basket.

She moved it out of reach and scanned the area

around them. "It's not how much…it's what."

"But we're only getting toothpaste, toothbrushes, mouthwash, and…oh."

"I want to pick out my 'oh' by myself."

"Sure you don't want my suggestions?" He gave her a toothy grin.

"Maybe in a few weeks, but definitely not tonight."

"You know, maybe it's a good thing we got stuck out here on the peninsula tonight. I learned some new things about you. Like it embarrasses you when—"

"That's enough. I've learned some things, too. That I'm very happy and very blessed. And that you need to let me go down the next aisle by myself."

"I've got one of those aisles, too. I'll go find it now. Meet you by the toothpaste."

They left the store and splashed across the parking lot.

Jennifer tossed the bag with their purchases in the back, and then started the engine. "Are we ready to head for the other end of town?"

"After you answer a question."

"OK, what is it?"

"Einstein really doesn't know?"

"Twice today. That's enough Einstein. Just tell me, Lee."

"What names will we use when we check in?"

"Oh." She paused. "I hadn't even thought—"

"But I have…Jennifer and Lee Brandt, brother and sister."

"That's really a stupid idea. They would have to think one of us was adopted. I'm Asian-Polynesian and you're, well…as Caucasian as they come."

"Not really. I'm one-eighth Cherokee."

"You never mentioned that before. You said your great-grandparents were German immigrants."

"They were, but my other side of the family came from the Indian Territories—outlaws and half breeds."

Her eyes widened at the word outlaws.

"You look surprised. You're not prejudiced, are you?"

"You know me better than that."

"Then what were you thinking?"

A smile spread across her face. "About our kids."

"What? That's not a subject to bring up tonight—especially tonight."

"With our bloodlines, can you imagine what they will look like? They're going to be beautiful, Lee."

"I'm sure the girls will. But the boys...they might slice you up with a samurai sword and then scalp you."

"The Cherokees didn't do that. But, you're right. Tonight's not a night for kids—I mean as a discussion topic, or for—"

"Sweetheart, I know what you mean. Tonight's a night to think about finding some kids, not about—"

"I think we need to change the subject." Jennifer pulled out and headed towards the far end of town.

Lee grinned.

She was blushing.

7

When they walked into the office at the inn, Lee made eye contact with the tall man standing behind a small counter. He wore a plastic badge with the word *Manger* on it.

"What can I do for you on this beautiful evening?" The manager quipped.

"Manger, huh? Any room at the inn for two weary travelers, or do we have to sleep in the hay?"

"That depends. Is your wife pregnant?" The man grinned.

"No...she's not. I mean she's not pregnant, and she isn't my uh...what have you got available tonight?"

That went well, you idiot.

Jennifer's glare reiterated his sentiment.

"The badge gets a lot of remarks." The manager pulled out a registration form. "I made the spelling mistake when I ordered the badges—all twelve of them. Since we had to pay for them, my wife makes me wear them. She's a real penny pincher. But about the room...this used to be an apartment complex, so all we have are one and two bedroom suites, all completely separate units, lots of privacy."

"We need a two-bedroom suite." He glanced at Jennifer.

She nodded.

"You're in luck. I have eight of them. Probably ten

by tomorrow night the way the weather's been going. All without any hay, just comfortable beds." He met Lee's gaze. "Name, please?"

"Lee Brandt."

"Just the two of you for one night?"

"Yeah."

Jennifer slid her left hand behind his back like she was hiding her engagement ring.

How would that help?

The manager looked at Jennifer then at Lee. He looked at Jennifer a second time and cocked his head.

The guy was obviously trying to decipher their relationship.

A couple of minutes later, they stood under the overhanging walkway sheltering the door to their suite.

As the door swung open, she stuck out a thumb and pointed into their room. "This wasn't a good idea, was it?"

"You tell me." He needed to do this right. He scooped Jennifer up and lifted her into his arms.

She gasped. "Lee?"

He carried her across the threshold.

She glanced out the open door, and her mouth fell open. "Lee, that man thought we were…"

"Jenn, I don't care what he thinks about me right now." He was still holding Jennifer and the door still stood open, but in the grand scheme of things, it didn't matter. What mattered were those brown eyes he could drown in and her full lips only inches from his, only millimeters, only sweetness when they met his.

Evidently, she forgot about the door. Jennifer returned his kiss with something far beyond mere warmth. When they followed the kiss with their ritual of peering into each other's eyes—both pairs of eyes completely unmasked, revealing everything—he saw a lot more than he bargained for.

He lowered her onto her feet. "You were right. Maybe this wasn't a good idea. Go lock yourself in your room. Put some of that white cream all over your face—the stuff old ladies use on TV—or something else repulsive."

"Can't do that. I didn't buy any makeup. But don't worry. You won't be tempted beyond what you can stand." Her smirk turned to a frown. "We have some important work to do this evening. We need to find a safe approach to the remaining mill sites. One of them will have people with guns...and girls who need us."

For the moment, the evening took on somber overtones as they fled from temptation to reality, a reality where the stakes were high. Life and something worse than death.

****

The grocery bag. They had forgotten it.

Lee grabbed Jennifer's car keys from the table and turned towards the door.

"No. I'll get the stuff from the car." Jennifer said as she tried to cut him off.

He stepped ahead of her and ran out the door to her car, grabbed the grocery bag, and scurried back inside the room.

Jennifer met him at the door. "Can I please have the bag with my things in it?"

"No, because it's also the bag with *my* things in it."

She grabbed for the bag.

He deftly moved it out of her reach.

"Lee, please give me the bag."

"Flip you for it. Winner gets to take their stuff out first."

Jennifer seemed to relax, and then lunged for the bag. She ripped it from his hand, tearing the bag and spilling its contents onto the floor.

He dropped to the floor and snatched his underwear.

Jennifer reached for her underwear, now fully displayed in front of him, including the tags. It was an interesting bit of information.

"Well, well, well. Jenn, I would have never guessed—"

Jennifer scooped up her bra. "That's enough. So now you don't have to guess." She looked up at him.

"You know what?"

"Whatever it is, I don't want to know." Her cheeks displayed a deep rosy color.

"Well, you need to hear this. I think you're a keeper."

She avoided eye contact. "You think I'm a keeper based on my...based on the tag you read? What kind of a guy thinks like that?"

"A normal, red-blooded, American guy."

"And that, Lee, is why we shouldn't be staying here in—"

The game was over. He sighed. "There's an important reason why we're staying here. Let's eat, then we need to plan for tomorrow."

She took his hand. "After that, we need to have a serious talk."

"A good serious talk or a bad serious talk?"

"Mostly good."

Her face conveyed a different message.

"Are you OK, sweetheart?" He studied her face. "Let's eat. Then we can talk."

8

Lee's nagging worry about the developing storm returned. "While we eat I'm going to check out this storm. The wind shifted around 4:00 PM, earlier than I thought it would."

He opened her laptop and waited for it to wake up. The WiFi connections showed only one router. He connected and opened a browser, pointing it at the University of Washington weather information web site, and then the forecast page.

On it, he found the link to NCAR's research applications and perused the numerical model output charts, looking for deviations from the storm analysis he had performed on Friday for his company's client.

Jennifer leaned towards him and looked over his shoulder. "You know, I worried about you switching career fields when we started courting. There's always computer systems work, but right now I'm thankful that you're back up to speed on weather forecasting." She pointed at the lower left corner of the screen. "I see a lot of concentric circles to the south of us. That's not good, is it?"

"No, it's not. The jet was already structured for rapid cyclogenesis...uh, storm development. The embedded remnants of an old Western-Pacific typhoon have increased the effect. It's so similar to the Columbus Day storm of 1962 that it's scary. What we're seeing here is called explosive cyclogenesis, and the results could be devastating to the entire peninsula."

"It won't stop us from finding the girls, will it?"

"Not if we get started early. My gut says we'll see wind gusts up to one hundred fifty miles per hour in the exposed areas by tomorrow afternoon. I'm drawing a line in the sand. No matter what, we need to be well inland by noon tomorrow. Before the Pineapple Express transitions to a hurricane-strength storm, and before driving down a forest-lined highway, like 101, becomes deadly."

****

After Lee's news about the storm, half of her sandwich was all she could eat. They needed more preparation and part of that was creating a map of Braithwaite's mill site.

"I'm going out to my SUV to get the map and satellite picture of the site we missed. It's near Braithwaite's mill. I think we can use them for both locations, all but the satellite close-up."

When she returned, Lee was wolfing down the second half of her sub. He cleared the table and tossed the wrappings in the waste basket. "Here, spread the map out on the table."

Jennifer folded the map in half, exposing the area from Kalaloch southward, and placed the satellite picture beside the map. She scooted behind the laptop and brought up a satellite picture of the area south of Kalaloch. "The mill Braithwaite told us about is three miles down the highway from the mill site we missed. I'll zoom in on that location."

She panned to the south. There was only forest.

She panned further. "Look, Lee. I'll bet that's the mill." She zoomed further, but the picture lost resolution before the buildings became clearly visible. "Well, we know where it is. We'll have to take Braithwaite's word about its condition. What's your gut feeling about where they're holding the girls? The mill we missed, or Braithwaite's?"

"If I was betting money, I'd put it on Braithwaite's mill. His description fits the criteria better than any other mill site we've found out here."

"I agree." Lee's hand was warm and comforting. She intertwined their fingers. "But we've got to be careful even at the other mill. We'll be sneaking up on some dangerous people. I want us to think about all the contingencies tonight."

Lee rubbed his chin for a few seconds. "Contingencies. How about this? If we're spotted by anyone who takes an interest in us while we're parking, we'll immediately head towards the nearest cell reception and call Peterson."

"That sounds good to me, but can we assume we've found the holding site if that happens?"

"Jenn, if they make any move towards us, I don't think we have any choice but to make that assumption, even if we haven't visually verified that the girls are there."

Jennifer took a deep breath and let it escape slowly, preparing for Lee's protest. "There's another possibility I want you to think about. And I want an answer." She paused. "It's my turn to take the point at the first mill. What if they spot me, they shoot, and I go down?"

"I won't let that—"

"You can't say that. Tell me what you'll do."

"If you go down, I'll carry you back to the car. Maybe I'll use your gun to hold them at bay until we can get—"

"No, Lee. If I go down and don't get up immediately, you've got to get away and notify the FBI."

"A good soldier never leaves a comrade behind."

"This isn't like war. There *are* no reinforcements. If I go down, promise me you'll get away and find help. We've got to stop this trafficking of young girls and make sure the girls being held are rescued." Tears tickled her cheeks and spilled into her lap. "You've got to *promise* me."

"You know I could never leave you behind. Why are you doing this?"

Now her eyes and her nose were running. She swiped at them. Would he understand or think she was crazy? "Because it's necessary."

"Tell me what's going on." He reached for her.

When Lee slipped his arms around her, the floodgates opened. The tears were driven by a voice inside that wailed like a frightened, orphaned child, lost and without hope. It shredded her heart. But no matter what she felt or what she wanted, she could never convince Lee to do something she wouldn't do, to leave the other one behind.

"Remember this morning when I told you I felt terrible because it seemed like these people held my own daughter?"

"I remember. Is that what this is all about?"

"It's like someone, a young girl, has been crying out for me to help today. Not an audible voice—I'm not losing my sanity—but someone needs me…desperately."

"It's me." He laid his cheek on her head. "I'm the one who needs you desperately."

"Someone else needs me too, and, Lee…" She looked up into his eyes. What was he thinking? Did he believe her and did he understand? "I think they need you, too."

"Do you really believe God is laying this on your heart?"

"I wish I could answer that." She wiped her eyes again. "I think so, but I'm not sure. I'm still learning things about my relationship with Him. Maybe my signals are crossed or something."

He cupped her cheeks and pulled her face in front of his. "Here's what we need to do. We're a pretty good team, so I know we'll find the girls tomorrow. With Peterson's help, we'll set them free. If God wants something more of us, He'll show us. Remember that verse in Psalms about committing our way unto the LORD, trusting in Him and letting Him bring it to pass. I think it's time to do some committing."

****

Lee tried to cover all the bases in his prayer, but he ached inside when Jennifer poured out the agony she felt in her heart.

After she finished praying, he gently pulled her into his arms. "Too many things have happened for this all to be coincidence. Even the delays today may have been for a purpose. If God wants to use us, we're already more than willing. Let's put the outcome in His hands. He'll show us if there's a girl out there who needs us, and He'll show us how to meet those needs." He paused. "Now there are some things I need to say to you, if you don't mind me changing the subject."

"I don't mind, but first—I know I've said this before—you are a very good man, Lee Brandt, and I love you more than I can tell you. No matter what happens tomorrow, please remember nothing can ever change that."

No matter what happens tomorrow, she had said. Tomorrow he would take Jennifer into the domain of an intense storm. Storms he understood. He had respect for them. But tomorrow he would also take Jennifer into the domain of human traffickers. He had no respect for them and could not understand them. When the two domains combined, he could only wonder what he was actually taking her into.

Her forehead, beautifully tan and intelligent, was only inches from his lips. He kissed it. "Taking you into danger scares me to death. But please remember this, there's no one I would rather have by my side when our lives are on the line than you. And there's no one else I'll ever have by my side in this life. I don't have any more room for love. You filled it...completely."

She was frowning now. "What about our children? We've talked about—"

"That's different." He managed a smile. "Whatever size house you live in, you always find room for your next child. Our hearts are like that when it comes to family."

"Then you do have more room for love?"

"For family, it's more like a shoehorn. You slip them in. Our kids will be partly you. Love for a wife and kids—it's atomic." He frowned. "Split it and you get a big explosion—E equals M C squared—divorce."

"But if something did happen to me, something

tomorrow, I wouldn't want you to live your life alone. You should—"

He put his finger on her lips. "Maybe I would prefer to live alone, in that case. But why the morbidity? Nothing is going to happen to you. I won't let it, and I don't believe God will, either."

When Jennifer set the travel alarm clock for 6:00 AM, she felt a measure of peace in her heart for the first time since she discovered the trafficker's message.

Their prayer time had calmed some of her fears, and Lee had drowned the rest with two kisses. Maybe he was right when he said with God and Agent Peterson on their side, Trader was toast.

She hoped so. But it took heat to make toast. Wherever that heat might come from, she didn't want them to get burned in the toasting process, and tomorrow there would be many, many ways to get burned.

9

Sunday Morning, November 3

Jennifer sat up in bed.

The "William Tell Overture"? You've got to be kidding.

Her rule was no upbeat music before coffee and no exceptions. Where was the button to shut off the annoying thing? She randomly pushed buttons on the clock's keypad until, mercifully, the tinny rendition of the classical piece stopped.

The clock read 6:00 AM, and they needed to be at Kalaloch by 7:30.

Despite the ominous unknown awaiting them, she had slept soundly.

Rustling noises and the sounds of footsteps came from the other side of Lee's door. He was up.

"It's 6:00 AM. I'm going to kill you for picking out that stupid clock. We've got forty-five minutes to get out of here, provided you live that long."

"I love you too, Jenn. Make sure you leave me fifteen minutes of bathroom time to brush my teeth and shave."

"Please do both. Yesterday you had some personal hygiene issues."

"After leaving in a panic yesterday morning, we both did." Lee stepped out of his room fully dressed. "You'd better get your clothes on unless you intend to wear those sweats all day."

"They're my pajamas. Just like yours, and I'm not planning to—"

"No, not just like mine. Mine are already folded and in my pack. I'm taking my bathroom time now while you get dressed."

She shuffled back into her room to dress.

Today they would find the girls and possibly encounter some of the most evil people on the planet. A case of nerves was incubating. Buttons misbehaved in her trembling hands. So did her boot laces. It took several extra attempts to tie their ends into bows.

When she collected her things to take her turn in the bathroom, the clock read 6:20.

How were they doing for time? With a mouthful of toothpaste, she ran a mental timeline. Out at 6:30, coffee, prayer at Kalaloch, mill number one by about 7:35. They were still on daylight savings time, so it would barely be light when they approached the first mill.

What would their world look like in twelve hours? The nagging question wouldn't leave her mind. It was a simple question to ask, but did she really want to know the answer?

The possibilities were exciting, but they were also frightening. Lee's arms. She needed their strength, comfort, and security.

He stood in the living room of their suite.

"Please hold me, sweetheart."

He pulled her head against his chest. "Worried about what the day might bring?"

"You know me too well."

"Not possible." He squeezed her. "I just assumed you were doing the same thing I am, wondering what's going to happen."

"Tell me we're not being fools—that this will all turn out good in the end."

"I'm not the final authority on that. But the One who is said all things work together for good for people like us. At least, that's what the end ultimately looks like. And your question about fools…" He cupped her cheeks so they stared into each other's eyes. "If those girls knew what we were attempting, and they knew we were the only ones attempting it, would they look at us as being fools?"

She pushed forward and kissed him. "How do you do that?"

"Do what? Cure the morning mouth I had when you picked me up yesterday? That's easy. Toothpaste."

"No. I mean how do you come up with a question that answers my question?"

"It's genius. Pure genius."

She poked his ribs. "I hardly think so. But right now, I need to focus on making something happen rather than wondering what's going to happen, so let's go. And, Lee?"

"What, sweetheart?"

"If you promise to keep using toothpaste, I think I can handle the next sixty years."

****

Lee looked at his watch, 6:32. "Good-bye, Olympic Suites."

"Should we tell anyone we stayed here together?"

He certainly didn't plan to. "It wasn't our first choice, and it shouldn't be our first choice to tell anyone. It might have been necessary, but was really out of character for us."

"It was kind of nice staying under the same roof, though, even if we were in separate rooms, wasn't it?"

"Yeah. It was nice." He gave her a smirk. "But I've heard that after you're married, it gets even better."

"I think we need to talk about coffee."

"I think I'd enjoy a quad venti mocha."

"No, I think you enjoy embarrassing me."

"Until this weekend, I didn't even know that was possible. But I've got to admit, with a little color in your cheeks, you could win any beauty pageant on the planet."

Jennifer took his hand and drove in silence to Mocha Motion, the drive-through espresso stand in the center of town.

"It's not raining as hard." Lee craned his neck to look upward through the passenger-side window. "But the wind is picking up out of the southwest. This shop may be open for business now, but I'll bet it closes early."

Jennifer's window slid down, and she placed their order before the female barista could greet them. "Two quad venti mochas. Extra hot, please."

"Anything to eat for you two? Muffins, maybe?"

Lee leaned to see the menu. "I'll have a poppy seed muffin and one of those breakfast cookies," he said, as he leaned across to shove a twenty through the driver's window.

Jennifer grabbed his hand. "You have a few things you need to pay for, but this isn't one of them." She glanced at the barista. "I'll have the same as my fiancé." She handed the barista her own twenty.

The young woman smiled warmly. "Fiancé. That must be nice. I've seen you here occasionally. What're you doing out here in such nasty weather?"

He looked up. "We—"

"We're staying at the inn." She blocked his view of the barista with her head. "We had to take a two-bedroom suite, because our wedding is still a few weeks away. It was nice to have some time together, but I've heard it gets better after you're married."

He groaned and lowered his forehead into his hand.

"Well…moving right along, here are your muffins and cookies. The drinks will be ready in a minute." The barista disappeared from the window shaking her head.

"Jenn, what do you think you're doing?"

"I know exactly what I'm doing—getting even. And it worked. You ought to see yourself."

"But we agreed not to—"

"No, Lee. You suggested. I never agreed. What's more, I think I'm going to tell Jim Williamson and let your men's accountability group at church deal with you."

"But, Jenn, they won't un—"

"And I won't, either…tell them, that is. But I'll bet they could really tighten down the thumbscrews if I did."

The barista, apparently still at a loss for words, shoved their two drinks at them.

Jennifer grabbed the two large cups. With her eyes on the barista, she pushed a cup at him. "Keep the change and have a nice day." She smiled at the girl and closed her window. "Well, one mission accomplished, and now we can focus on the next one."

"Please do," he said between sips of steaming hot coffee.

****

Shortly before they passed Braithwaite's shop, Jennifer hit the power button on the stereo. Two days before, she had positioned the player to begin at the song she now needed to hear. The song provided the answer to her doubts, fears, and Peterson's warnings.

Today she would to listen to His voice, the voice of truth from her favorite Christian singer.

Lee's head was tilted forward and his eyes were closed. He was deep in silent prayer.

She joined him, except for the closed-eyes part.

When the song finished, she hit the power button and held his hand as she guided the vehicle through the winding road that would bring them to Kalaloch.

In a few minutes they reached the Hoh River bend.

She released her grip on Lee's hand to steer through the steep, never-ending turn.

When the road finally angled back, Lee craned his neck, and then opened his window and stuck his head out as they crossed over the narrow bridge.

The Hoh River drained the wettest rainforest in North America. The roar of its water sounded loudly above the rain, wind, and road noise. The deep sound of awesome, raging power rumbled, resonating in her chest.

Lee closed his window and pulled the satellite picture and map from the side pocket of his door.

He would probably study their approach plans until they reached the sites, analyzing each detail for ways to improve it. That was Lee, analytical. But, like her, he also used his intuition. As Lee said, together they made a great team. She wished it wasn't a team facing life-threatening danger for the second time in seven months.

The voice of truth did indeed say to not be afraid, however, that didn't take all the fear away. But God provided courage for those who trusted Him. Enough courage to act despite their fears. That's what His word said, and that's what she needed today, cour—

Smack! Something hit the right side of the car. The unknown force shoved the vehicle over the center line.

She jerked the wheel to the right, barely preventing them from running into the ditch.

Lee looked at her. "The wind's picking up. You'll need to watch the gusts each time you pass an opening to the beach."

"It caught me by surprise. I didn't realize we were so close to Kalaloch and to the beach." She took a deep breath and blasted it back out.

"Are you OK?" He put his hand on her shoulder.

She reached across and squeezed his hand. "Yes. Just deep in thought...and in prayer."

"Me, too. We intended to stop in Kalaloch, but the Beach 4 parking area is coming up. Why don't you pull in there?"

"Good idea. And don't worry. I won't let the wind blow us off the road." She placed her hand back on the wheel.

"Jenn, you're the best driver I know, but we've got to make sure we're not driving this stretch of road this afternoon, or you might not be able to prevent that."

The next blast of wind sounded like someone whacked her car with a baseball bat. It splattered so much rain she couldn't see the road ahead. But she had anticipated the gust and managed to keep the SUV in the right lane.

When the Beach 4 sign appeared, she turned in.

The trees surrounding the paved parking area swayed like demonic dancers in the gusting winds.

Where was the safest place to park? Probably the center of the vacant parking area.

She stopped there and scanned the trees. If they fell, they couldn't reach her vehicle, could they? What if the wind picked up a tree? Could it carry the tree far enough to crash into...it wasn't the time for such distractions. They had a lot pray about.

"Lee, will you start, please? I'll finish. And please pray for me. The storm is barely starting, and I'm already battling the willies."

When Lee finished, he had verbalized every concern on her heart.

Jennifer thanked God for the unity that enabled him to enumerate her requests by simply speaking what was on his own heart. But the words in her heart needed to be spoken, too. They spilled out like water from opened flood gates. Protection for Lee, petitions for the girls and for the arrival of the FBI when they were needed.

At 7:30, they drove out of the parking area, exiting between two large, swaying trees, and pulled onto Highway 101. The prayer time had given her a measure of peace.

Lee shifted restlessly in his seat.

She wanted to take his hand, but the wind gusts were too strong and unpredictable. "Sweetheart, what's wrong?"

"We're running out of time. The worst of the storm will hit us shortly. We need to short-circuit our plan and—"

"And go straight to Braithwaite's mill?" She

glanced his way. "We both know that's where we'll find the girls."

"Yeah."

"Maybe the right timing is being worked out for us...by the One who really is in control here. Just think about it. Nothing has happened on schedule since we got out here."

"That's an understatement. So now, we go to Braithwaite's mill. But it's too dark for me to see the map. Let's stop at Kalaloch and use the overhead light to take another look at our approach plan."

By 8:00, they had finished re-examining the map and their approach to the mill site.

What if the girls weren't there? The thought ambushed her, attacking the confidence built during her prayer time. A storm surge of doubt rolled over Jennifer like a thirty-foot wave. "Lee, I don't think I can handle it if we strike out here."

His arms drew her close. "Remember Who's really in control? If that's what you b—"

"It *is* what I believe...but sometimes I need to be reminded." Jennifer shifted back into her seat and pulled out onto the highway. "Eight miles to the mill, right?"

"Right as rain."

"That was totally unnecessary. After the past two days, I'm ready to move to Death Valley."

"Death Valley? Couldn't you have picked some other desert location?"

"You mean like Tombstone?" She shot him a smile as she accelerated. But all humor had its roots in truth, and the truth was, as she had stated yesterday, what they were doing wasn't safe.

By 8:20, they were searching for the timber access

road a quarter mile west of the mill site. The recently planted trees waved like wheat in a breeze-swept field.

What would they look like when they began their violent dance to hurricane-force winds? She prayed she wouldn't be here to watch it.

Lee's voice startled her. "Fifty yards ahead. Let's hope there's no gate on it."

"Gate? Are you being your usual worrying self, or trying to get me to join you?"

He grinned. "Misery loves company."

No vehicles in the rear-view mirror. Good.

She slowed.

Lee pointed to the mouth of the road. "Great! There *is* a gate. Pull up to it and let me take a look."

"It's not a good idea to sit out here exposed."

"I only need a few seconds. Besides, the mill road is still a quarter mile up the highway. They couldn't have spotted us yet." He stepped out, opened the rear door, and pulled something from his pack.

He reappeared carrying a hatchet.

A handy tool for splitting firewood, but for unlocking a gate? She didn't think so.

Lee set the hatchet down on the steel cylinder protecting the lock on the gate.

What was he doing?

His hand reached up into the bottom of the cylinder and came out holding something. He picked up his hatchet and set something on top of the cylinder. A padlock?

Lee pushed the gate open and motioned for her to drive through. After she passed through, Lee closed the gate, put the padlock back inside the cylinder, and scampered to the vehicle.

"The lock was hanging there, but it wasn't locked.

What are the odds of that? Makes you wonder, doesn't it?"

"Yeah. I hope the rest of the day is as wonderful." She steered onto the small dirt road. This was the moment they'd been waiting for since Saturday morning. Her pulse shifted up a gear. But the accompanying adrenaline rush would erode her caution. She took a deep breath, exhaled slowly, and tried to calm down.

Lee looked at her and nodded. "Me, too. It's hard to stay calm and think things through."

The fuzzy images in the rear-view mirror told her they were out of sight of any traffic on the highway. "I'm going to park behind the small trees on the left."

She steered towards the parking spot, but the steering became mushy when she turned off the dirt road. The vehicle slowed to a crawl. Her reflexes kicked in. She pressed on the accelerator. The car stopped moving, all but the wheels.

She pulled her foot from the gas pedal and slammed her hand on the steering wheel. "I've gotten us stuck."

"Not your fault, sweetheart. The ground looked fine until we sank in. There must be underground seepage from all the rain. Let me get out and take a look."

He circled the vehicle and slid back in. "I'll find something to give us some traction. Be right back."

Lee disappeared around a cluster of small trees.

Jennifer took a deep breath and tried to relax, but her pulse pounded in her fingers, her head…in every part of her body.

Lee came out of the trees with a large armload of wood. He distributed the wood evenly to all four wheels and motioned for her to roll the window down. "When I get the wood under the tires, try to back out of the hole. I'll stay out here and watch the wheels."

On her first attempt, the car rolled backwards about a foot. But when the tires hit the back edge of the hole they'd sunk into, the wheels spun.

Lee gave her the slit-throat signal. "The wood is just sinking into the mud. No progress. We need to dig a gradual incline for each wheel and try again. Do you have anything we can dig with?"

"Nothing. I don't even think the jack has any parts we can use for digging."

"The jack…that gives me an idea. Wait here."

"Lee, we're losing a lot of time."

"Some. But sit tight while I get some more wood. There's a pile of old slashings beyond the trees. I can find something to dig with."

She waited.

Five minutes passed and Lee hadn't returned. Maybe he needed help.

As she opened her door, Lee reappeared carrying another large armload of wood.

It was 8:50 AM. Desperation grew, spreading through her body until her legs and arms grew weak and shaky.

As Lee approached the car, his eyes widened. He dumped his load of wood.

That wasn't a good sign. She rolled her window down when he stepped to the driver's side.

"Bad news. I created a bog around each wheel."

"We don't need this, Lee. Let's walk to the mill, now."

"You know we can't do that. If this is the holding location, and they detect us, we'd be creating one of the scenarios we discussed—where we have to run eight miles through the woods to Kalaloch. They would know where we were headed, and they'd be waiting for us. That leaves no us and no help for the girls."

"Tell me what I can do. I need to do something."

"Let me think for a minute." He stared at the wheel nearest him. "I need to see the base of your jack."

She pushed the button to unlock the rear door, slid out into the rain, and headed for the back. At least she remembered how to get the jack. "Will this work?"

Lee took the base. "I think we can make it work. But we'll need a wide base for it, something that won't sink. If the base holds up the jack, I can raise each wheel and fill the holes with wood chunks. If the wood holds up the wheels, you can back out to the road."

She shook her head. "That's too many ifs and too much time."

"Only two ifs and, yes, it will take some time. I'm open to other ideas."

"I don't have any. Let's divide the work and shorten the time. It's already 9:00. The wind is getting stronger."

"C'mon, then. I'll show you where to get the wood, and I'll look for a base. We should be able to move the car in less than an hour."

Over the next forty minutes, Jennifer jogged back and forth nearly a dozen times.

The wind drove the heavy rain so fiercely that, even with her hood up, the huge drops stung when they pelted her face.

When she dumped her last pile of wood, Lee shook his head. "We've got to jack up all of the tires again and add more wood. We raised the car about a foot, but now we've lost six inches of it."

She threw her hands up into the air, while her heavy breathing created small clouds around her head. "Are you sure this is going to work?"

"Eventually. We've made a lot of progress."

"OK. I'll bring more wood." Fifty yards to the pile of slashings...again. One delay after another. What was happening here?

Twenty-five minutes later they were ready for another attempt to free the SUV. The panic fluttered in her queasy stomach as she fired up the engine, hoping it was the car that came out and not her breakfast.

The SUV's clock read 10:30 when she gave the gas pedal a gentle push.

The rear wheels rolled out of the mud and onto the dirt road.

Fearing some other setback, she backed completely onto the road, pushed the lever to drive, and rolled forward onto higher, firmer ground.

She would leave her SUV parked on the small road rather than risk getting stuck again.

The lost time, the wind, and fear for the girls...she was losing it. Panic, worse than her attacks of acrophobia, screamed its alarm in her mind.

"Are you OK?" Lee stepped to her side.

"Not at the moment. What if they aren't here? I keep—"

"We can't allow that kind of thinking right now." He took her by the shoulders and peered into her eyes. "Jenn, look at me. The girls are only a quarter mile away. So are one or more goons. Those thoughts must be the basis of everything we think, say, and do, until we're done here."

She had never seen his deep blue eyes so intense,

so piercing.

"Listen, I want you to burn that bit of logic into your EEPROM and throw away the burning software. We're going to stand right here until you can tell me you've done that."

The girls were being held at this mill site. They had to be. Jennifer closed her eyes and pictured a room where several girls were tied and guarded by armed thugs. Somewhere deep inside of her mind, or her heart or her soul, a young voice cried. It wailed hopelessly.

She gasped and grabbed Lee's arm. "We need to go now."

****

The rapid transformation of Jennifer's face from a frown to a clenched jaw, from mental engagement to response, concerned him. "Whoa, Jenn. Remember, we need to be cautious as we move in. I didn't know that little pep talk would affect you like that."

"Thanks for your encouragement, but there's more to it than a pep talk. She's crying for help again. Would God do that to me?"

There was a lot going on here he couldn't explain—the delays, Jennifer's awareness of a girl in trouble, the intense storm. He exhaled sharply, blowing a cloud of mist from his mouth. "I can't answer for God. But if He wants you involved in rescuing those girls, He can use any means He chooses to motivate you. Think how he motivated Jonah. He had—"

"Lee, I'm not like Jonah. I'm running towards the girls, not running away."

"Sorry, bad analogy." He paused. "You know, we skipped your site, so I have the point for this site. Are you ready?"

"But—"

"That's how it needs to be. I'll be careful. You with me?"

She nodded.

His watch said 10:55 and his line in the sand said they should be well inland by noon. He strode out towards the mill site, knowing that meeting their deadline wasn't likely, wondering if it was even possible.

They emerged from the dense, dripping foliage of recently planted trees into a small opening. Ahead lay a stand of older trees. These overshadowing trees limited the undergrowth, allowing them to pass quickly through.

The urge to check his watch was impossible to ignore. 11:00 now. From the moment this storm began developing, a fuse had been lit. Now the fuse burned short. Before the explosion of wind came, they had to find the girls and get out of here. He broke into a jog.

Jennifer caught up with him and grabbed his arm, pulling him to a stop. "Whoa, Lee. Remember, we need to be cautious as we move in."

His own words thrown back at him, but she was right. "Sorry. I'm worried about the wind. Over the next couple of hours, it will become a major factor in everything we do."

They reached a small stand of old-growth timber. It was dark under the forest canopy, but a lighter spot appeared less than a hundred yards ahead.

"That's the mill." He gestured towards it. "Let's stop for a second."

He took her hands. They were trembling.

He pulled her close.

Jennifer's whole body was shaking.

He kissed her forehead. "Are you OK?"

"I think so. Just so full of adrenaline that I'm shaking."

"Then it sounds like you're ready. Time to execute the plan."

They approached from the south, the least likely direction from which anyone would come. When they neared the clearing, he slowed and surveyed the site. The mill yard looked open, recently used.

Braithwaite had given them a good description.

Jennifer tapped his shoulder. She was pointing ahead, to their left, where thick bushes lined the edge of the trees.

"Good idea," he whispered in her ear.

They moved to the edge of the forest, leaving a single tier of the bushes for cover.

"Wait here, while I take a closer look."

"Be careful, Lee. No heroics, remember?"

He took her hand and squeezed it. "No heroics, I promise."

He pushed his head through a bush until he could see out the far side, and then jerked to a stop when the buildings came into view.

10

Lee watched the smoke rise from the chimney of the only enclosed building on the property. The down rush accompanying the heavy rain brought smoke from the chimney to the ground, where it spread out around the building. There, the synergism of the wind and the rain quickly washed the smoke away.

How convenient for the goons. No passersby could tell the mill was occupied unless they came into the site.

No vehicles visible in the area. Either they hid them, or they were in use.

The building had probably been a millwright's shop. It had only one window and one door, both on the front side of the building. A single glance in that window should provide enough evidence to bring the FBI.

But he would have to circle around to approach it from the windowless side bordering the forest. From there he could peek in the window and move back to the trees.

Now for the hard part, convincing Jennifer this wasn't a hero tactic.

How should he give her the news?

She stood a few feet back in the trees, eyes wide and expectant.

Two thumbs-up would tell it all.

Jennifer's smile widened as he saw his signal. She

bounced up and down on her toes and reached for his hands when he got closer to her. "Tell me what you saw."

"This has to be the place. There's an inhabited building with smoke coming out of the chimney. No vehicles in sight, but that's not surprising."

"So what do you think we should do next?"

"I need to get in close. Maybe I can listen through the walls and hear the girls. But most likely, I'll need to look through the window on the front of the building."

"No way." She shook her head so hard her hood fell down.

"Jenn," he adjusted her hood. "Before you get dogmatic on me, please listen. We can mitigate the risks here."

"OK, I'm listening."

"Come with me around to the south side of the mill, and you can see exactly what needs to be done."

She pulled back and shook her head again.

"All right. We'll drive to Lake Quinault, and you can call Peterson with the facts we have and try to convince him to send a SWAT team out here. Come on, let's go."

Would his bluff change her mind?

"Lee…" Jennifer ran to catch up with him as he walked back towards the car. She grabbed his arm. "Lee, wait. Show me what you've got in mind." Her expression contained fear, mixed with torment.

He hated to hurt her like this. It cut him to the quick. "I'm not trying to do anything risky. But we need evidence that Trader or his goons are there holding some girls. We need to see the girls, or at least, hear them. We don't have the option of going inside and searching for evidence."

"I know you're right. But—"

"She's still crying for help." The words just slipped out. He desperately wanted them back because he hadn't fought fairly. In trying to draw the confrontation to a quick close, he had only hurt Jennifer again.

She was on the verge of tears. She bit her lower lip, and then her body slumped in surrender. "OK, show me what we have to do."

He wanted to hold her, comfort her.

Jennifer backed away from him.

"I shouldn't have said that. I'll do anything if you'll forgive me...anything."

She stepped forward, wrapping her arms around him. "I know you didn't mean to hurt me. I should take you up on your offer, but I'd rather just forgive you."

Who was this woman? Certainly not the unforgiving Jennifer he'd met last March. This woman was the product of God's love which had free course to work in her heart for the past seven months.

He returned her embrace. "I really am sorry."

"You should be, but—" She put her hands on the back of his head, pushing his hood forward as she pulled his lips towards hers.

Jennifer gave him a kiss more intense than any he could remember. For a few seconds, nothing else existed in the world but the sweetness of her.

When their lips parted, she stepped back, revealing an incredibly beautiful woman whose eyes were wide with excitement, but fierce in their intensity.

They were both ready now. Maybe the timing really was perfect.

"Now you can show me what we need to do.

We've got some girls to save, before we all blow away."

The intensifying wind changed from a moan to a drone that howled at them from the treetops. The ominous, tornadic sound signaled the closing of their window of time. They would now battle deadly winds, as well as deadly people. When they reached a position south of the mill, they crept to the edge of the trees near the windowless end of the building.

The droning of the wind grew louder.

She wouldn't be able to hear him unless he placed his mouth next to her ear.

"The window is around the corner, so they can't see me when I approach. See the small bushes?" He pointed ahead. "They'll give me cover to within twenty-five yards of the side of the building."

Jennifer turned her mouth towards his ear and lifted her Smith & Wesson .38 from her coat pocket, and then slid it back in. "Lee, if you're spotted, I can cover you for a few seconds. But you'll need to get out fast if I start shooting. They'll have more firepower than we do."

They stood cheek-to-cheek, mouth-to-ear.

"I can get to the side of the shop without being seen. From there I can listen through the wall."

"And if you don't hear them?"

"Then I'll need to move to the front of the building and look in the window. If they spot me, I'll run back to a point in the trees to the east of you. If anyone comes out to take pot shots at me, pin them down for a few seconds while I round the corner of the building. That will give me enough cover to escape into the trees. Then we both should circle back to the car as fast as we can. I'll make sure to catch up to you before we reach it."

"And if you don't see the girls?"

"If they come after us, our agreement was we tell Peterson they've got the girls. That's the only logical conclusion to draw, especially if they start shooting. But if I look in and don't see the girls, and they don't come after us...there's nothing more we can do until they leave the building."

"That's not so, Lee. We can be on the beach by midnight—the place where they made the last exchange—and try to break it up."

Jennifer didn't understand what the beach would be like, why the two of them could not go there. "First, the wind has gotta die down, or nobody can be on the beach and survive. And second, I'll only agree to intervention if we can get Peterson to commit to bring an FBI team out here."

"If we need to convince Peterson, let me handle him. He treats me like a daughter. I can come up with something to get them out here."

"I've never seen the manipulative side of you. Where did that come from?"

"I got you to start courting me, didn't I?"

"You sure did. Now, are we ready to do this?"

"Yes. I'll hide behind the last tree and keep my .38 ready. We'll react to their response."

"Sounds good. You should see me move from the trees to the last bush in about sixty seconds. I love you, Jenn. There's nobody I'd rather have watching out for me."

She reached a wet hand inside his hood and cupped his cheek. "Promise me you'll be careful."

"I promise. See you, after I see the girls."

In a few seconds he reached a point even with the

end of the millwright's shop. By lining up his approach with the front wall of the building, he could watch the door, but couldn't be seen through the window.

Even knowing where Jennifer was, he couldn't see her through the rain and vegetation. *Good. She is as safe as possible.*

He ran to a position behind the lone bush that provided cover, less than twenty-five yards from the building.

The mill yard was still empty of vehicles and people. Time to run to the end of the shop. He stood.

The door of the shop swung open.

He dropped to his knees in the mud behind the bush.

The door shut.

He resumed breathing, not even aware he had stopped.

Something moved near Jennifer's location. Probably her aborted shot at the person who opened the door.

A few running steps brought him to the windowless side of the shop. This was also the windward side and water ran down the deteriorating cedar boards and into his ear when he pressed it against the outer wall.

Through the boards came an occasional crackle and pop of burning wood and a few muffled sounds of human voices. The words were indistinguishable, as was the sex of the speaker. Lee needed to look inside.

At the corner of the building, his pulse quickened as the danger of detection intensified.

He scanned the mill yard. There were numerous tire grooves in the mud. Vehicles had been stopping near the door of this building. But right now, there were no vehicles and no people. Time to move to the window.

The rough boards rasped against his back as he slid across them. Only a couple of feet to go.

He swiveled to face the window and inched his way to it, keeping his eyes focused on the door that lay beyond.

This was the moment they had been waiting for since Saturday morning. But looking in the window at this acute angle wasn't providing visibility into the interior of the room. He took a deep breath and slid his face in front of the window. A huddle of bodies—

The door flew open. A man stepped out carrying a pan.

Lee had to get to the trees before the pan was replaced by a gun. He swiveled to run. His feet slipped. He gasped, and then blew it all back out when his back struck the ground, knocking the breath out of him and sending his body sprawling only a few feet from the open door.

The pan clattered on the doorstep. The man whirled and leaped back into the building.

Lee kept his gaze locked on the doorway as he pulled his feet under him. But what had he seen in that brief look into the room? He tried to recall the image captured by his eyes, tried to record it permanently in his memory. Two or three bodies and heads with long hair.

He sprinted towards the trees, angling around the corner of the building.

The look on the man's face said he would return with a weapon. Now the man would have to come several feet out of the shop in order to shoot past the corner.

He needed four or five seconds.

Jennifer would have to buy him that time.

****

Jennifer held her breath as Lee looked in the window. Her hand gripped the .38. She gasped and pulled the gun from her pocket when the front door flew open.

No. Lee fell down by the door.

She stifled a scream, and then took a two-handed shooting stance, cocked the hammer, and aimed.

The man in the doorway disappeared.

Lee sprinted along his planned escape route. He was fifteen yards short of the trees when the man burst through the door holding an assault rifle.

She fired into the top of the doorway.

The man's weapon fired a single burst in automatic mode. The gun wasn't aimed at anything. The guy had panicked when her bullet splintered the boards above his head.

Her second shot cracked the top edge of the door frame.

The gunman jumped back into the building.

She kept her shots high to miss the girls, the girls she was now certain were inside.

Lee had said he would circle the mill to meet her. She rushed through the trees towards the car, praying he would catch up with her.

He overtook her with a hundred yards to go.

His heavy breathing sounded above the noise of the wind and rain.

"Did you…see them…Lee," she managed between breaths.

"Yeah, I think so…we need cell reception."

She pressed her key fob, unlocking the door before they reached the SUV.

"Drive to the gate. I'll open it for you." Lee sprinted the seventy-five yards down the old timber access road to the gate.

After she pulled through the gate, he jumped in, splattering mud on the carpet.

Normally she would have scolded him. But this wasn't a normal time.

"To Lake Quinault?"

"Yeah. It's the closest cell service." He reached for his seat belt.

She wheeled the car to the right.

"Doggone it!" The tires kept spinning as she tried to accelerate through water standing on the pavement.

"Take it easy, sweetheart." He fumbled with his seatbelt, unable to latch it.

She slammed on the brakes, sending Lee crashing into the dashboard as the big SUV slid to a stop.

"Not *that* easy, Jenn. Go!"

****

Lee saw a white SUV emerge through the rain and fog. It must have pulled out of the road to the mill.

The vehicle sped towards them.

Jennifer floored the accelerator and cranked the steering wheel hard left. The car spun a half doughnut on the highway. In a blur of hands and arms, Jennifer straightened the wheel. They accelerated down the road towards Kalaloch with the white SUV on their tail.

"Just like old times, huh, Lee? Except Trader's in

the white car and we're in the black one."

"How can you even think about—just go, Jenn!"

"My right coat pocket."

He reached in and pulled out Jennifer's .38. "Where's the safety?"

"It's a Smith & Wesson—no safety. Pull the trigger it shoots. I shot twice at the mill."

He looked at the gun in his hands. "So I have four shots left?"

"Three."

"A five shooter? This is no time for jokes."

"Three shots, Lee. Make them count. I forgot to bring my box of ammo. By the way, what's the plan?"

"We didn't make one for this contingency."

She shot him a glance. "Don't you think we ought to?"

"OK. You drive like crazy towards Forks, and I'll try to hold them off until we get cell reception."

"Not good enough. We could get cell reception, get Peterson on the line, and still get killed."

"OK. Here's the plan."

"I've heard that line before."

He ignored the reminder. "You try to stay ahead of them. Don't let them cut us off. If they get too close, I'll try to blast out their windshield. If we can hold them off until we contact the Forks police, we'll be OK."

"What if they start shooting...like those goons last March?"

The road spray behind them formed a swirling cloud of mist.

"The storm will help us. As much as I'd like to, I probably can't take out the shooter."

"Hang on. No telling what I may have to do."

"I've heard that before, too." He had, but this was different from last March. Much different.

Rain still came down in sheets. It built up on the road surface.

Her SUV slid to the left. Jennifer pulled the wheel to the left. She over-steered. Her vehicle swung like a pendulum from left to right until it reached equilibrium.

"Well, that's the limit. At fifty miles-per-hour we start hydroplaning. I hope Trader and his goons in that white SUV are having the same problem."

"They're keeping up with us. But so far, they're not sticking any guns out the windows. I'm not sure how to interpret that. "

A short way ahead, the highway turned ninety degrees and ran parallel to the beach.

Jennifer cut to the inside of the sharp turn.

The vehicle skidded out of control. It crossed the centerline and slid sideways into the left lane.

She coaxed her SUV out of the slide, regaining control at the left edge of the roadway, and then eased the vehicle back to the right lane. "Sorry."

"Are you OK?"

"As good as I can be."

"You don't look as panicky as you did seven months ago."

"It's called experience. I'm going to try to open up a lead while the road is straight."

They sailed past Kalaloch at sixty miles-per-hour, on the verge of losing control. The windshield wipers slapped out an allegro tempo, but couldn't clear the driving rain from the glass.

At the first gap in the trees, a gust of wind pushed them onto the right shoulder.

Jennifer slowed and coaxed the vehicle back into the middle of the lane.

The white SUV took advantage of the wind gust and closed within a few car lengths.

"It's almost noon. We're nearing the onset of the hurricane-strength winds," Lee said. "Watch the gaps. A big gust could push us into the ditch. Maybe flip us."

"I would drive in the left lane, but I can't see far enough ahead."

"Hug the centerline and brace yourself for the gusts. That's all you can do. I'm watching the guys on our tail. So far they're just sticking close, not sticking out guns."

"Please keep the gun ready, Lee. They won't wait forever."

A muffled gunshot sounded. The ripping sound of lead tearing through metal came from inches above his head.

"Lee, what's going on? I don't see the shooter."

"Oh, no! They have a sunroof—rather a rain roof. A lot of rain in his face, but he can aim better up there than hanging out a window."

"I'll keep him busy," Jennifer replied. "You take him out."

Jennifer slowed, but swerved from side to side, trying to spoil the gunman's aim without losing control. Her tactic seemed to be working.

The gunman hadn't fired a second burst.

"I've got to stop him, or we won't make it much farther. I'll try the windshield."

"Remember, you've only got three shots."

"I'm well aware of that." He powered his window down, and then leaned out, offering his head as a target. He prayed he was hidden by the heavy spray created by the wheels and the turbulent wake of the vehicle.

The white SUV drew nearer.

Lee aimed for the windshield.

The gunman popped up from the sunroof.

Lee squeezed the trigger. His shot went into the top of the windshield.

The gunman's hands flew to his face.

The rifle disappeared through the rain, the spray, and the fog.

"I hit the top of the windshield. The glass sprayed his face. I think he dropped his rifle."

"Good job. But I'll bet they have other guns."

"If so, they might only be pistols. They'll need to get closer to use them, but that gives me a better shot."

"There's the Ruby Beach sign. I've got an idea. Hang on tight. Really tight."

What was she up to? A sharp right turn lay directly ahead, and then a hairpin turn angled back the other direction. He waited for her to slow down.

She didn't.

"Our spray is killing their visibility." Her gaze darted from the windshield to the side mirror. "I'm going to sucker them into the turn."

"Jenn, please don't overdo the sucker part."

Her SUV flew into the curve on the right edge of the pavement at much too high a speed. She didn't turn the wheel or slow until she reached the turn. It was a calculated risk, but a clever tactic.

Using the full width of the road, all the way to the far left shoulder, she would gain about fifty yards of paved braking room. At this speed, was that enough?

When she entered the turn, she shifted down to low range, throwing Lee forward in his seat.

Smart girl. No brake lights to warn them.

Jennifer pushed hard on the brakes.

He prayed her vehicle's tires and its anti-lock braking system were up to the task.

They slowed, and then went into a slide. Jennifer corrected for the slide but over-steered. They skidded back to the other side. One quick correction and Jennifer had them sliding straight again. But the drop-off beyond the left edge of the roadway rushed at them. Jennifer held the wheel straight as they continued to slow.

"Jenn, no!"

She pulled the wheel to the right and hit the gas. With wheels spinning, the rear of the car swung to the left. She pulled her foot from the gas pedal leaving them safe on the inside of the coming hairpin turn.

Behind them, the white SUV spun end-for-end.

Lee lost sight of it before he could tell how it fared.

At best, the thugs would stay on the road, probably facing the wrong direction. At worst, they'd roll down the steep bank.

Jennifer had bought them at least a half-mile lead with twenty-nine miles to reach Forks and twenty-six to reach cell range.

"Good job, sweetheart. Now let's leave them in the dust."

"Dust? You've got to be kidding."

He looked at the sheets of windblown rain and the cloud of spray behind them, still wondering about the fate of the white SUV.

11

Lee's arm hung down to the floorboard like a wet noodle with a revolver hanging on it.

What Jennifer had just accomplished was incredible.

But they would need more than witty heroics to make it to Forks alive.

Jennifer blew out a blast of air. "Why do you suppose there was no more gunfire?"

"I'm guessing there were only two people in the car and only one shooter, because he stopped after I shot at him. Maybe I blinded him with shrapnel, or hit him with a ricocheting bullet. Regardless, you need to—"

"I know. Keep our lead all the way to Forks."

The loud smack of a bullet hitting the back of Jennifer's SUV drove him down in his seat like a nine-pound sledge. "Make that temporarily blinded him. Tell me when there's a right turn coming. That'll give me a good shot."

"I won't know until we enter it. I can only see about thirty—we entered it."

He powered his window down.

The white vehicle was off to his right.

He aimed for the windshield and squeezed off the shot.

The SUV fell back out of sight, obscured by the driving rain and the heavy road spray.

"Where did they go? I can't see them in my mirror."

"Dropped back. I hit their windshield, but I think we just slowed them down. We've got a bit of lead now."

"Check the bullets. We can't afford any one-off errors."

He pushed the latch and inspected the open cylinder. "There's only one left."

"If they get close again, you better use it. We've been lucky so far. They haven't hit anything vital."

"You mean like us?"

"Or our gas tank, or tires, or—"

"I get the point. I'll shoot before they do."

"Please do."

****

Jennifer concentrated on navigating the wet, winding road for several miles. When they approached the last straight stretch before reaching the Hoh River, a white, ghost-like image of a vehicle appeared in the side mirror. "I think I saw them. I'm guessing they'll try to stop us on the bridge."

She would have to reach the narrow bridge before the white vehicle. How hard could she press on the accelerator? Only a slight push and the vehicle hydroplaned. "They're closer now. But I'll make sure we beat them to the bridge."

"Please do. Last bullet, Jenn. Do you want to hit the brakes and let me have a really close shot?"

"I don't want to do that. They would get a close shot, too, and they're not leaning out trying to shoot behind them."

"OK. Let's pray this one hits right in front of the driver."

When the white SUV moved within three car lengths, Lee leaned out the window, aimed, and fired. The undulating road bounced, spoiling his aim.

Their pursuers didn't fall back. Instead, they sped up.

"I missed. They're still gaining. It's all up to you now."

"Thanks. I didn't need any more pressure."

"I trust you, Jenn. We both trust God. We need to lose them. So go for it."

"That's easy to say from the passenger's seat."

The Hoh River Bridge lay in front of them. Jennifer accelerated towards it, but the car fishtailed. She pulled the gear shift down to low range, decelerating as they crossed the narrow bridge.

"The road goes right. Then the big bend back to the left."

"I know." She slid safely through the dogleg right, shoved the gear shift back to drive, and hit the gas when they entered the horseshoe bend.

"There's a passing lane up the hill. They'll try something there, for sure."

"I know that, too."

Partway into the curve, the road began its ascent out of the river gorge.

"Lee, they're coming around us in the passing lane."

"Cut him off!"

"I'm trying!"

Her battle for position seemed like a slow-motion final lap in a car race. She was in the lead, but wasn't at all sure she had the fastest car.

When the road finally straightened, they were still climbing, but the white SUV had pulled alongside. Then, it moved ahead and nudged their car.

She anticipated the maneuver and bumped back.

Neither vehicle won the duel on the first joust.

The white SUV driver completely disregarded the possibility of oncoming traffic and stayed in the left lane after the passing lane ended. His gamble was paying off. Their driver engaged her SUV with its side, steadily shoving them off the right side of the road.

"Hoh Rainforest Road!" She jammed on the brakes.

Her maneuver disengaged the other vehicle. They slid onto the small, paved road that snaked nearly twenty miles into the Hoh Rainforest.

The brake lights of the white SUV disappeared into the rain and road spray as it overshot the turn.

The goons would turn around and pursue them.

Of that, she was certain.

****

They were safe, for the moment.

But Lee knew this road. Where it ended, danger began.

More danger than just a white SUV.

"Jenn, you just picked the rainiest spot in North America."

"Sorry. I didn't exactly have a choice."

"There's a dead end in eighteen miles."

"I know. I said I'm sorry."

Tears welled in her eyes. This smart, tough girl— the one who was all heart—was losing it, and he had only made things worse, like a stupid jerk.

A freaked out jerk, but still a stupid jerk.

"Jennifer." He draped an arm over her shoulders. "If I could pick anyone in the world to have behind the wheel in this situation, I'd take you. I love you. I've seen what you can do. Let's beat those idiots to the end of the road. If we can hack our way through all of the moss, we'll run up the trail and lose them on the mountain."

Jennifer grabbed his hand and kissed it. She gripped the wheel, clenched her jaw, and mashed the accelerator to the floor.

12

Lee ran through several escape scenarios as he watched Jennifer navigate the paved section of the Upper Hoh Rainforest Road.

She skillfully drove through the narrow, winding portion leading to the road's end at the Hall of Mosses.

A crash and a thump came from behind them. A large, cedar tree now blocked the road, evidence of the arrival of hurricane-strength winds.

Would the tree block the White SUV?

He powered his window down and stuck his head out to survey the situation. "It looks like they can drive around the tree, but it'll buy us a little more time. Hurry. There's the exhibit building."

Jennifer drove to the far end of the parking area and braked. She pulled up the hood of her raincoat and grabbed the keys.

He jumped out of the passenger door and raced to her side. He didn't want her to face any part of this ordeal alone.

Which branch of the trail followed the Hoh River? He wasn't sure.

Two hundred yards behind them, a white SUV wove its way through a stand of cedars as it bypassed the fallen tree.

"Let's go. They're closer than we thought."

She took his hand and they loped along the lower fork of the trail.

Louder than the droning of the wind and the splattering of raindrops, a deep, ominous rumble came from the direction of the river.

When they rounded a bend in the trail, the source of the noise lay a few yards down the trail.

Lord, help us.

The deluge dumped on the rainforest by the Pineapple Express tried to obey the law of gravity, using the Hoh River as its conduit. The water tore through the earth and vegetation like Niagara Falls turned on edge.

The trail became a raging torrent fifty yards ahead. The raging torrent became an earth-eating monster, roaring as it devoured a foot of riverbank every few seconds, exposing the roots of the towering Sitka spruce lining the riverbank.

Trees normally yards from the stream swayed in the fierce gusts of wind, and then gave up their claim on the soil when the remaining roots cracked sharply. Overcome by the raw forces at work, the trees fell, accompanied by a cacophonic symphony composed by a demon.

Or maybe, the devil himself.

Jennifer clung to him when the next tree died with a piercing crack. It fell with a deep boom—so deep Lee could feel it reverberate in his chest.

The crown of the tree splashed into the river, spraying water fifty yards to the southwest, into the wind. The howling gale blew it straight back at them.

The water stung his face, but Jennifer's face was buried in his chest.

Lee stood, staring in wonder at the sheer force of the wind and the roaring water until Jennifer looked up at him and shouted, "What now?"

Lee cupped his hands around his mouth and spoke into her ear. "Losing them on the mountain is out. We've got only a minute or so until they arrive with their guns."

He studied the fall of the next tree. "Jenn, are you willing to gamble your life on my gut feeling as a meteorologist?"

"If I don't, we're dead anyway. That's no gamble. I trust you."

****

"Only God or a madman could come up with that, Lee."

Despite their circumstances, her comment struck him as funny. "Well, it's clear what you think about me."

She clung to him as if she wanted her body to merge with his. "I know we have to try it. But please stay close, really close, to me. I'm not sure I can do this."

"I won't let go. Let's move behind the bushes so they can't see us."

His watch said 1:30.

Another big spruce crashed into the river.

He timed the falling of the tree with his second hand.

The teeth of the windstorm were now biting the Olympic Peninsula.

Noon on Sunday.

So much for my line in the sand.

Whenever Trader or his goons rounded the bend, they would be mesmerized for a few seconds by the fury on display in front of them.

He counted on that brief delay, the difference between life and death for Jennifer and him.

He pulled Jennifer's hood back, exposing her ear. "When I pull you, we're going to run behind those bushes. We'll hide there until the right moment."

She glanced at the river and her whole body shook. This was her worst fear, a phobia about wild, raging water.

"That's right beside the river. I can't do that."

He pulled her closer, until they were standing cheek-to-cheek and mouth-to-ear. "It's the only way, Jenn. And we believe God is with us."

"OK. I just won't look at the river."

"While we're behind the bushes, the bank will be eroding away. The river may get close to us, but don't move—"

"Stop! I don't want to hear any more. I don't want to think about it, either. You may think I'm crazy, but please, kiss me...now...before we do this."

How could she even think about—? The fear in her eyes cut him deeply. Nobody was visible on the trail. He kissed Jennifer.

Obviously, she didn't want the kiss to end.

He pulled his lips from hers, but held her close. "I love you, Jenn. You can do this. He's given you courage, and He's given us each other."

"Lee, remember the good times—"

"But this isn't one of them."

Two figures appeared at the bend in the trail.

"Here they come. Get ready."

The rapid erosion had assaulted the next tree within the river's reach. The wind howled even louder. This had to be the right time.

He moved his mouth close to her ear. "Please,

God, protect us."

The raging river had exposed the entire base of the big Sitka spruce. The tree twisted and groaned from the force of the water blasting through its roots. Like the others before it, the tree leaned over the river, into the wind.

Lee locked his hand around Jennifer's and pulled her with him. After they stepped into the open, he paused, and then pulled Jennifer with him to the bushes at the torrent's edge. They slipped behind them.

One of the men pointed towards them.

Good. The goons knew where they were.

They had made their move. They were in position.

In a moment the tree would fall. When it did, he prayed the big spruce would fall between the other men and them.

A cracking sound split the roar of the next wind gust. The towering spruce twisted, snapping its roots, and began its fatal plunge into the river. Another gust hit the crown of the tree, spinning it halfway around.

This is what he had prayed for.

Almost.

Now the tree fell directly towards Jennifer and him. They had no room to retreat. In a few seconds, the ground where they stood would be in the river. Ahead were two gunmen.

Jennifer closed her eyes.

He was thankful she couldn't see what was coming.

Another gust hit the falling tree, pushing it more in line with the wind, but still dangerously close to them.

With the foot of a giant, the wind stomped the tree

to the ground as if it was merely a weed. The spruce hit with a deep, earth-shaking boom and a splash.

Tips of branches stung their hands and arms. The tree's impact broke the earth loose beneath their feet.

They needed to run. But the crumbling soil made running impossible. With the sod, they slid backwards into the river.

Lee lunged forward on his knees, dragging Jennifer.

The ground around them dissolved into brown liquid and merged with the river.

With the current ripping at his knees, and then at his thighs, the river would claim their bodies in another second.

A foot away, a large branch waved in the wind.

Could he reach it? He lunged. His fingertips curled around it. He clawed his fingers into a hand hold.

Jennifer's wrist slipped from his other hand.

Their fingers locked.

He pulled on her, and then grabbed again, catching her wrist.

He squeezed her wrist and she squeezed his, while their bodies skipped along the current like a fishing lure pulled too quickly through the water.

He couldn't lose Jennifer now. Another surge of adrenaline hit and he pulled both of them into the crown of the tree.

Another branch, one above solid ground, hung almost within reach.

He lunged, dragging Jennifer, and grabbed the branch. His arm strength nearly gone now, Lee planted one foot on solid ground and pushed with his leg, simply trying to maintain his hold on Jennifer's wrist.

Both feet were on the riverbank. He hauled Jennifer up, and then fell with her away from the water.

They crawled forward several feet.

Lee collapsed, breathing deeply, thankful it was air and not water going into his lungs.

He looked up. Everything up to a height of twenty feet was hidden from the men chasing them by the crown of the fallen tree.

The words of Isaiah rang true. God *was* a shelter in the time of storm.

Thank you.

Barely visible through the branches, the other men appeared reluctant to move towards the raging river and the falling trees.

Thanks to the uprooted tree, the evidence would indicate that their bodies were gone, swept out to sea by the torrent.

Now they needed to move.

He kept his hold on Jennifer, using the fallen tree to shield them. Soon their shield grew into many trees and bushes.

He didn't have to worry about falling timber. They were moving on the windward side of the tallest trees, where the howling wind rode over the shorter deciduous trees.

A green blanket now coated the vegetation. The Hall of Mosses must be only a short distance away, and beyond it, the car.

He took a deep breath, smiled, and glanced heavenward. They had cheated death...with a little help from a Friend in high places.

And Jennifer had faced her worst fear, the raging water phobia. She still stared down at the ground, following as he pulled her along. Endured her worst fear was a better description.

"You can look up now, Jenn. Grab your car keys."

"I don't even want to know what happened back there. Let's just thank God we're alive and get out of here."

"What happened back there is quite a story. If you—"

"Save it for later." Jennifer pointed ahead through moss-covered trees. "There's the car."

"There are *both* vehicles." His mouth stretched into a smile, and his hand, fishing inside his pocket, grabbed his locking-blade knife. "In case they're closer than we think don't start the engine until I hop in."

"What are you up to?"

"Murder."

When he bent low beside the rear tire of the white SUV, anger at the ruthless attempt on their lives drove a savage blow, plunging the knife deep into the tire's heart. The tire popped, hissed, and died.

He jerked the knife, creating a long laceration. Now to kill the front tire. The knife went handle-deep into the tire. A pop and a hiss drained the air and a little more of his rage.

The passenger door of Jennifer's car popped open as he ran to it.

Behind him, the white car listed badly to one side.

He slid in beside Jennifer.

She hit the ignition.

The SUV started.

Thankfully, the traffickers were more focused on killing them than killing their vehicle.

She coaxed the car around the parking area.

Would there be more downed trees? Could they

even reach the highway? He needed to stop worrying. Hadn't they just been delivered from certain death?

Rain still fell, though it was no longer a downpour. But the wind continued its fierce assault on the vegetation. The whole forest seemed to dance wildly like a mob of demons to the rhythm of Satan's whims. Satan's whims? Perhaps.

But then, God had conquered Satan.

But I wish He'd put him completely out of business.

Jennifer braked to a stop when they rounded a bend.

The cedar tree across the road blocked their path of retreat, but muddy tracks marked the path of escape. She followed them.

After rounding the tree, Jennifer set a fast pace down the Hoh River Road. Her hood was down.

He looked at her face.

Her large, intense brown eyes pored over the road ahead. The back part of her long, dark hair lay on her shoulders, while the wet tresses in front clung to her cheeks. She was absolutely incredible.

"I'll keep my eyes on the trees in case we need to dodge one. But, Jenn, if I'm ever in a tight spot and need a getaway driver, I want you at the wheel."

"Where did you learn to slash tires like that? Did you belong to some gang?"

"No. It's hereditary. My great-great granddad came from England. His name was Jack."

"You're not funny, Lee. I'm a woman and—"

"We're getting married. It's about time you confirmed that."

13

Jennifer pushed the car hard to reach Highway 101. Each mile she put between them and the goons felt like a hundred. The terror-filled events a few minutes and a few miles behind her now seemed more like a nightmare than reality, a reality she feared might give her nightmares. "At least I have one consolation, Lee. I didn't look at the river when—"

"Go, Jenn! Hit the gas!"

She pushed the pedal to the floor. "What's—"

A piercing crack sounded, and then a thump on the back of the car. In its death plunge, a cedar tree's branches brushed the vehicle.

Still in panic mode, she kept the gas pedal to the floor. Her gaze froze on the rearview mirror and the reflection of the tree.

Lee jammed both hands against the dash. "Slow down!"

A sharp left turn lay only a few yards ahead. She wouldn't be able to slow enough. She tapped the brakes, cranked the wheel to the left, and pressed the accelerator. They flew safely through, though she had barely slowed for the turn.

"Like Dale Earnhardt." Lee exhaled loudly. "But you can slow—"

"Dale who?"

"A racecar driver. NASCAR."

"I'll assume that was a compliment. But that was

close. Is the wind still picking up?"

"It sure looks like it. From here to 101, we need to watch the south side of the road for anything falling."

"You watch for falling trees. I'll look ahead for anything that's already down."

"Sounds like a plan. And, Jenn?"

"Yes?"

"We stranded them for quite a while. We need to get to Forks in one piece and make that phone call to Peterson."

She slowed, pulled her right hand off the wheel, and squeezed Lee's arm. "I'm sorry. It feels like my heart is pumping pure adrenaline instead of blood. I'm still shaking."

"It did get a little intense back there. The tree didn't help matters." He was grinning.

"A little intense?" She scowled at him. "I never want to see the Hoh River again."

"You did great. We're almost to the highway, but we should approach it cautiously, you know, in case those guys have friends."

"OK. You check your side, and I'll check mine."

"Nothing towards Forks except a small tree down in the left lane," Lee said.

To the south there were no vehicles visible from the Hoh River Road to the turn at the edge of the bend. "It's clear my way."

They were now headed to Forks, towards cell reception and a phone conversation with Agent Peterson at the FBI field office in Seattle.

"Lee, it's 2:30. Trader could deliver the girls in less than ten hours, any time after midnight. We need—"

"There's not going to be any exchange tonight. For more than a hundred miles out, the sea will be so rough no boats will enter that area. The shore, well, no one would survive a walk on the beach near Hole-in-the-Wall during the next eighteen hours."

"We found the mill, and we got away, so Trader will have to move the girls immediately. I'll bet he's furious."

"He's probably roaring as loud as the Hoh River. But you're right, and I'll bet he has some sort of shelter—a staging spot—near the exchange point, north of Rialto Beach. That's probably where he'll move them."

"I think I know where that spot is."

"Have you been holding out on me?" No more grins. He was frowning at her.

"No." She sighed. "Some fragmented thoughts are finally jelling."

"Would you care to elaborate?"

"I think I told you about a fork in the trail to the scanner site." She paused. "Twice recently, I've heard strange sounds coming from the branch to the north. I thought it was some animal. Once I thought it was a bear and ran all the way back to the parking area."

"A holding place. That makes sense. It could be why your equipment picked up the call. They were close by."

"I've seen footprints along the path—footprints much larger than mine. I was worried someone might've vandalized my scanner site. Then, there's the van."

"You've never mentioned a van."

"Twice I spotted a gray van in the Dickey River Bridge parking area. It wasn't a typical fisherman's vehicle, and the windows were dark. You know how we often play road tag with other vehicles on that stretch near Kalaloch? The last time I drove over, I played road tag for a few miles with that van from the Hoh River Bridge to Kalaloch. Then the van sped up. When I got to the long, straight stretch a few miles below Kalaloch, it disappeared. That's near the mill site where they're holding the girls."

"So you think it turned in at the mill?"

"There are too many coincidences, too many details fit that scenario. The first time I saw the van coincides with the exchange my scanner recorded."

"I think you should mention it to Peterson. If you're right, Trader will move the girls there today. A van with dark windows would be perfect for transporting three or four girls through Forks."

"Now that we know there's trafficking out here, it's actually pretty easy to start putting the pieces together. But when you're not expecting something so ugly in a place that's so beautiful, you would never suspect anything."

"You've sized it up pretty well. But there are some corollaries to your logic."

"Corollaries like?"

"Like…Trader can't operate at any location very long or someone might do what you just did and get suspicious."

"That's another reason we've got to stop Trader and Boatman here and now—stop the entire operation and nail them. Otherwise, they'll simply move to a new location and continue selling girls."

"Correction, Jenn. That's another reason Peterson and the FBI have to stop Trader and Boatman. We're lucky to be alive after our first encounter."

She didn't reply to his comment. But a plan formed in her mind, one Lee would surely try to veto.

"My phone says I have cell service. But it's only a couple of minutes to the store. I'll stop there." Jennifer parked in the supermarket's lot and handed her phone to Lee. "Do you want to call Peterson?"

"No way. After what you did to him on Friday, you can clean up your own mess. I'm surprised he hasn't called you already."

She opened the missed-calls log. "Uh, he did call. Fifteen times since Friday."

"Great. He's going to be hopping mad."

"Here goes. You better pray this goes well. We need Peterson out here now." She punched the speakerphone so he could listen.

"And you had better tread softly, Jennifer, or he's liable to have the police put us in protective custody."

Peterson answered on the second ring.

"Jennifer, where are you and why didn't you return my calls?"

"We've been out of cell-phone range most of the time and a little preoccupied."

"A little preoccu—"

"Peterson, we found where they're holding the girls."

"Are you and Lee OK?"

"Yes, we're fine."

"And you actually saw the girls?"

"Well, actually it was Lee who saw the girls, before…"

"Before what? Tell me everything."

"Well, there was some shooting—only enough to get us away safely."

A loud expletive burst from the speakers.

"Same word he used before. Probably the only cuss word Peterson knows." Lee whispered, grimacing.

"They gave chase, didn't they? Of course they did. They would have to stop you two."

"But they didn't catch us. Well, almost, but the falling tree—"

"I don't want to hear any more of the details, Jennifer. Where are you two and are you safe?"

"We're in Forks and we're safe."

"Then where are the traffickers?"

"We think they're stuck on the Hoh River Road, where Lee slashed their tires."

Peterson roared again, exhausting his one-word, cursing vocabulary three times over. "I don't know what to do with you, Jennifer. But you need to go to the Forks police station and tell them everything. Then you need to stay there until the team arrives. I'm calling them to assemble as we speak."

Lee leaned hard into the passenger-side door with his palms out, protecting his face.

"We can't do that. Trader will have to move the girls now, and I think he has a holding location off Mora Road, near Rialto Beach. Lee and I have—"

"You and Lee have to back off and let the police take over."

"And when is that going to happen, Peterson?" One more stupid demand and she might tell Special Agent Peterson that he wasn't so special, using a word from *his* vocabulary.

"As soon as the FBI team arrives."

"And when do you plan to arrive?" Her voice rose to a crescendo. "We're running out of time. These girls are supposed to be sold sometime tonight."

"It's 3:00 now. I can get the team together by 5:00, but you're having hurricane-force winds out there, so we can't fly the team out. We'll have to use our vans. With the weather, we can't possibly make it until 11:00 tonight, maybe later, if there are a lot of trees down. Those are just the facts, Jennifer. You're going to have to live with them."

"If you aren't here by 10:00, we're going in to disrupt the exchange. Those are just the facts, Peterson. You're going to have to live with them." As Jennifer terminated the call, she interrupted another ear-splitting expletive from Peterson.

"Hey, Peterson does know more than one cuss word. But frankly, I prefer the other one." Lee put a hand on her shoulder.

Jennifer started the car. She drove out of the parking lot, turning towards the center of town. Instead of driving to the police station, she parked on the street across from the sporting goods store. "Lee, wait here. I'll be right back."

"What are you up to?"

"Trying to keep us alive," she replied as she slid out. She went straight to the counter inside.

"Can I help you?" the clerk asked.

"Do you have ammo for a Smith & Wesson .38?"

"Sure. But I only have the standard shells. No hollow points or—"

"Standard shells will be fine."

"Is everything OK? You look like you need some help."

"I'm all out of ammo. Forgot to buy some after my last trip to the firing range."

"Well, here you go. Only one box?"

"That'll do, and thanks again." She handed him a twenty.

The shopkeeper cocked his head. "You look

familiar. Have I seen you here before?"

"I made several trips out here this past summer." She hoped he didn't remember the news coverage from last March. Out here, anyone, even this man, might be the enemy.

"Maybe that's it. Well, you take care out there. This is a nasty storm. Highway 101 is blocked both north and south of town from downed trees. The National Weather Service says to stay home unless you live in an area that floods."

"Thanks for the info."

Jennifer went out the door and hopped into the SUV. She tossed Lee the box of ammunition. "We're not going to run out of ammo this time. Highway 101 is blocked in both directions. We didn't get to town any too soon. Peterson's going to be later than he thought."

While Lee pushed cartridges into her Smith & Wesson, she drove northbound through town.

When she crossed the Calawah River Bridge, heading out of town, Lee gave her a frown and a glance.

"What happened to going to the police station? You need to tell me what you're thinking."

"We have to check out the trail I told you about." She hoped for his cooperation. "There's a building or some kind of shelter along that trail. The girls may be there now while Trader waits for the wind to die down."

"Right now Trader's probably walking down Highway 101 looking for a ride or a couple of new tires. Besides that, he's blocked by trees."

"Don't underestimate a man who would risk so much to sell girls into slavery. He's clever and ruthless."

Lee was quiet for a moment. "A CB radio. Do you recall anything like an antenna on their SUV?"

"Yes. There was some kind of antenna on it. It stuck straight up from the center of the back and it whipped around in the wind."

"That sounds like a radio antenna. I was too busy looking for the shooter to notice. But if Trader could contact his partners by radio, maybe whoever drives that van could...Jenn, he could have wheels again. He could still be preparing to exchange the girls when the weather breaks."

"That's what I'm thinking. All the more reason for us to head towards Rialto Beach."

"Don't even think about setting foot on the beach during this kind of storm. It's sure death—thirty-foot waves full of that driftwood we walk on in the summer."

"I didn't mean actually going onto the beach. We can hide my car in Mora Campground and walk to the Dickey River Bridge. It's only two or three hundred yards below the campground. If they're using my trail, there'll be a vehicle in the parking area, or at least, some very recent tracks. They couldn't have moved the girls more recently than an hour ago, even if they have a radio to call for help."

"Suppose there *is* a vehicle parked there. What then?" He was obviously looking for a way to dissuade her.

"If there's a vehicle there, we have only one choice. We sneak down the trail and find where they're hiding the girls. Then we make sure they can't complete the exchange before Peterson gets here."

"That's crazy. That whole area is on a ridge above

the beach. With these winds, trees could be crashing down like bowling pins along that entire ridgeline. Besides, Petersen won't be able to find us, and it will be dark in an hour or less with these heavy clouds."

"But I told Peterson where I thought the holding spot was located." She paused. "OK, look. If we can locate the girls quickly, we can drive to the Quillayute Airport. It's only five or six miles away. There has to be a landline phone at the weather station or at the lodge just down the road from it. We can call Peterson with the updated information about the girls' location."

"We can also get ourselves and the girls killed by going in and being detected. Trader knows about us now. What you're proposing is more dangerous than checking mill sites. Besides, he might kill the girls and run if he thinks his operation has been compromised."

"If we can't rescue the girls...if I can't rescue them, I couldn't live with myself."

"You can't think that way. It's not true." His hand reached for her.

"Yes it is." She brushed the tears from her eyes. "I've been reading about what happens to these girls. Most are sold into sexual slavery. Some girls are sold to men in Saudi Arabia—men who want a twelve- or thirteen-year-old wife to add to their collection, or should I say, harem. Then there are those rich princes. They pick a girl and fly them out of the country in their private jets. They keep the girls in their palace compounds, which the local authorities won't enter, and the girls are never seen again."

"Jennifer, listen to me. With these winds we can't stroll through a forest of old-growth timber. If we get killed or even injured, we can't help anybody."

"They're going to take the girls down the trail to

the holding location. If the girls can be taken down the trail, we can go, too. We have to."

Lee wiped a tear from her cheek. "I must be insane to let you talk me into this. OK, here's the deal."

She had won the concession she needed.

He was right about the possible cost. But if they were doing what was good and right, would God really exact such a cost from them?

What book was Lee reading aloud to her when she made him stop that day? Fox's Book of Martyrs. People did die. Sometimes *because* they did what was right.

"We'll go as far as the parking area to see if the van or any other vehicles are there," Lee said. "If we don't see any vehicles, we can check for tracks."

"We have three scenarios to plan for. What we do if we see—"

"No, Jenn." Lee's shoulders and voice dropped in resignation. "We have only one scenario. We just go down the trail and try to find the holding location. Regardless, we'll assume someone's there."

"So if we find the holding spot, we wait there?"

"Yes. We wait there. And if we don't find it, we hurry back to Forks, do a core dump of everything we know for the Forks police, and then wait for the FBI to show up."

She took Lee's hand. "I love you, Lee Brandt. I would do almost anything for you, but I can't abandon these girls. Please understand."

"I would do anything for you, too, Jenn. Even something as insane as what I'm about to do."

She lifted his hand to her lips and kissed it.

He looked upward through the top of the windshield. "Lord, I'm an idiot. If that's a sin, please forgive me."

Jennifer said nothing and kept driving, her mind working overtime on scenarios.

How could she park near Mora Road, but keep her car hidden? After turning into Mora Campground, she followed a camping loop that circled less than thirty yards from the road. She left the car near the back of a long, narrow, campsite.

Nobody could see the SUV unless they walked into this spot. But tonight, no sane person would be out. What did that say about her? She shoved the questions about insanity from her mind.

Her engagement ring. What if...?

I'll leave my ring here for safekeeping.

The small elastic pocket on the driver's seat would hide it well. Her gun and cell phone were tucked in her pocket, and her raincoat was zipped up. "Lee, are you ready?"

"As ready as I can be. We're going down the road to the parking area first, right?"

"Yes, but we need to make sure no one sees us on the road. We'll hide if anyone or any vehicle approaches."

They stepped out of the SUV into the light rain. The wind howled through the treetops, treetops which were bent sharply to the northeast and pulsating wildly with the passage of each series of turbulent wind gusts.

Lee gently wrapped her in his arms. "I love you, Jenn, and—"

"I love you too, Lee." She returned his embrace. "There's no other person I would want with me on an evening like this."

Lee lifted her chin, looked down into her intense brown eyes. He kissed her. "Let's be really careful. We stand to lose so much if—"

""Hush." Jennifer put her hand on his lips. "We have so much to gain. We can't afford failure tonight. Some young girls need us."

A piercing crack high above was followed by a loud crash somewhere nearby. Pieces of trees were breaking off and smashing onto the brush below.

She pressed tightly against Lee. "I'm going to need your strength tonight. The wind is more intimidating than I thought."

"It's not just intimidating. It's extremely dangerous. Clubs and spears can rain down on us. Whole trees can be halfway down before we see them falling. I'll watch the trees as much as I can. You watch for people. Now, tell me again what we do if we see any vehicles in the parking area."

"If no one is around, we skirt the parking area, staying close to cover, while we check it out. Then we cross the bridge and get on the trail. When we find the fork that branches to the north, we head down it and look for the holding location."

The drone of the wind suddenly intensified into a shriek.

Lee's head jerked upward. After a few seconds, he placed his mouth close to her ear. "OK, what if there are people in the parking area?"

"We hide and wait for a chance to follow them."

"Last question. What if the people are armed and they're guarding the parking area?"

"We...let's pray that doesn't happen."

"You're right about the praying part. But if it does happen, we've got to slip out of there quietly and get help."

"Only after we wait long enough to determine

they really are guarding the place. Now, are we ready to go?" Jennifer stepped into the bushes at the back of the campsite and worked her way to the edge of Mora Road. *Lord, please don't allow me to be a fool.*

There were no vehicles in sight. She prayed there would be no vehicles on the roadway for their entire two-hundred-yard walk down it.

A short distance from the parking area, they moved into the brush on the right side of the road.

The howling wind forced her to speak directly into Lee's ear. "It's about fifty yards to the parking area. Let's stay on the edge of the bushes while we move in."

Two minutes later Jennifer pushed her head through a bush to survey the parking lot. She gasped.

"What is it?"

"The gray van is there."

"Is anyone around?"

"No. They must have already taken the girls down the trail. Let's check out the van before we go."

Though the windows were darkly tinted, a short look through the side window of the van confirmed that the girls were not inside.

A loud crack felt like it pierced her body. She jumped. A series of crashing noises ended in a ground-shaking thump. A large tree had fallen while the ear-splitting noises had drawn their complete attention. As Lee warned her, walking through old-growth timber on this night could be deadly.

A white SUV sped around a nearby curve on the road and whipped into the parking area.

The tree had distracted her. Before she could react, they had been spotted.

The SUV braked to a stop and doors flew open.

"Run, Jenn! There are two men with guns!"

14

Lee charged into the bushes. The branches Jennifer pushed aside whipped him as he followed her.

Both of them stumbled as they ran recklessly through the tangle of vegetation, trying to put distance and trees between them and the gunmen.

No shots yet. That was encouraging.

Fifty yards in, Jennifer shoved her .38 at him. "Take it. Cover us from behind. I'm going to circle around to get back to the bridge so we can cross over and get on the trail. There are places along the trail to hide until we can go back for help."

He took the gun and followed as Jennifer crept through the forest. Crashing noises in the brush sounded close behind them. It was difficult to judge distances with the droning wind.

Jennifer stopped. "They're deep into the thickest brush, not moving fast, but they have us cut off from my car. There are a lot of ponds and marshes in here that we can't cross and don't want to fall into. Then there's the river. It's too dangerous to ford. We need to double back to the parking area."

He followed her lead. From her research out here, she knew this area better than he did.

It took Jennifer a couple of minutes to circle back to the road. She stepped onto it, scanned it in both directions, and then motioned for him to follow.

They sprinted safely across the bridge, but when

they approached the trail head, a man emerged from the brush a hundred yards up the road.

His rifle belched a staccato burst of shots, shredding the bushes on their right.

Jennifer plunged through the foliage. The trail was hardly distinguishable. More like a deer path. The dense foliage along it forced them to slow to a jog.

Trader could sprint down the road unimpeded and close the gap.

When they reached the far end of a straight stretch of trail, another burst of automatic weapon fire pruned the bushes on their right.

Jennifer yanked him around a sharp bend in the trail. Two large trees shielded them from a second spray of bullets. "Hurry, Lee. We've got to keep our lead for about fifty yards more. We'll jump off the trail near the fork."

Despite their situation, he smiled at Jennifer's shrewdness.

Trader would have to guess which fork they took.

After her maneuver, either guess would be wrong.

Jennifer took his hand and pulled him off from the trail into a dense area of forest. She was tough, smart, and he was growing comfortable following her lead.

"There's a lot of moss on the rotting timber here. Don't kick any of it loose. Make it hard for them to track us."

She was using his words about the limestone rocks from last March. "Where have I heard those instructions before?"

A brief smile flickered across her face, and she squeezed his hand.

If only tonight could turn out as well as the events of March.

Jennifer turned and headed directly towards the ridge.

The knot in his stomach tightened. The strongest winds on the entire peninsula would likely occur where the southwest winds accelerated over the ridge above the Hole-in-the-Wall.

He dropped the .38 into his deepest coat pocket and scanned the forest canopy for anything falling.

The wind volume cranked up several decibels, sounding like a crowd of demons rooting for the devil.

Jennifer cupped her hand over her mouth and his ear. "They're going to pass by us on the trail in a few moments. When they're beyond us, we should get on the trail. We can move faster there. We'll make a run for the car."

"That's a good plan if they pass us. But what if they're no-shows?"

"In that case, we stay hidden for a while. If we don't see them, we walk hidden in the trees, parallel to the trail, and work our way back."

"OK. But we've got to watch the trees. They're being shredded by the turbulence. How many goons do you suppose we're up against?"

"Three, or four. Two were in the white SUV, and at least one drove the van to the parking area by the river, probably with the girls in the back. If they didn't incapacitate the girls, there may have been two in the van."

"Three, or four. My thoughts exactly. If we can get to your car and drive back to Forks, maybe the police can help us before the FBI arrives—anything to keep Trader from moving the girls again, or—"

Crashing sounds pierced his ears. They came from somewhere southwest of their position.

Jennifer clung to him. "It's getting stronger, isn't it? I didn't think that was possible."

"Yeah, the wind is stronger. The next two or three hours will be the worst." He put his mouth near her ear. "Do you know how far we are from the beach?"

"The top of the ridge above Hole-in-the-Wall is two or three hundred yards southwest of us."

"These southwesterly winds are accelerating over the ridgeline above the beach. If they get any stronger, entire walls of trees could start falling—wall, after wall, after—"

Jennifer clamped her hand over his mouth. "Stop. I get it."

Two more loud cracks sounded, followed by crashing noises, each punctuated by a ground-shaking thump.

"As each row of trees comes down, it will expose the next row, a row that's never been exposed to strong winds. Like a domino effect."

Her hand clamped over his mouth again. "You already told me that."

He pulled her hand aside. "We need to move away from the ridgeline, and we need to do it now."

"Back towards the trail?"

"We don't have a choice."

A staccato of loud cracks rose above the droning wind. It sounded like the first domino had fallen.

He grabbed Jennifer's hand and pulled. "Run!"

They sprinted towards the trail.

"Lee, behind us!"

When he glanced back, two large trees fell towards them.

He jerked Jennifer, diving for cover. Lee curled his body around her.

The outer bows of a tree slapped the side of his head. Though covered by a hood, his cheek and ear throbbed from the slashing blow.

"Are you all right, Jenn?"

"I'm OK." She stood. "But, Lee, we're back on the trail. We need to—" She gasped and pointed towards their planned path of escape.

Two men loped along the trail, guns in hand.

So much for hiding in the forest or running back to the car.

"Lee, they see us!"

Jennifer pulled him forward and they sprinted down the trail towards Rialto Beach, towards more falling trees, and beyond that, something much worse.

Somewhere in the western sky, above all the clouds, the sun was shining.

Until the sun set, they could be seen for nearly two hundred yards. That was another reason to avoid the beach.

"We can't go onto the beach. It would give them easy shots at us."

"We've got no choice."

"Then we have to create another choice." Lee pulled the .38 from his coat pocket and turned to face their pursuers.

Her wide eyes and drawn face displayed her horror. "Please, not yet. Don't give him the satisfaction."

She was right.

They would be gunned down where they stood.

He dropped the gun into his coat pocket.

There was another fear Jennifer didn't yet understand. It frightened him more than facing men brandishing assault rifles when he had only Jennifer's little weapon.

With all her strength, Jennifer was pulling him nearer to that fear.

He gave in and ran behind her down the trail towards—his mind refused to picture what lay ahead.

Trader and his cohort still pursued them, nearing gunshot range.

Somewhere the trail had ended, and now they plowed into the thick undergrowth. It tore at their legs and ripped their raincoats. When they stopped, Jennifer stood beside him on top of the rocky ridge above the Hole-in-the-Wall.

The deafening boom of the waves reverberated in his chest. The forces unleashed and the sheer violence of the scene couldn't be assimilated in one glance.

The driftwood logs normally lining the beach bobbed in the water. Eighty-mile-per-hour winds, with gusts probably to one hundred thirty, created thirty-foot storm-surge waves. When the waves broke at the shore line, three-ton logs flew into the air like toothpicks. When that happened, there was no more water visible, only a broad expanse of foam.

Jennifer buried her face in his chest. She shook so hard he feared she would collapse. Would she choose to turn and face the men with the assault rifles after seeing the huge waves?

He closed his eyes. "Please, God. Show us the way."

At his words, Jennifer's shaking stopped. She spoke into his ear. "I sought Him. He heard me and delivered me from my fears. It's His word and it's true. We have to go to the beach. We've got to trust Him to protect us."

Lee looked behind them.

Guns ready, their pursuers moved in slowly and deliberately for the kill.

He tried, but couldn't make the decision to run towards that violent scene on the beach.

But Jennifer pulled free and ran to the edge of the rock. Before he could reach her, she slid down the rock onto a high, partially sheltered section of beach on the south side of the Hole-in-the-Wall. She stood ankle deep in foam, but her position was momentarily sheltered from both the logs surfing the thirty-foot waves, and from the guns.

He slid down beside her as a wave washed around the edge of the large sea arch, burying them thigh-deep in water and white foam.

They had twenty or thirty seconds until the men above could move into position to open fire.

Several thoughts coalesced to form a plan, a plan as desperate as their situation. With his arms around Jennifer, he counted the time between successive waves. About eight seconds.

They had hiked this beach several times last summer. Split Rock, the next place of shelter, was about eighty yards away.

In ideal conditions, a good high-school sprinter could cover the distance on a track. This beach was anything but ideal. To save time, they would have to start running before the backwash of the previous wave.

"We've got to run to Split Rock between waves. We'll go right after the next one."

Her questioning gaze said she knew they couldn't make it before the next wave broke on them.

But maybe they could get close. Maybe there would be no logs in the part of the wave that would hit them. Maybe the current of the wave, as it washed around Split Rock, would carry them to safety. Too many maybes, but they were out of options.

The wave they would follow leaped up to its full thirty-foot height as its base encountered the ocean floor.

"Right after this one breaks!"

"I love you, Lee!"

He kissed her forehead and grabbed her hand.

The ground trembled when hundreds of tons of water pounded onto the beach in front of them.

The deep rumble resonated in his chest, making it hard to draw a breath.

The wave pushed water and foam up to Jennifer's waist and pushed them towards the beach, off their path.

He gripped her hand tighter and started towards Split Rock. His legs churned in slow motion in the waist-deep water. As the wave washed back out, Lee gained speed. Soon, they both sprinted on packed sand.

Hope surged.

A small log rolled down the beach towards them. Jennifer tried to jump over it. It clipped her foot. She fell, yanking Lee off his feet. The fall broke their hands apart. They jumped up to run, but the water now bore down on them.

The mountainous wave towered above them. It broke early. With a deafening roar, it claimed them. Then it buried them.

No logs battered, but an overpowering current of water pushed him under. Lee surfaced. He stood on sand in two feet of water. He scanned the foam and water for Jennifer. He spotted her floating on the water several yards behind him.

The wave's backwash pulled her farther away. It drew her towards the Hole-in-the-Wall, towards deeper water and the next wave.

The approaching swell hit the underwater sandbar and leaped upward more than thirty feet, sucking all the water from the beach, claiming the water for itself, claiming Jennifer. The wall of water contained logs of all sizes, entire trees recently taken down by the storm. The huge wave lifted Jennifer to its crest. Her body disappeared. Then the wave slammed onto the beach in an explosion of water, logs, and foam.

In the twilight, standing in a partially sheltered area by Split Rock, Lee scanned the foam and the logs while the wind and waves continued their assault on the beach.

Jennifer was gone.

The fuse for a guttural eruption, an emotional bomb, burst into flame deep inside. When the fuse was consumed, it exploded from his mouth. "Nooooo!"

He needed to find her. To help her.

He ran through thigh-deep water to the base of Split Rock and clambered up its sheltered backside.

A horrifying scene played in his mind. It threatened his sanity. A picture of driftwood logs pulverizing Jennifer and the storm surge hurling her broken body onto the beach. His heart rejected it, but the nightmare remained in his mind.

He scoured the surf for Jennifer, wave after wave. He felt no imminent danger from the waves or from Trader, only an incapacitating pain in his heart. A dark fog settled over him. The fog displaced all hope, robbing him of everything except the unbearable pain.

****

When Lee came to his senses, he had been sobbing. Darkness had fallen.

Where was God?

Where was Jennifer now? In His presence? No. That would be premature, wrong. She was so beautiful, so full of life, love, and compassion. Especially compassion for the kidnapped girls. All of that served what purpose? It made no difference now.

After a while, a measure of rationality returned. Only one thing could possibly salvage any meaning—the least bit of good—out of his loss. He must kill Trader and his henchmen and stop the girls from being sold.

Whether he died in the process or not, he would kill these men.

Eventually Peterson would reach Forks with his team, and the human trafficking and drug smuggling would stop. But Trader would die, and the scheduled exchange would not happen.

He would do whatever it took to accomplish that. It's what Jennifer, the only soul mate he had ever known, would do if she was in his place.

He reached for Jennifer's .38 in his pocket. It was gone. That placed him at a greater disadvantage, but it didn't matter. Without a weapon, he wouldn't survive.

But neither would Trader.

He was ready to die. Death was his only path to Jennifer. But he had to live long enough to see her mission through.

First, he needed to get from Split Rock back to the ridge above the Hole-in-the-Wall. From there, he could backtrack to the other fork in the trail and see if it led to the place where Trader held the girls.

The wind had decreased somewhat. Occasionally, beams of light from a half moon slipped through slits in the clouds. The sporadic moonlight, the shelter of Split Rock, and the eight-second wave interval would allow him to run directly away from the beach to safety.

Fifty yards would take him beyond the reach of the waves and the embedded logs that still battered the shore. The final twenty-five yards would take him through a tangle of bushes, shredding his clothes and raincoat. That was no concern now.

Moonlight shone briefly, illuminating a twenty-foot wave ready to break.

He crouched on the rock. The wave broke, and then passed his position. Lee jumped down onto the beach and ran towards the shore with the rushing water.

Clouds covered the moon. It was dark again, so he could only hope no logs were rolling towards him in the backwash of the wave.

Something ripped at him. He fell forward into the water. A large, rolling log tore the skin from his left leg. The abrasions stung sharply in the salt water.

He fell onto his face. Would a second rolling log bash in his head? That might end his misery, but he couldn't allow it. Not yet.

Instead of a second log, he felt only the rush of the backwash, a deep sense of loss, and a deepening resolve.

Trader was a dead man.

15

The rushing water ahead of the next wave captured Jennifer. The strong current pulled her seaward. "Lee! Lee! God, please protect me. For the girls' sake, and for Lee."

To fight the ferocious current would only waste strength. She turned towards the roaring sound.

A forty-foot wall of water bore down on her.

Jennifer swam hard directly into it.

The storm had embedded entire trees and large pieces of driftwood in the wall of water.

The verses from Saturday's devotions washed through her mind, cleansing it of panic and terror.

Lord, You alone are my rock and my salvation.

Her stomach flipped like on a carnival ride when the giant wave lifted her body to its crest. One moment she was on top of the monstrous wave, directly beside the Hole-in-the-Wall. The next, she was falling. Falling.

A stunning blow to her forehead. A flash like lightning—

****

Jennifer became vaguely aware of her body rasping against something…a rock. Some force pulled on her arm. It hurt, but she seemed detached from the pain. There were voices, and then everything reverted to blackness.

A bright light stabbed her eyes as it shined through her eyelids. Something, or was it Someone, told her she must keep her eyes shut.

She was cold and wet. Her head ached and her mind spun like a centrifuge.

The wind howled. Waves crashed and roared, and there were human voices.

Danger! The alarm sounded in her mind.

"You think this is the girl who spied on us? Are you sure?" the gravelly voice asked.

"She was with the guy. They were clever, resourceful. Dangerous. If she wakes up, we need to find out what she knows, and then get rid of her," the deep voice said.

The deep voice was one she had heard before, but where? As the fog in her mind dissipated, she matched the voice with a person. It was the voice from the cell-phone recording.

Trader's voice. The realization shot through her like electricity. Jennifer tried to steady her breathing. No startled gasp could escape her lips. Her eyes must remain closed…for now.

It had to be three-fourths of a mile to the place where the girls were held. How far would they be willing to carry her before they decided she was too much trouble—too much dead weight? Until they wanted her dead?

Trader threw her over his shoulder like a sack of potatoes and started walking up the trail towards the forest.

Her weight obviously wasn't an issue. What about being too much trouble? She needed to avoid causing trouble if she wanted to see the girls.

The gravel-voiced man spoke. "Did you take a

good look at her?"

"I inspected the goods. Top quality," Trader said. "But if you're talking about who she is, I'm sure she's the girl we saw at the mill and again in the rainforest. She's wearing the same raincoat."

Jennifer knew what they meant and was glad she was unconscious. She was barely beginning to understand the filthiness and moral depravity of human traffickers, but even that bit of insight was enough to turn her stomach.

"If we cleaned her up, she's more than top quality. The other three aren't even in her league. I'll bet she's sixteen, maybe seventeen, at most. I know a certain prince who would pay a small fortune for her. If he won't commit to the deal, Boatman will pay the usual amount."

The gravelly voice confirmed what Jennifer thought. Goods to sell to a middleman, or perhaps a consumer like the prince. That's all young women were to them.

It was providential that she left her ring in the car. She needed them to continue believing she was sixteen, frightened, and naïve. The frightened part she didn't have to pretend.

"You might be right," Trader spoke slowly. "Getting rid of a body isn't easy. Even knocking her in the head and tossing her back into the surf has certain risks, especially if her body is found anytime soon."

"More risk since we're not absolutely sure the guy died. But it looked like that big wave got him. If we sell the girl, we're home free," the gravelly voice said.

They had to be wrong about Lee. She survived the big wave, and he was in a more sheltered spot than she'd been. She had to believe that, otherwise her heart would be broken. *Lord, protect Lee...*

"Home free, unless they called someone when they passed through Forks." Trader voiced a legitimate concern.

"We need to get her to talk. I can manage that without damaging the goods."

What would they do to her? The realization that they could do anything they wanted brought panic, panic that threatened to overwhelm her.

"How do you plan to do that?" The gravelly voice asked.

"If she wakes up, I'll demonstrate my methods when we get back to the shack."

Trader's words verified Jennifer's suspicions. She would soon see the girls, become one of the girls, at a place they called the shack.

She must conceal her age, her knowledge, and her experience. If she was going to help rescue the girls, she would need those resources, plus the element of surprise, plus Him.

You alone, Lord, are my rock and my salvation. You are my fortress, I will never be shaken. You saved me from the waves when I should have died. Now show me what I need to do.

Her chest was pressed against the back of Trader's shoulder. Less than twelve inches from her heart another heart was beating. A heart with a completely different nature, unregenerate, bent on evil of the worst kind, enslaved by its own proclivities and the forces of darkness—Trader's heart. She had told Lee she wasn't into irony. But here, irony reigned supreme.

Jennifer tried to formulate a plan to save the girls. Lee escaped the big wave that the gravelly voiced man mentioned. She would operate on that premise, that her soul mate was alive and would be doing something to rescue her and the girls, if he could. Did he see Trader pull her from the water, or did he believe she was dead? What would he do next?

It was a silly question. Lee would try to save the girls. Knowingly or unknowingly, he would also be trying to save her.

That thought brought hope. It surged in her heart. But what must she do? Only one answer crystallized in her mind. Buy time. The longer she could keep the girls alive and in the shack, the better their chances of rescue.

Peterson's team was on its way. Though they didn't know its precise location, within a few hours, the FBI would find them. Lee would come, too.

Before tomorrow night, there would be an attempt to rescue them. She needed to be ready to assist whoever made the rescue attempt. The girls also needed to be confident and ready. That's what she must do. Instill hope and prepare them for the rescue. Any further details would have to wait until she saw the shack and the girls.

Lord, please don't allow Trader to isolate me from the girls. Maybe it's time for me to wake up now.

16

The rolling log swept Lee off his feet. He plunged headfirst into the cold water, shoving his hands out to protect his face. He caught himself with a jarring impact that threatened to break his wrists.

He came down on something hard, bruising the heel of his hand. It wasn't a rock. His fingers had closed around a familiar object. When he stood to run, he held Jennifer's gun. But would it fire, or blow up in his face?

In the darkness, he stumbled away from the violent water. Probably away from Jennifer's body, too. But he couldn't dwell on that.

The gun wasn't cocked, so he slipped it into his raincoat pocket.

Now out of the cold water, thorny bushes shredded his raincoat and ripped deep scratches into the backs of his hands. When the thorns ended, he stood at the base of the hill. He followed the hill towards the ridge, praying that when he reached it, he could find the trail.

A shaft of moonlight beamed down between the clouds flying across the night sky. The light was too brief to help him, so he stumbled ahead through the low bushes until he reached the base of the ridge.

He climbed to the top and stopped. Now what? He had a gun. The ammunition box still rode in his coat pocket. But first, he needed to resolve his questions about the gun's usability. To do that, he needed a light.

The cell phone in his pocket was supposedly water resistant. It could be dead forever…like Jennifer.

He pushed that thought from his mind, knowing it would return to haunt and hurt.

Lee pressed the on button. The phone lit up and booted. There was no service here, but in the cell he had a makeshift flashlight for as long as the battery lasted.

He pulled out the gun, unlatched the cylinder, and removed the cartridges. After he had wiped away all traces of sand on the exposed parts of the gun, he ripped a shredded piece of fabric from his clothing, pushed one end through the barrel with a twig, and pulled it back and forth several times. He pointed the barrel towards his cell light. When he peered through it, the barrel looked clean. It wasn't bent or dented.

Should he test fire it? Even with the noise of the wind, Trader might hear a gunshot. He couldn't give up the element of surprise—surprise that he was alive and surprise that he had a weapon. He decided to assume the gun would fire and trust God for the results.

The windstorm gave him a twenty-four hour window to rescue the girls. When should he make the attempt? Where should he make it?

Jennifer said the exchange was scheduled for a beach about a mile north of the Hole-In-The-Wall.

Jennifer. Warm thoughts of her smile, her eyes, and her touch flooded his mind. He stifled them before they could derail his mission. He needed to pull himself together, to do what she would want him to do.

He took a deep breath, but choked on a sob before he could exhale. A growing anger rescued him from being completely overcome by the sense of loss. He would hold onto the anger. It drove both him and his plan forward.

With the gun, he could kill Trader and his henchmen. But to do that, he needed to separate the goons. Deal with them one at a time.

During any surprise attack, he must keep the girls safe. That was paramount. His best chance to free them was tonight, before first light.

Peterson's team could be in the vicinity before daylight. But he couldn't count on them. Too many uncertainties. He would take the girls and hide if any goons were left alive.

As Lee stood to begin his search for the trail, the surges of adrenaline were gone. He shivered from the wind and the wet clothing. He needed to keep moving.

He opened his cell and, shining the light downward, walked a line he thought paralleled the beach. Soon he discovered the small trail and some footprints.

He looked up into the dark sky. *Thank You.*

If he was truthful, only part of his heart felt gratitude. The feelings in the other part weren't good, but they were now easier to justify, because killing Trader and freeing the girls were becoming synonymous in his mind.

He clenched his teeth and pictured himself taking Trader to the top of the sea arch, shooting him in a shoulder and a knee, and then shoving him into the surf to drown like Jennifer.

Like Jennifer? He wasn't thinking like Jennifer. She couldn't love a man filled with anger and hatred. He couldn't allow himself to become such a man.

If freeing the girls required killing Trader, he would do it. But this was Jennifer's mission, not his vendetta. Whatever he did must honor God and her wishes. He prayed it would also rescue the girls.

17

What would happen when she told Trader that she was awake? Jennifer hesitated before speaking.

Please show me what to do.

She lifted her head and spoke softly, "May I walk now?"

Trader jerked to a stop.

His partner flashed the light in Jennifer's face. The gravelly voice spoke again, "Eyes wide open, boss. Let's see if she can walk."

"I think I can walk if—"

"You only speak to answer my questions." Trader's deep, harsh voice boomed out the order. It was a voice skillfully tuned for intimidation. "Do you understand?" He swung her down and set her on her feet.

"I understand." She wobbled, and then caught herself as her sense of balance returned. But she was disoriented. "Which way are we going?"

"You didn't hear me, did you? Only when I ask. Have you got that, you little..."

Jennifer shrank back in horror from the string of vile, demeaning words that exploded from Trader's mouth. He crafted his words to shock, assault, intimidate, and to remove all sense of self-worth. He was good at it, and that infuriated her.

She wanted to glare into his eyes, to stare him down, to show him what she thought of him.

Someone deep inside spoke inaudibly, saying, "No."

She followed the prompting.

After sucking in a deep breath, she blew it back out, and then turned towards Trader, careful to avoid eye contact. She must emulate a sixteen-year-old girl, frightened, intimidated, and docile. Head bowed, she nodded.

"That's better." Trader's voice relaxed. "Jacko, lead the way with the light. I'll be the rear guard."

Jacko stepped ahead of her on the trail.

She wanted to look around and memorize their path to the holding location.

Keep your face down, girl. She let her shoulders droop. Anything to appear subservient. But her gaze would rove, taking in her surroundings and memorizing every part of the trail.

The wind blew through her wet clothing and soon her teeth chattered. Her sudden chill brought a revolting thought. The warmth of Trader's body had kept her from shivering while she rode on his shoulder.

Jennifer's stomach churned. She almost vomited on the trail, but managed to reach the bushes before she demonstrated her feelings about Trader and his disgusting business.

"Are you sick?" Trader's voice sounded menacing. "If you are—"

"I'm not really sick. Just swallowed too much seawater."

"Forgot already?" Trader shoved her from behind, snapping her head backward.

She stumbled, but regained her balance. "No, sorry."

"That's better."

Total submission to Trader. That's the only thing he thought was better. As she took that thought to its logical conclusion, Jennifer feared for the girls in the shack and for herself.

When they came to the fork in the trail, Jacko led them down the north fork until they reached the shack, a prefabricated utility building with a single door and one small window.

"Ivan, open up." Jacko banged on the door.

A large man with a gun in one hand opened it.

When Trader pushed Jennifer into the light, Ivan's leering gaze roved over her.

"Where did you get a beauty like her on a night like this?"

"Caught her swimming by Hole-in-the-Wall. She was the girl with the man at the mill and at the Hoh River."

Ivan's grin disappeared. "She nearly shot me," he growled. "Looks familiar, but I can't seem to place her. Too young to be a cop, or a Fed. Maybe I saw her picture in the paper."

If they realized who she was, her situation would likely go from bad to much worse.

Ivan's dull, brutish look and hungry eyes told her his interest in her was fast becoming an obsession. He wouldn't remember who she was. But he was still dangerous. He had the same look as the stalker, the one she was forced to shoot two years ago. Evil exuded from the man. Ivan was completely driven by the forces of darkness.

The thought of standing in the presence of such evil made her shudder.

Please protect me from these men, Lord.

"Boatman will be happy," Jacko said. "Last time we were one short. We would have been one short again without this lucky find. We'll definitely keep *her* away from her shoelaces."

At Jacko's words, Jennifer's rage surged. She wanted to jump at him, plant her heel on his nose, grab his gun, and—

"Getting worked up, are we?" Ivan grabbed her wrists and crossed them. "These will calm you down, princess. Or is it queen? It's hard to tell with you Asian girls." He placed two sets of restraints around her wrists and cinched them tightly.

Jennifer studied the three girls huddled in the corner.

All three eyed her with interest.

They were beautiful young girls. One was about eleven, another thirteen or fourteen, and the third looked about fifteen.

Ivan checked her bonds, and then grabbed the back of her jacket and jerked her towards the three girls. "Sit down and be quiet. No talking from any of you, or else."

Ivan sat on a stool ten feet away watching them. But his gaze kept returning to her, where it rested most of the time.

If I had my .38, Ivan would be dead. Her thought shocked her. She entertained thoughts of killing another human being and only felt satisfaction. How could she do that? She wasn't like them. But maybe she wasn't as far from it as she thought.

The Bible's teachings about the fallen nature of man were a bitter pill for people to swallow, but in moments like these, they rang true, and she was thankful for God's grace.

Trader walked towards her. He grabbed her head with both hands, forcing her to look into his eyes.

Jennifer glanced at his eyes, and then dropped her gaze. He obviously wanted to read her emotions. She couldn't allow him to see the contempt and defiance.

"Old lady, have I got your full attention?" He relaxed his grip on her head.

She nodded, remaining silent.

"Good. Now tell me why you and the guy were snooping around the old mill and why you came to Rialto Beach after giving us the slip?"

The slip? She almost laughed. That was an understatement, a euphemism to avoid acknowledging the humiliation they had caused him.

She knew this moment would come, but felt unprepared for it. "I...I was only along for the ride. My boyfriend kept that mostly to himself."

"OK. But remember, this is all your doing." Trader spoke calmly. "Her pain is your fault." He walked to the huddle of girls, pulled out a stun gun, and shoved it into the eleven-year-old girl's back.

The girl screamed. She collapsed on the floor, shaking and sobbing.

Jennifer barely managed to stifle her sobs.

Please help this young girl. Give me wisdom and words. Show me what I need to do.

Trader's large, meaty hands forced her to look into his eyes.

Jennifer's streaming tears helped masked her anger, her defiance, and her desire to kill him

"Old lady, you did that to her. Look at me!"

She looked into his eyes. They were angry eyes, but lifeless. Trader was a walking dead man, and he didn't even know it. "Dead in trespasses and sins" became more than simply a phrase in her Bible. It became death incarnate, and it stood in front of her.

"Good. I've got your attention. Now, why were you and your boyfriend snooping around the old mill, and why did you come to Rialto Beach?"

"I promised him I wouldn't tell anyone. But I'll tell you, if you won't hurt her again."

"You'll tell me without condition. Start talking, and if I believe you, maybe the outcome will be a little less…shocking. If not, we'll see if something else might be more *apropos*." Trader turned to Ivan. "Which one of these dogs do you want, Ivan?"

Without hesitation Ivan said, "Her." His mutilated index finger, cut off at the first joint, pointed at Jennifer.

She felt the urge to vomit again.

"We'll see," Trader said, obviously toying with her emotions. "Why did you to come to the mill and then to the beach?"

"My boyfriend is a new reporter for the *Tribune*. He researched a story about a missing girl from our area. He said he found evidence linking missing girls to something on the peninsula. He didn't want to get scooped, so he decided to come out here to investigate. He asked me if I wanted to come along and help him." Jennifer could see he was thinking, considering the plausibility of what she'd said. She had fabricated the story on the fly, and now prayed there were no obvious holes in it.

"Suppose I accept your story, as far as it goes." He studied her face. "I still have no explanation of what led you down Mora Road, or who was the source of the information." He looked at Jennifer and then at Ivan. "If your story is true, you're still holding back information. So perhaps I should grant Ivan's wish."

Please give me the words.

"My boyfriend got a partial description of a van that might have been used to take a girl near Seattle. He has a friend who lives part of the time in the village, you know...La Push. They were talking, and his friend mentioned seeing a van like that near Rialto Beach. Said he saw it by the bridge more than once. Then his friend told him about one of the fishermen from the village coming in late one night. He saw a large boat offshore, a few miles out from the Hole-in-the-Wall. The fisherman saw the boat on the same day his friend saw the van parked by the bridge.

"My boyfriend also talked to people who live along Highway 101 from Lake Quinault to near Forks. He described the van and asked if anyone had seen it. I saw a map that he drew. It had some circles on it. One circle covered an area southeast of Kalaloch and the other was around the area where we are now. We came over to check out those areas. That's all I know." Jennifer had just told more lies than she could ever remember doing. But she lied with a clear conscience, and she lied without compromising the true source of their intelligence or her identity.

But...did Trader buy it?

"Old lady..." Like bullets from an assault rifle, his mouth belched out a long burst of gutter language. The words assaulted her mind and emotions, as Trader intended. "You're either the best liar I've ever met, or you're telling the truth. Either way, too much has been compromised to far too many people." Trader turned towards the man called Jacko. "We need to attend to some other business. I'll finish dealing with her later."

Finish dealing with her later? She couldn't let

Trader's statement paralyze her with fear.

Jacko and Trader discussed the storm's disruption of their plans. They needed to charge their cell-phone equipment and would use their van and SUV to charge the batteries for the next exchange, scheduled for sometime after midnight on Monday.

That meant she had to keep the girls safe for possibly twenty-four hours. But how could she do that when she wasn't allowed to talk to them?

Before Trader and Jacko left for the vehicles, Trader stepped outside and called for Ivan to follow.

Ivan stood outside the door, holding it partially open. "Watch the girls closely, Ivan." Trader was angry and loud. "Notice I said *watch*, not touch. Do you understand?"

"Of course. I'm not stupid, you know." Ivan's words came embedded in a growl.

"We'll not debate that now." The tone of Trader's reply was caustic. "But remember this, if you go out for any reason, tie them to the steel ring. And, Ivan, we always deliver unspoiled goods to Boatman, otherwise we don't get paid. Do you understand what I mean?"

"Come on, you know me. I look sometimes, but I want to get paid, too."

"If you don't do as I say," Trader's voice rose, "you will get paid, Ivan. You most certainly will get paid. Now, we'll be back in about two and a half hours. Can you handle things here for that long?"

"Yeah." Ivan backed into the shack and slammed the door, his body language sullen.

Jennifer glanced at the dim lantern providing the only light in the shack. Maybe she could use the poor light to her advantage.

A heavy layer of dust and dirt covered the

plywood floor. She scooted a few inches away from the oldest girl, opening up a square foot of floor space between her and the girls.

Ivan sat across the room, moping and oblivious.

She drew her right index finger across the floor. It left a visible line. She wiped the dust. The line disappeared.

The blonde girl watched each movement of her hand.

She scrawled out, "I'm Jenn."

18

When Jennifer finished writing her name, she looked up into the blonde girl's beautiful blue eyes.

The girl's expression was hopeful, as if resurrected. The dead hopelessness had vanished with a single word...hope.

She looked at Jennifer, studied her face. Slowly, almost imperceptibly, her head dipped once. The girl's hand casually wiped out "Jenn," and, over the next minute, replaced it with "Katie."

Jennifer read the name and mimicked the covert nod. She glanced at the girl's face again.

Katie's expression brightened at the small victory of exchanging names and there was a fire in those intense blue eyes. When their gazes locked, Jennifer felt a bond form between them.

Katie wiped out all of the writing over the next minute or so. Then she drew an arrow pointing to the girl who appeared to be about thirteen. Her finger wrote "Kirsten."

Jennifer met Katie's gaze and dipped her head.

Kirsten scanned their crude blackboard on the floor.

Katie drew an arrow pointing towards Jennifer and wrote "Jenn." She held Kirsten's gaze.

Kirsten nodded

Over the next few minutes, Katie drew another arrow towards the youngest girl and wrote "Melanie."

After Jennifer read it, Katie wiped out the final four letters leaving, "Mel."

Jennifer acknowledged the shortened name.

This was a critical moment. Jennifer fired a short prayer heavenward, and then wrote, "Help coming."

Katie's face lit up, then tilted towards the floor, obviously trying to hide her reaction.

Kirsten also tried to mask her excitement, but she had apparently attracted Ivan's attention.

Staring at Kirsten, Ivan rose to his feet.

Jennifer dragged her hand across the floor, wiping the writing away.

Ivan approached them carrying two large nylon ties. He stopped and his eyes roved over Jennifer for several seconds. "All of you, slide over to the post. You're going to get hitched." He chuckled as he gestured to a steel ring attached to a large post. "I'm going out for a few minutes. Put your hands up here."

Ivan threaded the heavy-duty nylon bands through the restraints around each girl's wrists, and then through the large steel ring attached to the post. He zipped up the two large bands binding all four girls to the ring.

Jennifer tested the post by pulling and pushing on it. It was firmly set into the ground, possibly in concrete.

"Pull all you want to, old lady. That post isn't going anywhere and neither are you. And remember, I'm still listening. So don't do anything stupid." He scanned the four girls, and then headed towards the door.

When Ivan opened the door to leave, the wind howled outside. It would drown out whispers, once he closed the door.

When the door shut, Jennifer turned to the girls. "Listen, the FBI knows approximately where we are, and they're trying to get here through the storm. We need to be ready for a rescue attempt, but we can't let Ivan or the others see any change in us."

"How do you know help is coming? Nobody saw them take me." Katie's face was filled with doubt.

"I know because I'm the one who discovered what Trader was doing and where he was doing it."

Kirsten's eyes were full of suspicion. "Then why are you here like us?"

"Because I took one too many chances. I wanted to know where the shack was located so I could tell the FBI exactly where to come. They know it's in this area, but we weren't certain it was along this trail. I made a big mistake, and they caught me."

Jennifer carefully omitted details for their protection.

Katie and Kirsten were frowning.

Mel scooted around the post, closer to her. "Please don't make him hurt me again."

"I'll try not to do that, Mel. But remember, I didn't make him do anything. Trader chose to do it, because he's an evil man, the very worst kind."

"I'm afraid, Jenn. It hurt so much when he shocked me." Mel's tear-filled eyes overflowed.

Jennifer lifted her elbow and draped an arm, as best she could, around the small girl's shoulders. "Mel, I know you're afraid. But we don't have to give in to our fear and let it overcome us. For people like us, people held captive, God wrote some very special things, things I believe with all my heart. Talking about captives like us, God's Word says 'when these people were oppressed they cried out to God. He heard from heaven, and because of His great compassion, He sent deliverers, who rescued them from their enemies.'"

Mel leaned against her shoulder. "Did He really say that…to us?"

"He said it to some other captives many years ago, captives He set free. Then He made sure it was written down in the Bible for us to read. I read it earlier this week."

Mel nestled her head against Jennifer's neck. "I hope He sends our deliverers soon."

"Me, too. But in the meantime, we don't have to let fear overcome us. God said nearly four hundred times in the Bible to the people who trust Him, do not be afraid. He also said, the people who love Him, He will deliver. He will protect the people who trust in His name. When they ask for help, He answers them. He's with them when they're in trouble, and He will rescue them and honor them. All we have to do is trust Him, love Him, and ask Him to help us."

Katie stared at the wall across the room. "If God is so good, why did He let Trader take us, and probably other girls, too?"

Jennifer slid her hand around the bands, placing it over Katie's. "What God wants, Katie, is to be a personal God to every individual. He wants the relationship to be based upon love. So He doesn't make people love Him. That would be a false love. Some people, like Trader, choose the opposite of what God wants. They choose to do evil. If there is going to be any real love, there has be a choice for each person to make. Some people make a bad choice—a very bad choice. But in the end, God promises to punish the people who choose evil, instead of choosing Him. So for right now, we get to love God, but we have to put up with some evil people. Does that make sense?"

Katie stared at the wall. "Let me think—"

The door opened.

Mel lifted her head from Jennifer's shoulder when Ivan entered the shack.

He walked directly to the girls and checked their bonds. He smiled, cut the bands holding them to the post, and studied Jennifer.

The moment Ivan began surrendering to his own proclivities, Jennifer saw it in his eyes. He stared into her face. She also read his facial expression, and what she saw frightened her. His gaze began systematically exploring her. It turned her stomach and made her feel contaminated.

Ivan stepped closer.

Jennifer steeled herself for what was coming.

19

Lee crept along the trail, occasionally using his cell phone for light. Out-manned and out-gunned, he needed to surprise them.

In the darkness, nothing about the trail looked familiar, but judging by the distance he'd walked, he should be near the fork. Sounds. Barely audible sounds, but they didn't belong to the storm. They were human voices. He slid behind a bush.

Two men stepped onto the trail. They must have come from the north fork, and they appeared to be walking towards the vehicle in the parking lot.

If, as he and Jennifer suspected, there were three men, only one man would be guarding the girls. This might be his best chance to free them.

Knowing where two of the men were changed everything.

After he gave the two men a minute or so to clear the area, he would take the north fork and find the holding location. If he could move close enough, he would incapacitate or, if necessary, kill the guard, take his weapon, and flee with the girls. Even if the two heard his gunshot, it was nearly a half mile to the parking area, four or five minutes of jogging along the trail through the trees. He would have time to hide the girls in the forest.

It was a good plan.

He headed down the north fork. Nearly a quarter

mile down the trail, it curved to the right. When he rounded the bend, a light shone through the trees.

The source of the light was a small building. It had one window and one door.

He prayed there would be a shooting angle from outside the window, one that did not endanger the girls. But before taking any action, he needed at least one glimpse inside.

The end of the building provided a safe approach, one that kept him out of sight.

He stopped and checked the trail behind him. There were no signs of the other two men.

He dipped his hand into the muddy soil. The dark mud oozed between his fingers as he applied it to his face.

He checked the .38. It was fully loaded.

From the edge of the window he could only peer in at an acute angle. It was enough to see the shadow of a man projected onto the wall beyond the door. But which way was the man facing?

Lee inched forward and slid his mud-covered face in front of the glass, then pulled his head back to process the image.

The man sat on a stool, his side exposed to the window. He was looking at the back left corner, probably at the girls. An assault rifle lay across the man's lap.

Lee could shoot the lone guard through the window before the man could raise his weapon. But he needed to be certain of the girls' positions before firing any bullets into the room.

He slid his entire face in front of the window and peered into the room.

The man stood, rifle in hand. "I said strip, old

lady!" The gunman barked the order.

The urge to kill this brute grew until it was almost uncontrollable. He took a calming breath and assumed a two-handed firing stance in front of the window.

The brute faced a huddle of bodies in the back corner of the room.

"Stand up now!" The man snarled.

One of the girls moved to stand, but the man's body hid her.

She was directly in the line of fire.

He needed a safer shooting angle, but somehow he had to intervene before this brute could have his way.

"Start undressing, old lady."

"No!" A single-word reply came, clearly audible above the wind.

The voice was unmistakable. Jennifer.

The reality hit him like a slap to his face. His hand shook as rage replaced rationality.

The man moved forward.

Lee's hand stopped shaking. His thoughts cleared.

The gunman reached for the girl's shoulder. When he did, his body moved to her right.

Lee was staring into Jennifer's face, fighting to control an explosion of emotions. His finger tightened on the trigger, but Jennifer was still too close to the line of fire. He would have to use his knife.

The man shoved Jennifer downward onto the floor.

When she hit the floor, she swung her right leg up, landing a strong, well-placed kick.

The brute roared in anger and pain.

Lee pulled the trigger twice. Two loud pops sounded above the noise of the wind.

Bullets ripped two holes in the man's upper torso.

The shots knocked the man against the back wall. The brute slid to the floor, writhing.

Lee burst into the room. When the goon tried to get up, Lee used a savage, chopping motion to smash the handle of the .38 into the man's head, driving it down until it bounced on the wooden floor.

Blood exploded from the guy's head wound, splattering across the floor and onto the wall.

The man lay still.

"Lee!" Jennifer scrambled to her feet. She tried but failed to put her bound arms around his neck.

Lee wrapped his arms around her as muddy drops fell from his cheeks.

Jennifer was smiling through her tears. She struggled to wipe the mud away with her bound hands.

Those restraints needed to come off. He opened his knife and sliced through the nylon bands, slinging them across the room.

They landed on the wounded man's bleeding head.

"Jenn, I thought the wave—"

"Hush," Jennifer whispered as she pulled his muddy face to hers,

It was a passionate, gritty kiss from a gritty woman, and it tasted like dirt, but it was a kiss he would never forget.

After the kiss, reality returned. "Let's go, Jenn. We've got to get the girls out of here before the other men return. They probably heard the shots."

20

The girls weren't moving. Were they bewildered, because he had punctuated such violence with a kiss? "Jenn, help me out here."

Jennifer turned to the girls. "Come here, girls."

The first girl was a beautiful, tall, blonde teenager.

Jennifer raised the girl's hands.

Lee slid his left hand between her bound wrists, exposing the nylon bands, and sliced them with his knife.

"Lee, this is Katie. Katie, Lee is my fiancé."

"Your fiancé?" Katie's brilliant blue eyes opened wide in surprise. "But you're—"

"Katie, I'm twenty-six years old and I work for the National Security Agency."

"But...I thought you were one of us."

"I am, Katie. We're in this together. My fate would have been the same as yours."

"Hello, Katie." Lee noted her intense blue eyes.

The next girl, a stunning, dark-eyed brunette, shoved her hands out.

"Lee, meet Kirsten."

"Hello, Kirsten."

The smallest girl, with light-brown hair and large, innocent, blue eyes, extended her hands.

"And this is Melanie. You can call her Mel."

"Hi, Mel."

The man on the floor remained still.

"I'm taking this goon's weapon. Girls, grab any flashlights you see and any ammunition. Don't leave them anything they can use against us. Jenn, do you still have the keys to your car?"

Jennifer slid her hand into her jeans pocket. "I've got my keys," she said as she grabbed a flashlight sitting against the wall. When she looked over at the man on the floor, her voice grew thick with revulsion. "Lee, that's Ivan. He's still breathing, but I'm not sure how I feel about that."

Lee grabbed the rifle and the full clip of ammunition sitting by the door. "Well, it makes me feel better. If he lives, he'll get to serve his entire term in the federal pen. Now let's get out of here. We'll hide along the trail. Girls, try to be as quiet as you can and don't be afraid regardless of how close Trader and what's his face—"

"Jacko," Jennifer spat the name.

"No matter how close they get. We have weapons as good as theirs. If we're quiet, we also have the element of surprise. And we have God on our side. Now follow me."

The path leading to the shack was dark. No bouncing flashlight beams and no sounds except the wind. He led the group down the trail.

Jennifer held the .38 in her right hand and extended her other hand back to Mel. The three girls walked single file, hand-in-hand behind her.

He noticed Katie had taken on the role of rear guard. Because she was the oldest? No. There was something else about her.

Jennifer had watched him scrutinize Katie. "She's smart, Lee. That's the best place for Katie, watching our backside."

"Good. But from now on, let's whisper until we know they're nowhere near." He pointed the light back towards the girls. "Did you all hear?"

Three heads nodded in unison.

He slowed their pace from a fast walk to a cautious amble. If he could keep the girls out of Trader's sight, he could keep them safe. As he watched the trail ahead, he also monitored the bushes alongside for a hiding place.

A flashlight poked him in the ribs. "Lee, I thought I saw a light up ahead. Probably Trader and Jacko."

"Turn our light off and follow me. Calm the girls, Jenn." He veered off the trail to their right.

Despite the darkness, they negotiated the first few feet easily, but then the forest floor became littered with rotting logs and bushes. They stumbled over the obstacles, and Trader's light grew brighter.

A large bush lay directly ahead. He huddled the group of five behind it.

Though the wind had diminished some, it still whistled through the treetops, effectively muffling the low-pitched sounds of human voices. They were well hidden, safe, while Trader passed by them.

A sharp crack sounded.

Kirsten gasped and recoiled in horror from the branch she had broken.

Trader's light swung their way. Then it lit up the area around them.

Jennifer's arm curled around Kirsten's shoulders.

Lee leaned close, taking in part of her whispered words, "… don't be afraid for I'm with you. I'm your God. I'll strengthen you and help you…"

The light moved on. Trader was moving up the trail again, with Jacko following.

Lee's gunfire, when he shot Ivan, would force Trader to go back to the shack. From there, even if Trader moved twice as fast as them, they should be a few minutes beyond the parking area before Trader could reach it.

"Jenn, you can turn the light back on, and what do you think about this?" He whispered his plan to her as they moved. "Keep in mind that Peterson's team could be here soon to rescue us if we have to remain hidden in the forest near the campground."

"It sounds good. But what about their vehicles? They can use them to catch us."

"What vehicles? I'll slash their tires when we go by. I won't leave them enough good tires for even one car."

"OK, Ripper, let's do it. When do we start?"

"In another thirty seconds, we won't have to worry about them hearing us if we break any more twigs." Lee put his arm around Kirsten and gave her a hug.

Jennifer pulled the other two girls close.

They stood like a five-man football team, huddled, arms around shoulders, heads nearly touching, as the quarterback called the play.

Katie, Kirsten, and Mel seemed alive again.

No one can survive without hope.

He would give as much hope in the next few seconds as he could.

21

Lee spoke softly to the girls. "In a few seconds those goons will be safely out of earshot. That's when we'll start running to Jenn's car." He outlined their plan, including the risks that might leave them hiding in the forest short of the car. "We're all in this together, and we all must depend on each other to escape. But we have Someone else on our side, Someone Trader doesn't have. God. Let's pray to Him now." After Lee finished his short prayer, he stood silently for a few seconds, and then lifted his head. "It's time. Let's go."

Kirsten slipped her arms around Lee's neck and gave him a firm hug. The other two girls followed her lead.

What he hoped for, prayed for, had happened. They were a team now.

When all five stepped onto the trail Lee set a fast walking pace, and then increased it to a jog. As he loped down the trail, his fingers ran over the gun he'd taken from the shack, planning his actions if he needed to fire it. Would the weapon be in automatic or single-shot mode if he pushed the safety lever down? He would have to defer that, and other determinations, until later.

Lee lowered the gun and patted his jeans pocket feeling for his knife.

Jennifer poked him in the back with what felt like the butt of her .38. "Still the worrier, I see."

"I've just got, you know, concerns."

"Déjà vu? Seven months ago?"

"No, Jenn. Don't even think that."

"I wasn't serious. I only noticed you checking for your knife."

"If Ivan had played his little game a few seconds longer, you would have seen me slash something other than tires."

"You stopped him with my .38. Let's forget about Ivan."

A short burst of automatic-weapon fire sounded from far behind.

"That was Trader. We can forget about Ivan now," Lee whispered. "We're getting close to the parking area. When we arrive, take the girls and run to the campground. I'll slash their tires and sprint to catch up."

"OK, but hurry. Don't spend one more second there than you have to."

"If you think I'm taking too long or if you see lights behind you, get the girls off the road on the campground side and hide them."

"I will, but you'd better not take any chances, Lee, or I'll kill you."

"With your .38?"

"No. With my bare hands."

When they crossed the bridge, Lee pointed to the left side of the road. "There's the parking area. Let's hurry."

He trotted off the bridge and into the entrance to the parking area.

What was this?

"Jenn, three vehicles." Lee heard something in the bushes to his right.

The lights of the third vehicle came on, blasting their eyes with intense light.

A raspy voice came from near the lights. "Put down your weapon, or I'll take you all out, starting with you, Mr. Gunman." A dark figure moved ahead of the vehicle, off to one side.

The bluish lights now revealed a gunman with his weapon trained on them.

There wasn't supposed to be another goon. Who was this man? Since he hadn't gunned them down, he probably had the same question about them.

Lee needed a good answer. He slowly bent down and placed his rifle on the ground. As plans to use the weapon came to mind, each was discarded because of the danger to Jennifer and the girls.

"Your light, too."

Lee set the flashlight down, pointing it towards the gunman. It was a very small advantage, but he would take anything he could get.

"Hands in the air, all of you. Spread out and take two steps forward. Now!"

Jennifer stood on his left. On his right were Kirsten and Mel.

Katie was gone.

"Who are you, and where were you going with my three girls?"

Three girls? *His* girls? This must be Boatman.

If Lee couldn't make something happen, he was dead, and soon the girls would wish they were.

Except Katie. She was smart and to Boatman, invisible.

Hopefully he wouldn't notice that there was no blonde in the group.

"I'm going to ask you one more time. Who are

you?" The raspy voice became more abrasive.

Lee was running out of options, so he decided to roll the dice. "Boatman, I thought it was time for me to take over Trader's business."

"So you know I am, and you told me who you want to be. But who are you?"

"I'm Weatherman. I can run this business more efficiently and more securely than Trader. And I don't use sexually incontinent goons like Ivan."

The silhouetted head cocked to one side.

Jennifer had slipped over a few inches, so her right arm was partially hidden from Boatman's view by Lee's shadow.

He gently rocked while he waited with his hands in the air, inching to his left, shading more of Jennifer's right arm.

After a long pause, Boatman replied, "Trader was useful because there was trust between us...most of the time. With you, I have no trust. How do—"

Something crashed into the white SUV. The vehicle alarm wailed.

Boatman whirled, pointing his gun at Trader's SUV.

Lee dove, taking the two girls to the ground. He covered them with his body, and then looked up knowing what he would see.

Jennifer had already drawn her .38.

Boatman swung his rifle back.

Three shots cracked above the alarm and the wind. Three familiar sounding shots.

The element of surprise, a two hundred IQ, a marksman, and a heart that wouldn't quit—Boatman had no chance.

"Jenn, hold your gun on him." He spoke over the

wailing alarm. "I'll check him."

He spun towards a rustling sound in the bushes.

Jennifer swung the .38 in that direction.

"It's Katie." Her voice was barely audible over the car alarm. "Please don't shoot."

"Wait right there, Katie." Jennifer's alto voice carried the authority of a battlefield commander.

Katie stood motionless.

The wailing alarm stopped.

Boatman's neck was warm to his touch. But it wouldn't be warm much longer. "He won't be making any more exchanges." Lee pulled the clip from Boatman's gun, stuffed it in his pocket, and then slung the weapon far into the thick bushes.

"OK, girls. Come to me now," Jennifer ordered, but her voice had softened.

"Jenn, take the girls and run. I'll catch up when I'm done."

Jennifer wrapped her free arm around Katie. "Thanks, Katie. You saved all our lives."

Katie returned the hug, and then they all disappeared into the darkness.

Lee's fingers fished through his pocket, and then closed around his knife. He had twelve tires to slash. With adrenaline still coursing through his body, Lee dealt ten devastating blows to ten tires before a light beam appeared, bouncing wildly through the trees on the far side of the river.

Trader and Jacko.

His feet pounded the pavement as he sprinted towards Mora Campground, the girls, and Jennifer.

The battle with Trader would come later. How much later?

He wished he knew.

22

Mel wasn't a runner.

Trying to compensate, Jennifer shortened the distance by running the inside of each turn on Mora Road as it snaked through the forest.

Rapid footsteps sounded behind them.

"Keep running, it's me." Lee pulled alongside of her. "How are the girls holding up?"

"At this pace, they're doing fine. Did you see Trader?"

"Yeah. He showed up before I slashed the last two tires. Don't think he saw me."

"Doesn't really matter though, does it?"

"About the tires? He'll know who it was. Second time today. Should make him really mad, maybe a little crazy."

"Crazy sounds good."

"Yeah. But he and Jacko…are probably running up the road behind us."

"Any sign of them and we go into the trees, right?"

"That's the plan."

They rounded the final turn before reaching the long, straight stretch. It continued more than a half mile beyond the campground.

"Jenn, I think we need to get off the road now." He motioned to their right. "Behind the big tree on the right."

"Girls, here's where we're going." Jennifer illuminated the tree with her flashlight.

"Good." Mel spoke between gasps.

Jennifer kept the flashlight beam low to the ground, lighting their path only enough to get the girls safely off the road.

When they reached a secluded spot thirty yards into the trees, Lee stretched out his arms, inviting the girls to step close to him. He waited until the five formed a tight circle. "Turn out the light, please. Trader and Jacko will soon come into sight on the road. Here's our situation. They don't know where we are. Jenn's car is nearby, but they don't know where it is. Probably think we're trying to reach one of the houses up the road to call the police. Now, we can't use the car to make a run for Forks unless we're certain Trader and Jacko aren't waiting to ambush us."

"So what are you proposing, Lee?" She had disagreed with Lee's risk taking before and stood ready to do it again.

"Let's move further into the trees, and we can talk about it. The wind is still strong enough to cover our voices. We'll go slow and move without the light."

"I'll lead." Jennifer extended a hand to Mel. "Katie, please keep your eye out for Trader's light along the road."

"No need to do that," Katie pointed behind them. "I see it now."

"You've got good night vision. Let's hide behind the bushes. And Katie, please track Trader's light as best you can. Let us know if it stops or changes direction."

"I will, Jenn."

Katie needed to be needed. But Jennifer sensed her

motivation went much deeper. She was selfless to the point of risking her life to save the rest of the group.

As they worked their way behind a large group of bushes, Jennifer decided she would coax Katie's story from her at an appropriate time. There seemed to be something about this girl, something Jennifer was supposed to respond to.

Lee spoke softly, "We need a plan to get out of here. Keep in mind there may be disagreements, and that's OK. Let's speak openly and come up with our plan. Now, an FBI team led by a man Jenn and I know personally, Agent Peterson, is trying to get here. But they won't know exactly where we are unless we can call either them, or the Forks police. Jennifer's car is parked about two hundred and fifty yards to the east of where we're standing." He pointed. "I'm sure we can get to it without being detected by Trader and Jacko, but we don't want them shooting at us along the road if we try to drive back to Forks. It's a little after 2:00. In about four and a half hours, it will start getting light. Once it's light, Trader might find Jennifer's SUV...and us."

Where was he going with this? She wouldn't let him separate them, not like he did in March. "We should hide and wait for the FBI to show up," Jennifer said. "They can take on Trader and Jacko much better than we can."

"What if it starts getting light and they still haven't shown up?" Lee asked.

"We need a fortress to hide in. A place that gives us visibility of the area around us, some protection against bullets, and it should keep us hidden from view. We can wait indefinitely in a place like that. If Trader shows up, we gun him down and leave. Right now, I wouldn't mind giving him what I gave Boatman."

"OK. Plan number one is to hide in the campground. It keeps us safe for several hours and only gets dicey if Trader walks in on us or if we accidentally give away our position. It does mean we have to find a fort. Jenn, you know this area better than any of us. Do you have a place in mind?"

"The restroom in the campground near my car. It's heated enough to keep the water pipes from freezing in the winter. We'd be warmer there than out here in the woods. But we'll have to check it out to see if we have enough visibility to spot Trader if he approaches."

"Sounds good, provided we can be hidden and still see around us." Lee broke the huddle. "Let's check out the restroom."

"Have you got any other ideas, Lee?"

"I like what you suggested. But I would add one more thing to it."

"I'm listening."

Here it comes. The part where Lee splits off from the group and tries to —

"Jenn, no sacrificing anybody to the likes of Trader. I promise."

"Like I said, I'm listening." Her tone didn't change. She couldn't let it.

"You know the ranger's house at the east end of the camp? You mentioned it to me a few days ago. You said it was occupied during the summer and early fall, but not now."

"Are you thinking there might be a working phone in the house?"

"More like hoping. It's worth sneaking over there to check it out. But not until you're all settled into Fort

John."

Mel giggled at Lee's description and then slapped her hand over her mouth.

Jennifer mussed Mel's hair. "As much as I want us all to stay together, you're right. One phone call could end this ordeal. Are you going over to the house alone?"

"He should take me along to watch for Trader while he goes in." Even with the darkness hiding her body language, Katie's determination was unmistakable.

Brave, smart, athletic, a team player. Jennifer was rapidly accumulating a list of Katie's admirable qualities.

"Good idea," Lee said. "Katie and I need to check the house out soon, before Trader starts snooping around. Let's move to the restroom, get settled in, and then Katie and I will go to the ranger's place."

She took a deep breath and blew it back out. "I know Trader probably went beyond the campground to the first house on the road to head us off. But what happens if he comes back and cuts you two off so you can't get back to us?"

"Then we have Trader right where we want him, in a crossfire."

"Oh, yes. I remember now. You're Lee Brandt, the optimist." She couldn't hide the sarcasm.

"You're the one who said 'to the beach' if I remember correctly." Lee cleared his throat. "I'm sorry. There's so much we stand to lose if something goes wrong. I know it scares you. It scares me, too. But I love you, Jenn. That's part of the reason Katie and I need to go. We'll be careful, very careful." As Lee spoke, he drew her close.

When Lee kissed her on the forehead, she smiled.

It was good for these girls to see how love worked. It was even better to feel it. But the thought of Trader and Jacko ambushing Lee and Katie scared her.

"About your concern." Lee paused. "If we were to get into a firefight with Trader and Jacko, which gun would you want?"

"My .38."

"Are you sure? The automatic shoots eight rounds a second."

"I know more about the .38, and it hits what I aim at. Plus, it doesn't jam."

"OK. Katie and I will take the automatic. Now let's move out to Fort John."

23

The brief shafts of moonlight squeezing between the racing clouds gave Lee moments of visibility. But the intermittent light also prevented his eyes from adjusting to the intervening darkness.

"Your night vision is better than mine, Jenn. Will you lead us from here to the camp?"

She stepped in front of him. "Sure, I'll lead."

In a few moments, Jennifer brought the group to a stop. "This has to be loop C, and I think I see the trail."

The restroom building loomed in front of them.

"It's the off season, like the lights...off."

"That's probably best for us, Jenn. Our eyes will be adjusted to the dark and we won't be lit up like a lantern for Trader to see. Let's go inside and check out the visibility."

"We can go inside and check it out, but we're going into the women's side."

He shrugged and stepped towards the men's door. "Does it really matter?"

"Yes it matters. Men's restrooms are gross."

"Is that based upon statistical analysis? What's your sample size?"

"It's what all the ladies say."

"Yeah," three voices replied in unison.

Jennifer was using her battlefield commander's voice again.

He needed to give on this issue. "OK, we'll use the

women's side."

"He's going to be in *our* restroom?" Mel's tenor voice leaped up to soprano.

"Look, everybody," he scanned their faces. "This is first and foremost a fort, not a restroom."

"But what if one of us needs to, you know…" Mel stopped.

"OK." He gave a concessionary sigh. "When one of you needs to, you know, I'll leave, banished to the men's room until you knock on the wall."

"Lee, would you please go to the men's room until we knock?" Mel pointed towards the door.

"I'm outta here," He slipped out the door and entered the men's side.

When three knocks on the wall sounded, he walked back to the women's door. "You knocked three times, so I'm coming in. At least it wasn't on the pipes."

Jennifer giggled as he stepped in.

Mel cocked her head. "Knocking on pipes? What does that mean?"

"Means you aren't gonna show." Lee and Jennifer answered in unison.

He turned towards Mel. "We'll explain later. Right now, we need to check the visibility. We can only see to the west from the men's restroom, but let's see what we've got in here for the other three directions."

After breaking a small pane in the frosted-glass window and prying some wooden slats loose from a vent on the wall, he was satisfied with the visibility on three sides. "We need to decide on some ground rules for—"

Jennifer stepped close and put her arms around his waist. "I think we all understand the advantages and shortcomings of the fort. But, Lee, I keep getting urges to take us all to the car and make a run for it. It's only about seventy-five yards away."

"Trader is watching Mora Road. He'd do anything to stop us. We need to stay here until Peterson arrives. It's nearly 3 AM. He could be here any minute. But since we can't count on that, Katie and I should go to the ranger's house now."

"You're right. We're safe and warm for now. Maybe I'll even dry out."

"Katie, before we go, you need to learn to shoot an AK-47." In the dim light of the cell phone, he watched her eyes widen.

Katie watched him as he set the assault rifle on the floor and positioned his cell to illuminate the gun.

"You need to know a few things about this gun."

"OK. But you're going to do the shooting if it comes to that, right?"

"I'm showing you this in case I get hurt or, you know…"

"But, Lee, that's not going to happen, because we'll be careful and, well, Jennifer said God will rescue us from our enemies."

"Sometimes He surprises in the way He helps us. I'm showing you this just in case the worst happens. So watch closely, because this could save our lives. Here's the safety lever. Pull it up and the gun won't fire. Push it down and it will be in automatic mode. I finally figured out that part."

"What?" Jennifer blurted. "You're giving Katie on-the-job training for a weapon you're clueless about?"

"If you've fired one of these things, Jenn, you show her how it's done."

"I haven't fired one." Jennifer lowered her voice.

"But I've had several fired at me."

He shook his head. "That's not what we want Katie to learn. I've got this thing figured out, so let me finish." He paused. "OK, Katie, put it in automatic mode."

Katie moved the safety down, and then quickly back up.

"If you fire in automatic mode, the barrel will try to rise. You have to pull it down with the barrel handle."

After he showed her how to load and clear a jam, Katie grabbed his arm.

"I get it, Lee. I'm good to go if you really need me to shoot. But I hope we don't need to do any shooting…only make a phone call."

****

Lee led as he and Katie stepped into the darkness.

Only when the moon made its brief appearances could he see anything on the ground. He inched his way down the trail, but this was taking far too long.

Katie tapped his shoulder. "My eyes are adjusted. I can see pretty well. Do you want me to lead?"

"Yeah, please. My eyes need a little more time," Lee whispered. "You lead for a while. Be sure to stay near the right edge of the road. If we see or hear any signs of Trader, step into the bushes."

"Got it." She stepped in front of him.

When they passed the loop B road, he could make out the white letters on the sign. In another fifty yards, they reached loop A.

"Katie, I'll take the lead from here. I think there's a shortcut ahead that will take us through the trees to the ranger's house."

Katie followed down the right edge of the road.

He stopped and scanned the trees on their right.

"What is it?"

"It's OK, Katie. This is where we cut through the woods." He stepped into the trees.

Soon a lawn came into view and beyond that, a building.

"Is that the house?" Katie whispered from behind.

"That's it. Are you ready?"

"Shouldn't we walk around it first, to make sure no one's around?"

"Good idea." He pointed ahead. "We should circle the storage building, too. Let's stay near the edge of the trees. You watch for Trader or Jacko, and I'll look for a place to break in."

Within minutes, they had circled the house and the adjacent building.

"In the back of the house, there's a window I might be able to force open. Let's go back to it."

When they reached the window he turned to Katie. "Here, you take the gun, now. I'm going to pry the window open with my knife. Hope there's no alarm. It would bring the police eventually, but—"

"But probably Trader first."

"Yeah. Let's pray that doesn't happen."

Slowly his knife pushed the sliding portion of the window up. He worked his fingers into the small gap he had created. When he stuck the knife into the upper part of the frame and pushed, the window slid open. He waited.

There was only silence.

"Good, no alarm, at least, not on this window. I'm going in now."

"I'll knock on the window if I see any signs of Trader out here."

Lee slid through the window and dropped onto the floor.

An explosion of light blinded him.

"Looking for this, Mr. Tire Slasher? You want the phone?" *This must be Jacko.* His voice was mocking. "It's been disabled. You might say *slashed.*" He held up the sliced cord. "Now, give me your hands and don't try anything."

Lee tried to fight off the panic that caused his thoughts to race too fast. Finally, he caught one. He needed to pray. *Please, Lord, help Katie.*

He slowly extended his hands.

Jacko zip-tied his wrists.

What would Katie do? He recalled her determined voice and her words, "He should take me along to watch for Trader."

Katie would do what she had to do, try to take out Jacko. Everything he had seen convinced him this courageous girl would fire on Jacko. But, if she tried and missed, Jacko would return her fire.

Help Katie. Keep her safe.

Once his wrists were secure, Jacko stepped back and pointed his weapon at him.

"Move into the living room." Jacko followed him until Lee stopped in the center of the room.

"Now, Mr. Tire Slasher, tell me what—"

The big window exploded. Shards of glass splattered against the wall and noise filled the night.

Lee jumped backward, creating more clearance from Jacko, giving Katie more shooting room.

It wasn't necessary.

Jacko hit the floor on his back.

The shooting stopped.

Silence. Except for the whistling of the wind.

Lee ran towards the living room door and leaped feet first into it, legs flexed to kick it open. He flew through the doorway as his feet hit nothing but air. But his back landed hard on concrete. Air exploded out through his mouth. Then came the agonizing attempts to suck the air back in.

Katie stood over him looking confused. Her gaze darted between Jacko's body inside the door and his on the concrete walkway.

"Knife...in coat pocket," he croaked like a bullfrog.

Her hands shook as she pulled the knife from his coat. The knife locked with a click.

He held up his hands.

She sliced through the tie. "Are you OK? I didn't hit—"

He managed his first full breath. "No, you didn't...breath...knocked out of me."

"I'm sorry, Lee. I didn't know the door would open, and I didn't—"

"I'm sorry too, because I was going to kick that door to kingdom come about the time you opened it." He chuckled.

Katie didn't.

"Give me the knife, Katie. I need to check on Jacko."

Lee bent over the motionless body. It was the second warm neck his fingers had touched, the second one without a pulse.

He picked up the gun and flashlight. "Jacko won't be chasing us anymore." He stepped close to her. "Katie, I know shooting him was hard to do. You might even have some bad feelings about it. But

178

remember this, you did the right thing in that situation, and you did it perfectly. Don't let anybody, even yourself, tell you differently. Now push the safety lever all the way up."

"I already did."

"Good." Lee wrapped his arms around her. "I'm so proud of you, young lady."

Katie held her head high, but she was shaking. Then tears streamed down her face.

He held her, and her tears turned to sobs.

"How did you ever manage—"

"Jennifer said He was there for us if we trust Him." She managed between sobs. "He was all I had to trust."

"And you put it in the right place, Katie...in the right Person."

Katie stepped back, swiping her face on her sleeve. Lit by the living room light, her brilliant blue eyes met his, and her chin rose. "I'm ready, now."

He reached inside and turned off the lights, and then returned to Katie's side. "We've probably attracted Trader. You've got your gun, and now I've got mine. A light, too." He popped out the clip from Jacko's gun, examined it with the flashlight, and popped it back in. "Come on, soldier. Let's get back to Fort John."

24

3:30 AM. Monday, November 4

Though Lee didn't want to overload her with responsibilities, he trusted this girl. In the few hours he had known her, Katie's clever and courageous acts had twice saved his life.

"Katie, will you lead us through the trees. After the lights back there, I can't see anything." He caught her arm. "When you reach the edge of the road, stop before anyone out there might see us...anyone like Trader with his flashlight."

"I will. After what we've escaped from, we can't let Trader catch us again."

"I'm not big on irony. But with three of his men dead, I don't think Trader has catch on his mind. It's more like kill."

"I'll be careful, Lee." Katie led him through the darkness of the trees for three or four minutes before stopping. "The road is about ten feet straight ahead."

"Thanks. I'll take the lead now."

"Why are you always taking the dangerous part? We're in this together."

"I do it because I'm the adult, and I have the responsibility for your safety."

"Then tell me, what was I when I held the gun while you went into the house? What was I responsible for when I shot Jacko?"

"You were fulfilling the role of an adult, and you did it perfectly. I know this may not sound fair, but I have to get you back to Jenn in one piece. If I don't, she'll shoot me. So, Katie, I need to lead now that we're going to be exposed on an open roadway."

"Go ahead." Katie sighed. "I wouldn't want to make Jennifer mad at you."

"Thanks for understanding." He looked both directions along the main road and stepped out.

Katie's arm yanked him back with a force that nearly slung him to the ground.

"What is it?"

"There's a car coming down the road. It's coming from the same direction as Trader's van."

"You're right. But Trader couldn't have—it's slowing to turn in."

He pushed her back into the shelter of the trees. When the car turned into the campground, two bright headlights swung in an arc, flashing across their hiding place. The vehicle stopped, illuminating the entire campground road in front of them.

"Katie," Lee whispered. "Something looks familiar about—"

"It's a van, Lee. A really big one."

"Yeah. Big enough for a whole SWAT team." He stepped from the trees into the lights of the vehicle.

"No, Lee! Don't do it!"

"It's OK. It's the FBI."

"You mean our rescuers finally got here?" Sarcasm had quickly replaced panic in Katie's voice. This girl had a lot in common with Jennifer.

"Something like that." He kept his gun in his left hand, holding it palm outward, pointing the business end towards the ground.

Katie stood feet spread, with both hands on her AK-47.

He hadn't anticipated this. Things could go dreadfully wrong. "Katie, don't raise your gun! Keep it down!"

A deep voice boomed from the van, clearly audible above the wind whistling through the treetops. "Is that you, Brandt? Who else would be fool enough to—"

"It's me, Lee Brandt. That is you, Peterson, isn't it? I really would like to put this gun down."

"This is Peterson. Put it down, Lee. And please tell me that isn't a teenage girl behind you holding an assault rifle."

"Can't do that, Peterson. Wouldn't want to lie to the FBI. She killed one of the traffickers with it."

Peterson was silent, probably digesting Lee's last bit of information. "Brandt, what in blue blazes did you and Jennifer stir up out here? By the way, where is Jennifer? Is she all right?"

"Jenn and I have the three girls. She's with the other two and the third is standing behind me, ready to take you on. Agent Peterson, meet Katie. Katie, you can put your gun down, or at least hold it like you're not about to shoot somebody."

Katie held her gun with both hands and remained in a firing posture. "Are you absolutely sure, Lee? No one is spoofing us or anything, are they?"

"No tricks, Katie. The nightmare's over."

Katie stepped forward, holding her AK-47 in her left hand as he had done.

"Secure the area, men." Peterson stepped out of the van and gestured in a circular motion.

Several men slipped out the van's door and

quickly disappeared into the surrounding darkness.

"OK, let's try this again. Katie, this is Agent Peterson, FBI."

No greeting from Katie. That worried him.

When she opened her mouth to speak, her deep frown and glaring eyes gave him more reason for concern.

"Aren't you a little bit late?" Katie threw the words at Peterson like the fastball rock she put through Trader's van window, but this pitch was high and inside. "We had to do three-fourths of your work."

Lee stared at Katie, wondering if he now had a fifteen-year-old Jennifer on his hands, and, if so, what he could do about it.

Peterson pulled his head back at Katie's redress. "What are you talking about, young lady?"

"If you had gotten here when you were supposed to, we wouldn't have had to—I wouldn't have had to—I just killed a man." Katie put her gun down beside Lee and reached for him.

A voice came from inside the van. "The area is secure, Pete."

Lee held Katie while she cried.

Peterson was silent.

So was Lee, but praying that all of the remaining fear, anger, and guilt would flow away with Katie's tears.

Please, Lord, don't let her carry it any further than this moment.

Peterson didn't speak until Katie released her hold on Lee and wiped her cheeks. "I'm sorry, Katie. But we couldn't get here any sooner. We had to cut through a lot of downed trees. We wore out two chains on our saw. You did a brave thing. I wish we could've gotten here earlier so you wouldn't have had to…" His voice trailed off.

Katie stood erect and faced Peterson. "And I'm sorry for dissing the FBI. But I wish you'd gotten here to kill those three guys, so we didn't have to."

"What do you mean killing three men?" He reverted to his booming voice. "Lee, just tell it to me plain. How many perpetrators are out here and what's their status?"

Lee kept his summary as concise as possible. "Things got pretty wild during the storm. We can tell you the long version later. But right now, we know of only four perpetrators here on land. Three of them are dead, the fourth—well when you turned in to the campground, Katie and I thought the fourth one had found us and we were going to kill you, until I recognized the van."

"Let me see if I've gotten this straight. You and Jennifer came out here looking for the traffickers' holding location and, against superior fire power, while outnumbered, you managed to kill three of the four perpetrators, taking their weapons and their captives. You were looking for the last man, to kill him, when we arrived."

"Those are the facts, but you make it sound—"

"I make it sound far-fetched and crazy, because it is! You two came out here against my direct orders—"

"Peterson, we don't work for you. You work for us, the taxpayers."

"Blast it, Lee! You know what I mean. You two came out here against my better judgment and—"

"And rescued all three girls!" Katie's strong alto drowned out Peterson's bass. "Killed three of the four perpetrators and, if you were the fourth man, the one called Trader, we would've killed you, too!" In the high-intensity lights of the van Katie's blue eyes glared like cold steel, while her tone burned like the molten form of that metal. "When you turned in, you drove right into a trap. Maybe Lee and I are the ones who should be in that van trying to rescue you."

"Brother." Peterson shook his head. "I believe you've made your point, young lady. See me when you graduate from college. I may have a job for you. Now, where did you say Jennifer and the other two girls are?"

"Uh…they're holding down the fort."

"What fort?"

"Fort John," Lee replied.

Katie laughed. That was a good sign.

But Peterson's blank stare contained no humor.

"Come on, Peterson. I'll show you. But you'd better let me go in first or Jennifer might shoot someone. She already killed the guy from the boat."

Peterson tossed his hands in the air. "Is this another perpetrator—a guy on a boat? So you killed four men?"

"No. This guy, alias Boatman, came to check on his buddies. He caught us escaping with the three girls, after I killed their guard."

"Kill, kill, kill. If this was a movie it would be X-rated for violence. Do you see why I didn't want you and Jennifer to—"

"Peterson," Lee interrupted, "It's the business these guys are in that's X-rated. Now, do you want me to continue, or not?"

"I'm not sure I do, but we might as well get it over with."

"Boatman got the drop on us in the parking area.

But Katie chucked a rock so hard it went clear through his car window. That set off the security alarm and gave Jennifer an opportunity to pull out her .38. She put him out of business...permanently. We only killed three men, Petersen."

"I'll remember that when I fill out my reports." Peterson shook his head. "You only killed three men, three measly little men, only three—creating mountains of paperwork for me and—"

Katie stepped toe-to-toe with the tall FBI agent. "I can give you some better things to call them than measly."

"I think what you'd better give me, young lady, is a description of the one who's still at large."

Katie gave him a description of Trader that an artist could have sketched. Was this what Jennifer's teenage sisters were like?

Peterson called the information in to the Forks police, and then closed his cell phone.

"Peterson," Lee cleared his throat, "There's something I should've asked you."

"What's that?"

"How many vehicles did you see in the parking area by the river?"

"Three. All with flat tires—flat, slashed tires."

"Good. Then Trader's on foot. Soon he'll need a vehicle."

"I'll pass that along."

"Also, Katie and I are at least a half hour overdue. Jennifer is going to be worried. You know how she can get. I need to let her know that you're here and we're all right."

"How can you be sure that Trader hasn't gotten to them?" Peterson frowned. "You can't go barging in on...Fort John, is it?"

"Jennifer is pretty well fortified and she's armed. We would have heard gunfire if Trader tried anything. Let me go in and make contact with her."

Peterson opened his mouth to speak.

"Look." Lee let out a sharp blast of air. "You know both of us, so you know this is the safest way to get her to stand down."

In the blue light of the headlamps, Peterson's face grew a reddish shade of purple. "Blast it all to blazes, Lee! I have to give an account, from this moment forward, for everything that happens out here. I'm the one who's responsible for everybody's safety."

"Then you'll let me go to the fort so everyone can actually be safe. She'll shoot you, Peterson."

"Yeah, and she always hits what she shoots at," Katie added.

Peterson took a breath and exhaled loudly. His voice softened. "This will not appear in the official report. But we will back you, hidden and out of sight, while you contact Jennifer. But you *will* stay well back while you communicate with her. Is that understood?"

"Understood. Now let's go. Jennifer is in the restroom on loop C, about three hundred yards from here."

"Hence, Fort John."

"You're pretty sharp." Katie fired her acrid comment at him.

"So's your tongue, young lady."

Lee glanced at Katie and shook his head. "Katie, please cool it while I tell Jenn we're all right."

"Yes, Lee," Katie replied. Her melodrama, sounding like the epitome of compliance, was not lost on Lee. Nor was the glare of her defiant gaze.

Peterson glared back and his face grew red again. "Young lady, I would handcuff those eyes of yours if that was possible."

"And I would tell you what you can—"

"Katie! Cool it! Jenn is already going to be trigger-happy. Do you want me to get shot?"

"I'm sorry, Lee. I lost my temper."

"Just like Jenn," he muttered.

Katie smiled at his comment, but she kept her mouth shut.

Now to cool off Jennifer.

25

Lee jogged down the road to loop C. He turned the corner onto the lane, and then slowed, knowing the dicey part lay a few feet straight ahead.

"Jenn, it's Lee. Are you and the girls OK in there?" He waited.

No response.

"Jenn, Peterson and the SWAT team are here. We got Jacko, and Trader's on the run. It's all over. You can come out now."

"We heard shots, Lee. What happened?"

"Katie had to shoot Jacko."

Lee could hear a cacophony of female voices.

Jennifer shouted something.

The voices stopped.

"How do we know this isn't a trap?"

"Come on, Jenn, this is crazy." Lee turned around, his back to Fort John. "Peterson, tell one of your men to step out in the open and shine his flashlight on his SWAT team uniform."

"Do what he said, Ruska." Peterson ordered.

After Peterson's command and the flash of the light, Jennifer opened the door.

Simultaneously, lights came on from several points in the bushes, illuminating the entire scene.

Jennifer ran into his arms. He kept them open until he could also wrap them around Mel and Kirsten.

While he tried to kiss Jennifer, Kirsten tugged on

his shredded coat sleeve. "Did Katie really shoot Jacko?"

Mel tugged on his other arm. "Did she do it in machine-gun mode?"

He heard Jennifer's voice rise above the pandemonium, "Rain check?"

"Most certainly," he replied.

"Katie mowed him down just like in the movies?" Mel stared into his eyes, and when he nodded, her whole frame relaxed.

It occurred to Lee that these girls' greatest fear had been the men who held them. Now that fear was gone forever. Except Trader. Lee'd have to see what he could do about that.

The van rolled towards them. "Lee, Jennifer." Peterson resorted to his voice of authority. "We need to get you two and the girls into the van for safety's sake. We don't want to risk any sniper fire."

Katie's voice came from somewhere inside. "Jenn, are all three of you OK? Trader didn't pay you a visit, did he?"

Jennifer swept Mel and Kirsten through the van door with her arm. "We're all fine, Katie. No signs of Trader."

Mel plopped down beside Katie on the rear seat of the van. "Tell us what happened. Where did you run into Jacko?"

Kirsten slid in beside them. "Yes, tell us."

Katie lowered her head, but said nothing.

Lee wanted to intervene, but stopped when she looked up at Mel.

"Jacko trapped Lee in the house. I was holding the gun and watching from outside. I did what I had to do. That's enough for now, Mel. Can we talk about something else?"

"What a girl," he whispered to Jennifer as they took the seat in front of the three girls.

"Yes." Jennifer leaned her head against his shoulder. "Without her, we might not have survived tonight."

In the backseat, Mel and Kirsten draped arms around Katie.

"I'm glad the bad men are dead," Mel blurted out. "This has been a horrible night."

"I'll certainly never forget it," Kirsten said softly.

"That's an understatement," Jennifer whispered to Lee.

"I love you, Jenn, and I'm glad to have you sitting beside me, safe and sound. That's an understatement, too."

Peterson climbed into the passenger side of the van and turned to Jennifer. "Where's your SUV? You mentioned something about being shot at when you called from Forks."

"Just go one hundred yards or so around this loop and you'll see it. We hid it before we went to the parking area by the river."

"We'll need to do forensics on it if there are bullet holes, and you'll need repairs."

"There are bullet holes...in all the right places." Jennifer snapped back.

"You mean there are *right* places to have bullet holes in your car?"

"Yes. The places where the bullets don't hit you on their way through."

"You do have a point, Jennifer. But my point is you're going to be without your vehicle for a few weeks. The FBI will pay their portion for the rental.

Changing the subject, based upon that Boatman character, I'm extending the investigation offshore. We'll involve the Coast Guard. If we get lucky and find something, we can use our agents deployed overseas."

"I hope you trace these guys all the way to where they're selling the girls. Maybe even rescue some," Lee said.

"Unfortunately that's a rarity. In other countries there are too many officials on the take, or too intimidated to talk. Some are paying customers who won't incriminate themselves."

"We've got to do something to put a stop to this trafficking business." Jennifer's voice rose. "I'm going to do something, whatever it takes."

Peterson turned back towards the driver. "Let's roll out for Forks."

Jennifer sat up, rigid. "My engagement ring! It's in the car. Does it have to be impounded, too?"

"No, it doesn't." Peterson said. "Ed, circle around to Jennifer's SUV."

"Why did you leave your ring, Jenn?" Lee asked, puzzled.

"I just had this feeling that I shouldn't wear it. Not having it on helped me fool Trader. The traffickers thought I was a teenager."

"If you'd have worn it..."

"Yes. Things might have turned out differently. Makes you think Someone was watching out for me." She gave him a warm smile.

"Someone was." He returned her smile, and then leaned forward between Peterson and Ed. "What about the FBI team? They're all over the camp and—"

"And a few other places, too," Peterson said. "Also, there are state police, Clallam County deputies, and some Forks police. Watch as we drive down Mora Road. The SWAT team will have plenty of transportation when they're finished out here."

After Jennifer retrieved her ring, the van left the campground.

While they drove back towards Forks, they passed police cars at strategic locations along Mora Road. The speed and comprehensiveness of the FBI response, once it began, impressed him. "You're really putting the squeeze on Trader, aren't you?"

"That's the idea. We have roadblocks along Highway 101 both north and south of Forks. If he doesn't decide to play mountain man, we'll nail him soon."

"And if he does?" Jennifer asked.

"I was afraid you might ask that." Peterson paused. "Then all bets are off, for us and for him. This is wild, unforgiving country. And about getting the girls back to their parents," Peterson paused. "I thought about holding the girls at Forks. But the roads may not be open until late in the day—too many trees down. I'm going to tell their parents to meet us at the field office in Seattle."

Katie shifted uneasily in her seat. "That's fine for Mel and Kirsten. But I have some special considerations and...and a request."

"Oh, and what might that be?"

Katie leaned forward. "My foster parents, and I use that term loosely, don't want me, and I don't want them. There has been attempted, well, attempted abuse several times. I was planning to run away if I couldn't get moved to a new home. But Trader caught me first."

"Who's your caseworker?" Petersen asked.

"Mrs. Barnes, in Seattle. She was recently assigned

to me. I've only seen her a couple of times, so we don't know each other very well, yet."

"Do you have her number?"

"Yes. I memorized her number in case I needed help."

"But you said you were planning to run away."

"Peterson, that was only if I couldn't get help. I hadn't called Mrs. Barnes about the...problem yet. Then Trader came along and gave me a bigger one."

"Katie, I'm sorry we got started on the wrong foot. I happen to know someone who works for the state, someone who can help us even at 5:00 AM. It so happens this someone also owes me a big favor. I'm about to call it in."

Katie's eyes widened. "I'm sorry for what I said, Agent Peterson. The way things worked out, maybe you arrived at the perfect time, because Trader didn't get another shot at us."

"That's as it should be," Lee nodded. "He already had more than his fair share of shots at Jenn and me."

"OK. Here's the plan for the next hour or so. I'm going to make a few phone calls, and then we'll be arriving at the Forks police station around 6:00 AM. There, we're going to take statements from each of you and ask a lot of questions. Then you girls can call your families and tell them you're safe. But before you call, I'll give you a list of details you should omit when you talk to your parents, things which might hurt our investigation. Then, it's five hours in the van back to Seattle, where your parents will pick you up."

"The only person who needs to hear that Katie's all right already knows. It's me," Jennifer said.

"And me too, Jenn," Lee murmured.

Jennifer pulled her head back and smiled at him.

"What about Katie, Lee? She has no one to call, no one she wants to call."

"That's a tough one."

The look he received from Jennifer translated to three words. She might as well have spoken them. Fix Katie's problem.

Lee put his arm around Jennifer and pulled her close.

How do I fix it?

You already know how.

He waffled between the two sides of his mind — the logical and the sensing. "Jenn, I'm so tired I can't even think right now."

Jennifer glared at him.

"I need coffee, Jenn."

She gave him twin laser beams.

He avoided them. "Hey, Peterson, is there any chance of swinging by the coffee shop on the way in? They should open before we get there."

"There's coffee at the police station."

"Correction." Lee shook his head. "There's black tar at the police station."

"Use cream and sugar."

"Have some mercy, man. I need espresso, multiple shots. They use the good stuff at the coffee shop."

"I can't believe I'm doing this." Peterson pursed his lips. "If it will get you to shut up so I can make another phone call — Ed, drive to the coffee shop, and then to the police station."

"Thanks, Peterson," Ed grinned at his boss. "You should try it. You'll like it."

"And then I would develop a one-hundred-dollar-a-month espresso habit like every yuppie in town," Peterson mumbled.

"Make that a hundred and fifty and you can have a gold card and a couple of free drinks each month." Lee grinned.

"Brandt, why don't you, uh, kiss Jennifer, or anything else that will plug your mouth for a few minutes."

"Jenn, did you hear that? Peterson wants me to kiss you for a few minutes. Who am I to disobey an FBI agent?"

Jennifer leaned closer to him. "Not until you answer my question."

"What question?"

"Don't play dumb. You know what I'm talking about."

He knew all right. There was what he knew, there was what he feared, and then there were the words of Elijah in 1 Kings 18:21, words that convicted him. *"How long will you waver between two opinions?"* His mind and heart had a heated discussion on that subject.

The context of that verse was wavering between God and Baal, not the custody of children. *Yeah, but Baal worshipers sacrificed children. Is that what you're gonna do?*

"Oh, man. Jenn, I really need coffee." He tried to make his voice sound pitiful, desperate.

Wimpy!

Jennifer glared at him again. "Lee Brandt, you need a lot more than what coffee can give you."

****

At 5:35 AM Lee's triple-grande caramel mocha was frothing from the steam applied by the barista.

Katie, Mel, and Kirsten sipped hot chocolate, and

Jennifer waited for her double tall mocha.

When they climbed back into the van, Peterson smiled and handed Jennifer his cell phone.

Excitement flashed in her eyes as she listened to the person on the other end.

"Yes, that's great," Jennifer paused, frowned, and then stated firmly, "I'll cross that bridge when I come to it. Thanks. Here's Peterson."

Though the three girls chatted as they sipped their hot drinks, Katie had eyed Jennifer during the entire phone call with a skeptical frown on her face.

Lee believed her expression was about to change. He also believed it was time to give Jennifer an answer. He pulled Jennifer's face close to his and whispered, "Katie goes home with you, right?"

"Yes, Mr. Brandt."

"Jenn, that's where she needs to be, now. I know that. I'm a little slow. After all, you've got at least forty-five IQ points on me. Will you please show a little mercy on—"

Jennifer's lips truncated his sentence. She kissed him long and meaningfully, while the three girls in the backseat sang, "Ooooh," in three-part harmony.

He placed his cheek against Jennifer's and whispered in her ear. "We're driving into the police station. Shouldn't you tell her now?"

Jennifer kissed his cheek. "Yes. She needs to know before Mel and Kirsten start calling their parents. And, Lee, you need to shave."

Jennifer unbuckled her seat belt and twisted around to face Katie.

Katie's gaze locked onto Jennifer's face like a heat-seeking missile on a jet fighter's afterburner.

"When we go inside, Katie, you don't need to call

anyone. That's been taken care of."

"So Peterson called for me?"

"He did. But what I really mean is the people who need to know you're safe already know. They're sitting in front of you."

Her eyes grew wide. "You wouldn't joke about something like that would you, Jenn?"

"No. We have the approval from Mrs. Barnes for you to stay with me, for now."

While Ed braked to a stop in front of the Forks police station, Katie unbuckled her seat belt, flung her arms out to Jennifer, and then hesitated.

"It's OK, Katie. I sometimes shoot, but I don't bite."

"I won't be any trouble for you, Jenn. I promise. I won't interfere with you and Lee—"

Jennifer pulled Katie into a tight hug. "You don't have to worry about any of the details, or about Lee and me. We'll all be talking to Mrs. Barnes when we get to Seattle. For now, you have a home, and Lee and I are delighted."

Lee placed his arm around her. "We are, Katie."

"Everybody, out," Peterson ordered. "We've got some work to do here."

****

The FBI and police worked well together as they elicited information from the girls and coordinated their calls to family. The biggest hitch was the inability to get consensus on a composite of Trader.

After the fifth set of eyes and mouths were discarded from the crude computer drawing, Mel became agitated. She grabbed a sheet of blank computer paper and a pencil from the desk. "No." She blew out a blast of air. "He looks like this." She drew quickly.

Katie pointed to the sketch. "That's Trader."

Jennifer mussed Mel's hair. "It sure is."

Kirsten put her hand on Mel's shoulder. "Who needs computers when we've got Mel?"

Peterson stepped behind Mel and studied her sketch. "Finish it up, Mel. It looks like we have something we can send out."

Lee patted Mel's head. "Good job, Mel. Trader's toast, now."

"I think I've heard that before." Jennifer looked at him. "But this time, I agree."

Eventually the questions from the police slowed to a trickle, and then stopped.

Peterson took Lee and Jennifer to a small table in a quieter corner of the room. "The Coast Guard just boarded a Saudi ship sailing a strange route for a freighter. We have no further details. But if it turns out this ship is involved, I'm guessing Trader's business was selling the cream of the crop to the highest international bidders, or filling orders for them. I can think of some likely customers in the Middle East."

Jennifer exploded from her chair and pounded on the table. "Just shut them down, Peterson! Whatever it takes."

"Whatever it takes? When cases go international, politics come into play. Then all bets are off. But I'll push as hard as I can for prosecution of everyone involved. Now, it appears—" His phone rang again, and he glanced down at it. "Just a minute. I've got to take this call."

Lee's head felt like he had a shot put inside.

Fatigue set in rapidly as the caffeine and sugar wore off. He looked at the girls from underneath his heavy eyelids.

They looked nearly exhausted, too.

When Peterson returned, he scanned the five. "We have some news about Trader. We got a report of a car stolen from a bed-and-breakfast off Mora Road. The description of the car went out a few minutes ago, as did Trader's picture." He paused and studied their faces. "Well, I can see that bit of news didn't perk you five up. I think we'd better get you into the van before we have to carry you out. Come on, Ed. All aboard for Seattle."

26

6:45 AM. Monday, November 4th

When the van pulled out of Forks, Lee and Jennifer sat in the second seat with arms intertwined.

Jennifer looked back at the girls, and then rested her head on his shoulder.

He rested his head on hers. Her hair was soft against his cheek. "You did it, Jenn. Mission accomplished. You got the FBI involved, stopped the exchange, and saved the three girls sitting behind us."

"But we didn't catch Trader. I'm afraid he'll move to a new location and continue his business. Speaking of the girls, look at them."

"They're all asleep."

"But look how they're sleeping. Katie's got one arm around Mel and the other around Kirsten. Both of them are leaning on her. Isn't she amazing?"

"She is. She's got a big, strong heart. But Mel was pretty incredible, too. I didn't have a clue she could draw like that."

Jennifer yawned and nestled her head against his neck.

He caught her yawn. "A week ago Trader was virtually unknown. But after Mel's sketch, he'll probably make the FBI's ten-most-wanted list. They'll catch him."

"I hope so. But about the girls. Mel's and Kirsten's

families will pick them up in Seattle, and they'll go home. It looks like I can take Katie for a few days, thanks to Peterson pulling some strings. But what's going to happen to Katie over the long haul?" She raised her head and studied his face.

"Why don't we see how it goes for the short-term first, and then—"

"You mean for the short-term, when we're planning a wedding and while we're on our honeymoon?" She smiled and once again nestled her head against his neck.

He ran his fingers through her hair. "Maybe the honeymoon would be a good time for her to get to know her great-granddad. It's a quick way to give him the great-grandchild he asked for. You do remember his stipulation about our courtship?"

"*Her* great-granddad? You mean you would really consider it? It wouldn't be for all that long. In three years she'll be off to college and the nest would be empty."

"Listen to what you're saying. Do you really believe that we'll have an empty nest in three years?"

"No, probably not. Katie might have a little sister by then. But we can decide about that after the honeymoon."

"Jenn?"

"Yes?"

"There might not be any decision to make after the honeymoon."

"Oh...." Jennifer's head popped up, and then a drowsy smile formed on her lips. She snuggled closer, put her head on his shoulder, and leaned against his neck. Her breathing became deep, slow, and regular.

As the van rolled along Highway 101, the

predawn twilight revealed the wind-battered forest and the road surface littered with broken branches. The events of the long, stormy night rolled through his mind, more as emotions than pictures.

The despair his storm-battered heart had felt twelve hours ago fled, chased away to some far corner of the universe by God's mercy and grace. Love moved in where hopelessness had dwelt, filling his heart until there was room for nothing else.

His heart felt full, but the love filling it came from an Infinite Source, so wouldn't it always have room for another person? A person like Katie?

****

"Time to wake up. We're on Third Avenue, almost to the field office." Peterson's voice pulled him out of some strange dream and back to reality.

Lee raised his head. His neck felt as flexible as a steel rod. He massaged it with his free hand and glanced down at his watch. 1:05 PM.

Jennifer raised her head from his shoulder and kissed his neck. She glanced back at the girls. "Look behind us."

Fully awake, Katie sat with her arms draped around Kirsten and Mel.

He smiled at her. "We're nearly home, Katie."

At the word home, a frown formed on Katie's brow. It vanished after a glance at Jennifer's smile.

Mel and Kirsten opened their eyes, but left their heads resting on Katie.

Peterson twisted in his seat. "When we get to the field office, there will be media people shoving mikes in our faces and asking all sorts of unpleasant questions. All of you should refer them to the FBI to get their questions answered. If they persist, tell them until this investigation is concluded, they must get their information from the FBI. Do you understand? No answering media questions."

Five heads nodded.

"Katie?" Peterson smiled at her.

Katie's chin rose and her eyes brightened.

"Your caseworker, Mrs. Barnes, will be there to meet you." Peterson refocused on Jennifer and him. "Jennifer, you and Lee need to go with Katie. Mrs. Barnes will want to talk to Katie and Jennifer. Because of an imminent wedding, if I heard correctly, she will need to talk to Lee, too. Katie, I spoke with Mrs. Barnes about an hour ago. Unless she uncovers some well-hidden skeletons in Jennifer's closet—not likely considering the security clearance Jennifer holds—your home for the immediate future will be with Jennifer."

"Thank you!" Katie leaned forward and threw an arm around Jennifer. She extended her free hand towards Peterson.

He took it and gave it a firm shake.

Kirsten yawned. "We're happy for you."

"Yeah," Mel added. "Kirsten and I get to go back to our mom and dad. You get to live with Lee and Jenn. But I hope we can see each other, sometimes."

Katie's expression morphed to a serious frown. "I've been praying that's also what Mrs. Barnes will say."

"Why don't we all do that together?" Lee scanned their faces.

Kirsten frowned and cocked her head. "You mean right here, right now?"

"Right here, right now." He stretched out his arms.

"Let's huddle up as best we can."

Five seatbelts clicked open. As the van rolled down 3rd Street, their heads met and five pairs of arms draped around adjacent shoulders.

Peterson looked back at the commotion. "Great. Now we have five traffic violations to add to this case."

When Lee finished the prayer, Peterson's voice boomed out. "Brace yourselves for the media blitz, everyone. Let me go first and try to fend off the vultures." When Peterson stepped out of the van, numerous mikes were thrust up at him.

Lee surveyed the scene and immediately thought of the quills of a porcupine.

Peterson scanned the media for a few seconds. "I'm Special Agent Peterson, FBI. And I'm pleased to announce the three abducted girls are here, safe and unharmed, thanks in a large part to a pair of civilians who risked their lives to save the girls. Because the investigation is ongoing, all information given to the media will come from the FBI. Please restrain yourselves, ladies and gentlemen. These girls have been through a lot. Let us return them to their families now."

Reporters shouted questions at them from all around the van.

"We've heard one girl has no family. Is that why she was targeted?"

"Is one of the girls really only eleven years old?"

"Have you caught all the perpetrators?"

Peterson raised his hand, palm outward. "The FBI will give you a statement later today summarizing all of the information we can release. No more questions, now."

But Lee heard more questions. Hundreds more

were flung at Jennifer, him, and the girls. Jennifer kept one hand tightly clamped on Katie's hand while Lee gripped her other hand.

Like an offensive lineman, Peterson opened a path for the five people following him.

****

Jennifer entered the conference room and sat down across the table from Mrs. Barnes. Jennifer's hands trembled. There was so much at stake, and all of it was beyond her control. She prayed silently, committing her relationship with Katie to God.

Mrs. Barnes stopped writing and looked up. "Katie can stay with you for the next few days. But what about Katie's next three years as a minor? Would you really be happy being a twenty-six-year-old mother to a fifteen-year-old girl?"

No nonsense. Cuts right to the chase. It was a good sign.

"Mrs. Barnes, you and I both know Katie is much more than a fifteen-year-old girl. She's extremely bright, mature. She's very special. If you give me permanent custody of Katie, I'll commit my lifetime to being a mother to her. I can give her the love she needs."

"How can you be so sure after knowing her for such a short time?"

Jennifer needed to relax and think. *Take a deep breath, girl, and blow it back out.* "As a wise man once said, shared danger has a way of compressing time. I know as much about Katie now as if she lived in my home for months. Besides, when you commit to someone, you don't ever walk away from the

206

commitment. If things aren't going well, you fix the relationship and continue."

"I see. Off the record, Miss Akihara, are you a Christian?"

Where was *this* going? She had heard about people who despised Christians so much they enjoyed making their lives miserable. Many held positions of authority, like Mrs. Barnes.

"I've been a Christian for the past seven and one half months. What I told you about commitment—"

"Miss Akihara, I understand the basis of your commitment. It's the Bible. I can't put that in the official record, but I can mention how you define commitment. For Katie, I believe you will make a wonderful guardian."

"Thanks for your confidence in me. I—"

"But there is another person I need to consider. Since you and Lee intend to marry soon, would you please ask Lee to join us? "

"Yes, ma'am." Jennifer stood. "Mrs. Barnes?"

"Yes?"

"The definition of commitment I gave you…I first learned it from Lee, before he showed me it came from the Bible."

"Thanks, Jennifer. If you'll bring Lee now, we can finish the preliminaries."

"You mean these aren't the finals?"

"Unfortunately, they're not. The finals consist of reams and reams of paperwork. I'll introduce you to it, and then let you take some of it home."

"Excuse me, while I find Lee."

In the lobby there were hugs being exchanged between the three girls. Final hugs? She needed to hurry. "Mel, Kirsten, wait for me."

"Jenn," Mel sounded excited. "Lee said we should celebrate each November 4th as our anniversary."

That was good, but she wanted to give them something even better. "That sounds great. But if your parents agree, I have an idea that might bring us together a lot more than once a year. I'll call your folks if it looks like a go. Now, I need a hug from both of you."

After their final hugs, both girls lingered in front of her, teary-eyed.

"Thanks for coming after us, Jenn." Kirsten managed between breaks in her voice.

Mel turned and cried.

"Hey, girls. I'll be in touch. You take care, and I promise we'll see each other soon." She gave them both an extra-long hug.

Two couples came into the room. Kirsten and Mel turned and ran. The joyful greetings with their parents were noisy and tearful, but love and relief were also evident.

Jenn turned away, knowing the girls were in good hands. Now it was Lee's turn in the hot seat. "Lee, Mrs. Barnes wants to talk to both of us...together."

"That's interesting. What about Katie?"

"Yeah, what about me?"

"You have to wait outside until Mrs. Barnes is through with us."

Katie grinned at her. "Can I listen through the door?"

"I don't know. What do you think?"

Katie's grin faded. "That she wouldn't want me to."

"And I'd say you're probably right."

"But is everything going OK, Jenn?"

"Don't worry, everything will work out fine."

Lee took Jennifer's hand as they walked together into the room where the caseworker waited.

Mrs. Barnes looked up from the forms. "Let's cut to the chase so we can get you two out of here. I heard you've been up for nearly forty-eight hours."

"Four hours of sleep in the last seventy-two, if you don't count the catnaps while we rode home in the van," Lee said, unable to stifle a yawn.

The short lady looked from Jennifer to Lee. "How soon do you intend to marry?"

"As soon as possible." They replied in unison.

A laugh escaped and Jenn reached for Lee's hand.

Mrs. Barnes smiled politely. "Realistically, when can we expect a wedding?"

"In about four weeks."

Lee pulled her close to him. "After what we've been through, we're not waiting a second longer than we have to."

Mrs. Barnes folded her hands on the stack of papers. "Are you planning a honeymoon?"

"Yes, three weeks in Maui, immediately after the wedding." Lee covered another yawn with his hand.

This was news to her. "But, Lee, you told me you could only get off for two weeks."

"I know, but I'm going to demand three. After what we've been through, I think Dale and Jerry will sacrifice a little to make it happen. We need some time together with no one shooting at us, running us off the road, bombing our car—"

"Goodness! You experienced all of that?" Mrs. Barnes gave him a wide-eyed frown.

Lee pursed his lips and nodded. "In the last eight months, yes."

Mrs. Barnes' frown transformed to a smile. "Are you sure Katie will be safe with you two?" She paused. "Tell me this. What happens to Katie during the honeymoon?"

This part was a slam dunk.

"Mrs. Barnes, Katie is going to acquire a great-granddad who wants great-grandchildren in the worst way. When he approved our courtship he—"

"So you two are doing the old-fashioned courtship thing?" The little lady raised her eyebrows. "No living together before the marriage?"

Lee put his arm around Jennifer. "Yes, we are. Courting, that is. That means nothing inappropriate until we're married, which will make everything appro—"

Jenn stuck an elbow in his ribs.

Mrs. Barnes grabbed her pencil and scribbled something on a form. "That answers several questions for me. But back to the great-grandfather. Tell me about him."

Lee spoke first. "He lives about two hours south of here. He wants great-grandchildren as soon as possible. It was one condition of the courtship."

"That you have a child now?" The caseworker's eyebrow rose.

"No." Jennifer laughed and shook her head, "Only that we don't postpone having children."

Lee chuckled. "He has a sixth-degree black belt in karate. He said he'd kick my head into orbit if I ever hurt Jennifer. If Katie wants to learn, he can teach her all the self-defense a woman needs in those three weeks."

"How old is, uh, is it Mr. Akihara?"

"It is," Jennifer answered. "And Granddad is

seventy-two, but he hardly looks a day over fifty."

Mrs. Barnes turned to Lee.

"Lee, tell me what is your general perception of Katie? Who do you think she is?"

"Katie's a very intelligent young lady. She's strong physically, strong in spirit, and she has a huge heart. She cares for people. She's also a very beautiful young lady. That made her a target. It will probably create problems for her throughout her teenage years, but she's a person I would trust with my life. In fact, I did that this weekend."

The caseworker's eyebrows rose at his last statement.

"Lee, tell me what you think Katie needs?"

"Katie needs to be loved by her parents and trusted enough to be given significant responsibility. She needs to be needed, and she thrives on coming through in the clutch. I've seen it. She also needs a father figure who will protect her from what I've already alluded to. And...Katie needs to know how much God loves her. I don't think she knows that yet."

"Lee, Jennifer, thank you for your candor in answering my questions. Will you both please step out for a moment and send Katie in?"

He stood, took Jennifer's arm, and led her to the door. When he opened it, Katie stood to the side of the door, out of Mrs. Barnes's sight.

"Were you listening?" He grinned at her.

Katie smiled and mouthed silently back, "Would I do that?"

"Get in there, you rascal."

What did Mrs. Barnes want to ask Katie at this juncture? Had she or Lee said something that alarmed her?

"Katie Lloyd, are you coming?" Mrs. Barnes's voice called from inside the door.

****

Jennifer waited for Katie, her child, to walk out of the caseworker's temporary office. This was a new kind of fear for her. No one was going to blow her away with an assault rifle, but they could blow away her hopes and dreams, or fulfill them, with a single document.

When Katie scampered out of the room, the joy on her face ended Jennifer's fear.

"Mrs. Barnes said I can stay with you—soon with both of you. She said she'll make sure I never have to move again, except with you."

Lee squished both of them in a hug.

Peterson walked their way. "Looks like you three got some good news. Well, I've got some more good news for you. The Coast Guard stopped a freighter in American waters off the coast, near Lake Ozette. They boarded the vessel and found one container configured to hold human cargo. We think the ship's captain may be involved in the trafficking operation. If so, we may be able to dismantle part of the international organization Trader worked with. Who knows, maybe we can find out what happened to some other girls."

Thoughts of the trafficking erased Jennifer's smile. "We'll be praying for that to happen."

"Yes, we will," Katie added.

Katie praying? It was a good start.

Jennifer's smile returned. No, it was a great start.

27

It was 3:30 PM on Monday afternoon when Jennifer walked up to her apartment door. Nearly sixty hours had passed since she left it early Saturday morning to analyze the scanner data. And now she was leading two people she loved through that door. What a difference the past two days had made in her life.

Lee gestured towards the car sitting across the street. "Looks like we've got police protection."

A reminder that Trader was still at large.

Her stomach tightened. But the manhunt was intensifying. They would catch him soon. "I hope we don't need them very long. Actually, I hope we don't need them at all."

Lee opened the door for her and Katie, and then he scanned the sky. "The storm has passed. The wind's coming from the northwest. You can say good-bye to our balmy, sixty-five degree weather and to the rain."

"It's a storm I'll never forget. And I don't care if I never see another drop of rain." Inside her apartment a room waited for its new occupant. "The Pineapple Express almost took our lives, but it brought us another life."

Katie looked uncertain.

She took Katie's hand. "Come on. I'll show you your bedroom."

"Good thing you rented a two-bedroom apartment, isn't it, Jenn?" Lee squeezed her shoulder.

"In hindsight, I doubt it was an accident."

Katie stopped staring wide-eyed down the hallway. "Was it an accident that I got here without any of my clothes or other things?"

She gave Katie a side hug. "Don't worry. Tonight you can use one of my nightshirts. It's too long for me, anyway. I have an extra toothbrush and anything else you might need in the morning. Mrs. Barnes said she would bring your things from the foster—"

"Can we not mention that place?" Katie's gaze pleaded with her.

She would help Katie bury those fears from her past. Beginning right now.

"Sure. As of right now, it's gone forever. Now get ready for bed. We all have some sleep to catch up on after being up for two days."

Lee relaxed on the couch.

And that's what she wanted to do, curl up beside him. She scurried to her room, slipped into her pajamas, and threw on a robe. When she came out of her room, she collided with Katie.

Katie wasn't complaining verbally, but her down-turned mouth and head said she wasn't comfortable in a nightshirt that advertised a movie, though it fit perfectly. Katie's blue eyes, blonde hair, perfectly sculptured face, and tall, slender body put movie stars to shame. She was going to attract every young man in Seattle.

Lord, please help me handle that issue for Katie better than I did for myself.

"Are you hungry?"

"Starved."

"I thought you might be. The bottom cupboard to the left of the sink holds my supply of healthy snacks.

Grab anything that suits your fancy. But then you'd better get to bed."

"Can I have a drink first, Mommy?"

Mommy. It was meant as a joke, but still the word touched a warm, sensitive spot in her heart. She forced a frown on her brow, and then gestured towards the refrigerator. "Grab some juice from the fridge, and then it's to bed with you. We've got a busy day tomorrow."

"Doing what?"

"For one, buying you some clothes."

"If it's such a busy day, why are you headed towards Lee in the living room?"

"Lee and I have a lot to talk about, a wedding and—"

"And me?"

"Katie, we've already talked about you."

"When was that? I've been with either you or Lee ever since—"

"In the van coming home."

Her frown remained. "But you two *are* going to talk about me, aren't you?" Katie needed a hug.

Jennifer circled Katie's neck with her arms. "If we do, you'll hear all about it in the morning. And don't worry. It will all be good talk."

Katie returned the hug. "You mean that, don't you?"

"Yes. Lee and I try not to say things we don't mean and…we don't keep secrets."

"Hey, what's going on here?" Lee stepped into the living-room end of the hallway. "Can I get in on it?"

Jennifer opened a spot for him in their huddle. "Three's not always a crowd."

"Without you, Katie, this would have been the

saddest day of my life—if I still had a life."

****

Thirty minutes later Jennifer and Lee sat side-by-side on her couch while Katie slept in her bedroom. They hadn't talked about those two hours when neither of them knew if the other was alive. But the scratches on Lee's hands came during that time. She caressed them with her lips.

The despair lay behind them. It was time to look ahead, to love, joy, and peace.

His eyes were sagging, nearly shut like hers.

"I'm going to need a rental car for a couple weeks. Can you come by in the morning and take us to the car lot?"

"I'll be here at 8:00 AM. They don't open until 8:30. That'll give us time for—"

"For something we've missed for several days," Jennifer sighed. "Coffee. And then I'm going to—"

His soft kiss punctuated her sentence. "What is it you're going to do?"

Good question. Did it even matter?

"I'm not sure. This man I met keeps changing my plans." She paused. Yes, it did matter. "I'm going to schedule the church. After that, I'm going to call my family and see if they can be here in three and a half weeks for a wedding."

"Aren't you going to schedule me?"

"Nope." She shook her head.

"You're not even going to check with me about my schedule?"

"Silly boy, you'll be there. I think we need to talk about Katie now. She thought we would. In fact, I'll bet she's full of thoughts tonight."

"Jenn, she's a teenage girl. You probably don't want to know all the thoughts running through her mind."

He wasn't getting it.

"But, Lee, Katie is like us."

His eyes scanned her face. "She's like you, spectacularly beautiful."

"No, I mean like both of us."

"In what sense?"

Sometimes he was clueless.

"I saw some of the papers Mrs. Barnes brought with her to the field station. Did you know that Katie's IQ is, well, it's higher than yours."

"Just spend five minutes with her and anybody would know she's bright."

"Lee, we're equipped to understand her better than most parents, because we're both, well…"

"Even Lee, the family idiot, with his 145 IQ gets your point." He paused. "I'm sure there are ways we can help her, ways other parents might find difficult."

"She needs us. Adopting her is the only way we can guarantee some future caseworker won't take her from us." There. She had dropped the load on her heart.

Lee could carry it now.

He rubbed his chin and thought for a moment. "How do you feel about having a daughter who's only ten years younger than you?"

"Sometimes it feels like there isn't even ten years between us. But it's fine with me."

He stared across the room. "You're probably right. But deep inside Katie there's still a little girl who has wounds and scars from being orphaned, placed in the foster-care system, and who knows what else. And she had to kill a man. That memory won't magically disappear."

"I know." His neck was warm against her cheek. She let her heavy head rest there. "But we both know a God Who can heal those wounds. Other parents may not have a loving Lord to introduce Katie to."

"It's not like I didn't see this conversation coming. Right after Katie threw that fastball through Trader's SUV window, I saw the bond between you two forming."

"What about you?"

"After the incident with Jacko at the ranger's house, I began thinking I'd be proud to have a young lady like her for a daughter."

"Then we've got to adopt her as soon as we're married."

"That would be a lot faster than waiting nine months to satisfy your granddad's demand for a great-grandchild."

"Men, they all have a one-track mind."

"No, I don't. I've got at least a two-track mind."

She brought a couch pillow down hard on his head.

He grabbed the pillow and tossed it out of her reach. "So are we agreed, then?"

"On what? Your mind or—"

"That we'll push the paperwork as far as we can and file for adoption after we're married?"

That was Lee. Like all men, clueless at the start. But he was a quick study.

"Thank you, sweetheart." She slid her arms around his neck. "We'll file when we return from Maui. But we probably shouldn't tell Katie until we've got the paperwork in the mill. You know, in case there's some obstacle we haven't anticipated."

"No, Jenn. If we're agreed to pursue this, we should tell her our intent. She needs to know we're committed to her. If she knows that, everything will be fine." He was right.

Maybe she had some clueless moments, too. "OK. Then we'll tell her together. How about tomorrow evening?"

"If you can hold her off that long." Lee chuckled. "If she suspected we'd be talking about her, she'll be full of questions."

"That's settled, then. Now, there's one more thing I want to talk to you about. I...want to spend some time speaking to parents and kids at schools, churches—wherever I can—about the child-trafficking epidemic. Whenever possible, I would like to have Katie, Mel, and Kirsten on the platform with me. What do you think?"

"Go for it, if their parents agree. If anyone can paint a picture of what's happening, it's you. You've been there." He gave her a hug. "I'll help in any way I can."

"Thanks for understanding."

Lee slid down in his seat on the couch and leaned his head on her shoulder. "I'm starting to fade. Do you have any other surprises to spring on me before I fall asleep?"

"Just this." She offered her lips.

He pressed his softly against them.

She intended it be a goodnight kiss. But afterward, instead of shooing Lee out the door and leaving for her bedroom, she thought it would be nice to lean her head against his for just a few moments...

28

Tuesday Morning, November 5

The sound of distant music woke Jennifer to a fuzzy state of semi-consciousness. The alarm in her bedroom played a soothing praise song. A hand rested on her shoulder.

Lee?

Through the fog a picture formed of Lee sleeping beside her on the couch, and then the fog returned, warm and fuzzy.

"Jenn, I think you need to wake up. You know, if we aren't careful this is going to become a habit that's impossible to break."

The fog cleared. "Good morning. What's going to be impossible to break?"

He kissed her forehead. "I was talking about sleeping under the same roof. Saturday, Sunday, and last night—"

"We didn't sleep Sunday night." She tried to raise her head, but her neck wouldn't cooperate. "There was a little too much excitement. But last night was nice, even if I do have a major kink in my neck." Her right arm was draped over a blonde princess sleeping beside her. "Katie thinks so, too."

"So I've noticed."

Katie opened her eyes and clutched Jennifer's arm. "No bad dreams, no bad people. It's really nice. I haven't slept like that since—I can't remember the last time."

Lee yawned. "Here we are like the three bears. Maybe more like two bears and Goldilocks."

Katie sat up, her body rigid. "Never ever call me that again, Lee, or I'll—"

"Or you'll kill me? That's what Jenn would say. But I'm sorry, Katie. If you don't like—"

"I'm sorry, too. I didn't mean to get angry." Katie's eyes were wide and tears welled in them. "But Mr.—I won't even mention his name—called me that when he harassed me. So please—"

"Vocabulary." Lee pretended to type on a keyboard. "Goldilocks—delete. It's gone. Are there any other words I should delete while my dictionary is open?"

"You can delete princess, too. Same reason."

At least Jennifer had only thought the word.

"It's deleted, Katie." He lowered his hands from his imaginary keyboard. "I think it's nice too, nice to be here together without having to worry about how we're going to escape, or about being shot."

There was work to do today. Women's work.

"It was very nice. Uncomfortable, but nice. Now, Lee, don't you have someplace to go? Something to do?"

"Are you running me out, without even offering me breakfast?"

"You need a shower and clean clothes, and I need a rental car. So get cleaned up and get back here, because I really need breakfast too, from our favorite coffee shop."

"I'll pick up breakfast on my way back. Orders, please."

****

The doorbell rang. It was a good thing she had shortened the drying cycle. Jenn handed Katie her clothes. "They feel dry enough. Jump into these, Katie. Lee's here with our breakfast."

Soon all three sat around Jennifer's table. "I'll pray this morning."

Humor had been in short supply over the past two days. But their favorite coffee had been missing entirely.

"And we thank You for providing these mochas and saving us from the black tar at the police station. Amen." Jennifer finished her prayer and looked up.

Katie frowned at her. "Jenn, do you always talk to God...like that? Flip, I mean, casually?"

Katie's hand was rigid, but it relaxed somewhat as Jennifer put her hand over it. "Not always. God is my friend. But then, He's also my Heavenly Father and the One I serve. He knows how much I like good coffee. Sometimes I speak in a humorous way with my friend. But the key in talking to God is to never forget He's also my Father and my Lord. Funny? Maybe, sometimes. Flippantly? I try not to do that. So how's your mocha?"

"It's my first one, but I think I'm addicted already." Katie sat her cup down. It produced a hollow sound.

Lee took a sip of his venti-sized mocha. "I've been addicted for ten years now. But don't drink your first one too fast. We don't want you bouncing off the walls."

Smiling, Katie eyed Lee's cup. "Too late, it's gone.

And don't take your eyes off yours, or I might not be able to restrain myself."

Lee laughed and shielded his cup from her.

When they finished breakfast, the three climbed into Lee's '62 Impala.

He started the engine and the exciting, syncopated rumble began, the sound Lee said came from his 283 engine with a racing cam.

He pulled out onto the street and headed towards the car lot. "So what do you plan to rent, a compact?"

"You've got to be kidding. It's too bad they don't rent muscle cars." She laid her hand on the gear shift. "The FBI is paying for my rental car. Since we did a major piece of work for them, without pay, I might add, I'm going for an SUV. If Peterson complains, I'll remind him of a couple of phone conversations we had this weekend. He'll pay the bill."

"I think you've got enough clout right now to manage Peterson. But, Jenn, he thinks of you almost like a daughter. He has ever since last March."

Katie sat up in the backseat and put her hand on Jennifer's shoulder. "Speaking of last March, you said sometime you would tell me about what happened."

She patted Katie's hand. "I'll let Lee tell you while I rent us an SUV. It's a story about terrorists, caves, and a life-changing kiss. Actually, two of them. A tale of two kisses."

29

The small SUV fitted nicely in her parking space at the apartment. Jennifer slid out. "I need to make some phone calls, Katie. After that, we'll go shopping. If you want to, you can shop online for a bit, and then show me the clothes you like."

"That would be great. But don't spend a lot on me. I don't need many clothes."

That was probably the story of Katie's foster-child life. Not many clothes. "This is as much for me as it is for you. You wouldn't deny me the enjoyment, would you?"

Katie smiled and shook her head.

"Well then, the computer is in the corner. Have fun. It may take me a half hour to make my phone calls."

"Do you want me to leave the room while you're on the phone?"

She was gradually picking up bits and pieces of Katie's life as a foster child, always on the outside looking in. Maybe the girl would tell her story when the time was right. "No, Katie. There are no secrets in this house, except around Christmas time."

She placed her first call to the secretary at Maplewood Community Church. "Kathy, this is Jennifer Akihara. Would you please look at the church calendar and tell me if anything is scheduled for Saturday, November 30th? Yes, I know it's only three and one half weeks away...you knew I was calling to schedule a wedding...great. I'm going to call some relatives, and then I'll stop by and pick up the papers."

One down, and so far no hitches. Please help this next call to go as smoothly.

"Hi, Mom. Have you got about five minutes? Good. Now here's the big question. Can you, Jess, and Julie fly over here a few days before November 30th? Yes it's for my wedding.

"Mom, you're going to be a grandmother soon. I know you raised me to be a proper lady. Yes, Lee's going to be the father. When's the baby due? She's no baby. She's sitting right here in the room with me. I'll explain later.

"You saw the news, huh? Lee and I are both fine, thanks in part to the young lady you'll be meeting when you get here. She's the granddaughter I'm talking about. What picture is in your paper? Katie is the tall girl in the middle. She saved our lives, Mom. I can't wait to introduce Jess and Julie to her. Jess and Katie are about the same age. The wedding will be Saturday afternoon, November 30th. I'll get back to you with the details."

Jennifer hung up the phone. *Thank you, God.* Still no hitches. Well, none of any consequence.

"So your mom thought you were pregnant?"

"Yes, it was probably terrible of me to tease her like that. She was horrified at the thought of me having a baby out of wedlock."

Katie swiveled the computer chair around to face Jennifer. "But I've seen you and Lee, how he treats you so respectfully. He would never—"

"Katie, you and I need to have a talk soon. For now, suffice it to say, no matter how good you think you are, there are still temptations none of us are immune to, especially when you're engaged. Now, I need to call Granddad, Howie at work, and then we're out of here."

Katie's expression was thoughtful as she swiveled back to the computer.

Jenn could tell she had questions, and smiled at the thought of teaching this young girl about God and family. She reached for the phone.

****

Jennifer hung up and drew a deep breath. "All done. Oh, Friday you're going to meet Granddad. Now show me the clothes you found."

Katie's preference in clothing was pleasantly surprising. Simple, clean designs. Katie would look wonderful in them. Thank goodness she didn't like tacky clothes or anything racy.

"My goodness, it's 11:00 AM. We can hit the outlet stores, and then it should be about lunch time."

"Lunch sounds good." Katie's voice was soft, but probing.

Teenagers and eating. Jenn had forgotten a lot in six years. "Would you like to have lunch first?"

"If you don't mind. Mel, Kirsten, and I didn't get much to eat while they held us. I was used to it, but I thought Kirsten might pass out a couple times. When they did give us food, well, Ivan was a bad cook."

Jenn dismissed her frown and tried to smile. "That's all we need to remember about him. Now, how about going out to eat?"

"Whatever you decide is fine with me."

"OK, I know a place with a big menu, It's quiet

there at noon, unlike the evenings."

****

By 11:30 Katie sat poring over the menu, unable to narrow her choice to fewer than five items.

"Five choices? Tell me which five and I'll see if I've had any of them."

Katie slid her finger down the large menu. "First, there's fish and chips, then—"

"Stop there. You can never go wrong with their fish and chips. How about a small salad on the side?"

"Are you sure that's not too much, Jenn?"

"No, it's fine. Do you like Italian dressing?"

"Yes. It's probably healthier than ranch."

"A little."

The waiter was walking down an adjacent aisle, obviously waiting for them to choose.

"We're ready now." Jennifer smiled at him.

The young man's gaze returned frequently to Katie while he took their order.

When the waiter left, Katie looked up at her. "He was watching me, wasn't he, Jenn?"

"That he was. But I can't say I blame him."

"I hate it when guys do that. They've caused me so much trouble."

"Katie, he wasn't looking in a bad way. For whatever reason, God chose to make you absolutely beautiful, and then He gave you a heart to match your looks. As long as the boys aren't rude or crude, you can't fault them for gazing at some of God's finest handiwork."

"They look at you, too. Do you like it?"

"I hate it." Her reply started a giggling fit. Great.

Now they had attracted the attention of several more young men who worked at the restaurant.

One of them carried a tray with two orders of fish and chips on it.

After their meal was served, Jennifer folded her hands on the table. "Katie, would you like me to ask the blessing?"

"Sure." Katie bowed.

Jennifer didn't want Katie to feel uncomfortable about praying in a public place, so she kept it simple, thanks for the food and for bringing Katie into her life.

Katie sat silently for a few moments while they ate. But she squirmed restlessly in her chair, frequently glancing at her. This young girl needed to learn that she could speak openly with her...Mom. *I'm her Mom.* Jenn took a second to delight in the wonder.

"Have you got something you would like to tell me?"

"Was I that obvious?"

"Truthfully, Katie, yes. So why don't you just tell me?"

"When you prayed, it reminded me of how I've begun to pray." Katie studied her eyes.

Jennifer dropped her fork. "When did you start praying?"

"I started regularly after I met you at Trader's shack. Before you came, I just cried out to God for help whenever I felt hopeless."

"When did you first start crying out to God for help?"

"Not long after Trader captured me." Katie's hand slid forward on the table.

Jennifer took it. "Do you remember what day it was?"

"It was when they put me in the building at the old mill. Early on Saturday, I think."

Jennifer squeezed Katie's hand tightly.

"Jenn, is there something wrong?" Katie stared at the tears spilling onto Jenn's cheeks.

"No, Katie. I think something is very right. You see, Saturday morning I discovered an encrypted, cell-phone call. When we decrypted it, we heard Trader and Boatman arranging an exchange, girls for drugs. I knew girls were being held at an old mill site, so Lee helped me search all of the old mill sites on the peninsula. The whole time we were looking, I kept hearing the voice of a girl—someone who seemed like my own daughter—crying out for help. It upset me so much I started acting a little crazy and desperate. Lee can vouch for that. So, what do you think?"

Katie stared across the room for a moment. "There's only one answer that makes sense. God heard me calling for help. He made sure you heard, too. Then He used you and Lee to answer my prayer. So is that what a relationship with God is like? You talk, He hears you, and then He does things?"

"That's only half of the relationship. When you have a friend, you talk and they listen. Then what?"

"They talk and I listen."

Jennifer nodded. "Yes, and so that begs the question—"

"You mean the question of how God talks to me. Well, He hasn't that I know of." Katie looked down and frowned. "Does that mean there's something wrong with me?"

Jenn hesitated before answering. "Yes, there is something wrong, but it's not only with you. It's with everyone. But, Katie, the good news is it can be easily fixed."

Katie looked puzzled. "But what if it can't? What—"

"Don't think that, not for one moment. God loves you very much, and He made you who you are."

"It sounds like He made me into somebody He can't accept."

"Please listen for a minute. Let me explain something, and then I think all your questions will, well, they will go away."

"OK, Jenn, lay the magic on me. Whatever it is."

She smiled at Katie. "It's not really magic. It's completely unselfish love. God revealed many things about Himself in the Bible, as well as in the universe He created. But when He described His character to us, He told us He's a God of justice and a God of love. However, because He's just—"

"I know what you're going to say." Katie's fingers tapped a snappy rhythm on the table. "We're not perfect. But does that leave any room for love?"

God as Judge, Jesus as both advocate and our substitute.

Katie had already demonstrated that she could understand that analogy.

Jennifer sent up a silent prayer, and then told the Story of all Stories to a young lady who was more than ready to hear it. As Jennifer drew the story to its redemptive end she prayed that its impact would continue on…for a lifetime.

"So, suppose…" Katie moved the salt and pepper shakers like they were pieces on a chessboard. "Suppose I wanted a two-way relationship with God where Jesus takes God's justice for me. How would I start it? Do I have to wait for God to, you know, make the first move?"

"God already made the first move by sending Jesus to earth. He invites us to come to Him. In fact, He says He's standing at the very door of our heart, knocking and waiting. If we open the door, He comes in and we are changed. We become His child, adopted into His family."

"Suppose I want to open the door." She paused. "What would I do?"

Jennifer studied Katie.

The public setting didn't seem to bother her. And one of the waiters was quietly keeping others away from their table. The young man smiled at her and gave her a thumbs-up sign.

Jenn took it as her go-ahead signal.

Please take her heart like You did mine.

"Katie, if that's what you really want, you simply tell God. Pray to Him and tell Him you want to become His child, to forgive you, and you want Him to be your Lord, you know, the One you try to please as you live your life."

"Jenn, we're only talking heavenly child, right? I can still be somebody else's earthly child, can't I?"

"Heavenly child only, forever and ever."

Katie bowed her head. Jennifer's last glance across the room revealed the young waiter, head bowed and lips moving.

Thank You that an appreciative audience can share in the joy of this moment. Jenn smiled at the young man.

In a few seconds Katie looked up.

"How do you feel, Katie?"

"Like everything is right in my life. Everything is the way it's supposed to be. I don't have to cry out and just *hope* somebody hears me."

"I'm so proud of you. So happy for you. But, you

know something?"

"We need to get going, right?"

"If you want any clothes, yes, we need to go."

"Can I tell Lee tonight?"

"Of course. He'll want to know. But now, to the outlet mall, and then we need to make one more stop before we go home."

"When we're done at the outlet mall, I won't need anything else."

"There's a place...it has something you and I are going to need very soon." Jennifer took a final sip of her lemonade.

"Both of us?" Katie's nose wrinkled. "Is it underwear?"

The laugh exploded from her mouth along with the lemonade. "Sorry, Katie. That's not what I was thinking." She paused and soaked up drops of lemonade. "I need a wedding dress, and you need a bridesmaid's dress."

"Are you sure you want me to—"

"Absolutely."

Katie's feelings of being outcast were something they needed to help her overcome.

"If it weren't for you, my family would probably be attending a funeral instead of a wedding. I want you and my two sisters with me when Lee and I say our vows."

Katie wiped her eyes and clamped her arms around Jennifer. "I can't wait to tell Lee tonight, and I can't wait to see you in a wedding dress this afternoon. Let's go."

****

Jennifer stood inspecting a long rack of wedding dresses, while Katie looked over her shoulder. "Much too bare." She moved on to the next dress. "Way too low in front." She scanned the next dress from the top to the bottom. "This short dress looks kind of odd where the hemline ends."

Katie laughed. "Maybe they made it out of odds and ends."

The next dress was OK, but there were still more choices. She moved down the rack.

Katie grabbed her arm and pulled her back. "Jenn, wait. I can totally see you in this dress, and it'll be beautiful."

"I don't know, Katie. It's fairly modest. Maybe a little low, but not too bad."

"Just try it on and you'll see what I see."

If Katie was this adamant, maybe she should humor her.

"Ma'am, would you help me pull this dress off the rack?" Jenn asked.

"Yes!" Katie's voice rang through the shop.

Several heads turned towards them. A few people walked their way.

Great. Now she would have an audience.

"Come on, Jenn. Try it on," Katie begged.

Two clerks spoke softly to one another.

"Get the camera. I'll grab a release form. This could be commercial-quality advertising."

A camera? This was becoming a show, and she did not want to be the leading lady. She wanted to hide. Jennifer slipped into the large dressing room.

The clerk followed her in, carrying the dress.

After five minutes of wiggling, pulling and fastening, she was properly in the dress. She wanted to see herself before anyone else, especially before that camera did, but she couldn't until she stepped outside to the large mirror.

"May I go out now?" she asked. "No more hooks, zippers, or buttons?"

The clerk examined her again. "You're good to go, though good seems hardly adequate."

"Katie, ready or not, here I come." When she pushed on the door, it swung open.

Horrors. There were at least a dozen people gawking. They all gasped in unison.

Was it that bad?

When the crowd moved to the sides, her reflection in the mirror appeared.

An audible gasp she couldn't suppress broke the brief silence.

"Katie, how did you do that? This dress is perfect. I couldn't see it, but you could."

"It's a whole lot more than the dress, Jenn. I've seen Lee look at you with bug eyes. But when you walk down the aisle in that dress, his eyes are going to pop right out of his head."

"If he goes gaga-eyes on me during the wedding, I'll kill him."

Katie's mouth fell open.

"It's only a figure of speech. If I really meant it, Lee would be dead and buried months ago. Now, for the bridesmaids' dresses. Will you please help me pick them out?"

"But they're for your sisters. I've never even seen them. I don't know if I can do that."

"Here's the deal. You pick out a dress somewhere near cranberry in color. One we can order quickly. If it looks good on you, it'll be fine. My sisters are a little taller and skinnier than me. Not as tall as you, but the store can alter the length. "

"Are you sure about this, Jenn?"

"Just try to do for you what you did for me. If you do, I'll be more than satisfied. You've got the eye for it."

"Maybe I've got the eye for the dress. But I think you've got all those other parts."

"Uh, thank you, Katie, I think. Now, not a word to Lee about dresses or colors, yet."

Katie made a lip-zipping motion.

Within thirty minutes, Katie found a cranberry-colored dress. It drew a small crowd when she modeled it. What were she and Lee going to do when she drew a crowd of boys?

As a last resort, we can tell the boys she mowed a guy down with an AK-47.

****

Jennifer lined up a row of four Styrofoam containers full of Thai cuisine alongside a row of four empty serving dishes. "Here's your scoop, Katie. You take two and I'll take two."

As Jennifer arranged the dishes on the table, Katie glanced at her. "Are you going to let Lee think we made this ourselves?"

"He'll know we ordered takeout. These are our favorite items on the menu."

Katie inhaled the aroma of stir-fry chicken and a wonderful blend of spices. "If it tastes like it smells, I think it's going to be my favorite, too." She closed her eyes and inhaled again.

As Jennifer tossed the last takeout container into

the trash, the doorbell rang.

She hurried, but Katie beat her to the door.

"Can I tell him now, Jenn?"

"Sure, tell him whenever you want to." Jennifer wanted to see Lee's reaction to Katie's news. Wonderful news that further confirmed Katie was where she belonged.

Katie opened the door.

When Jennifer stepped near him, Lee kissed her. "Hello, beautiful." He turned to Katie. "Hello, beautiful, who's on the front page of the paper." He hugged Katie and pulled the evening paper from under his arm. "Take a look. There are my two favorite ladies. Mel and Kirsten, too."

As Katie pored over the picture and the article, Jennifer's phone rang. "Let me get this, and then we can eat."

"Hello…yes…Katie, someone wants to talk to you."

"To me? Is it Mrs. Barnes?"

"No, it's Mel."

Fifteen minutes of chatter ensued. After the phone conversation, Katie hung up and sauntered towards Lee. "Mel is calling Kirsten now. She sure was excited about seeing our story in the paper, even if the reporters didn't get it right." She stopped, facing Lee. "I have something to tell you."

"You decided on a school today?"

She shook her head. "It's about a relationship."

"You talked to Jennifer's grandfather?"

"No." She looked into Lee's eyes. "Someone much older than he is."

"How's that possible? He's older than dirt."

"I'm going to tell Granddad what you said."

Jennifer gave him a warning look.

"I thought you wanted to marry me. Do you want a headless husband?"

Katie tugged on Lee's arm. "The relationship is with God, through Jesus."

Silence.

Lee was obviously trying to process the fullness of what Katie had so simply stated.

After a few seconds, he smiled and hugged Katie. "So now you're my sister."

Katie's wide eyes displayed horror. "Sister, I…I was hoping for something more like—"

He chuckled. "We can explain the sister thing later."

Jennifer stood beside Lee, her arm around his waist. It was the perfect time. "Katie, Lee and I have decided there's something we would like to do, but we want to ask your permission first."

Katie's gaze darted between them. "What is it?"

"Lee and I want to start completing the paperwork to adopt you as our daughter." She paused, partly because her voice choked and partly to gauge Katie's reaction. "And we want to file the papers as soon as we're married, if it's all right with you?"

Katie couldn't blink away her tears. They spilled onto her cheeks. Her arms circled Jennifer's neck, and her voice broke. "I…never thought I would be thanking Trader for anything. But I'm glad he brought us all together."

Lee joined the embrace. "What Trader meant for evil, God used for good. So, can we take it your answer is yes?"

Katie pulled her arms from Jennifer and slipped them around Lee's neck. "You should have known it was yes. But I hope you won't ever be disappointed."

"Katie," Jennifer asked, "why would we ever be disappointed?"

"I'm not perfect, not like you two."

She cupped Katie's cheek. "Remember our conversation over lunch? We're not perfect, either. And we won't be perfect parents. But Jesus already took care of our imperfections, so let's not worry about them unless He shows us they need some attention. Now, let's eat before our dinner gets cold."

Lee winked at Katie. "You mean before our cashew chicken take-out gets cold?"

30

Monday Evening, November 11

Jennifer watched the large entryway door of Maplewood Community Church. When it opened, a group of teenagers exited, full of joy from their time of fellowship at the Monday youth-group meeting.

There was Katie. The tall, blonde girl was a stunning beauty who would stand out in any crowd.

Katie stopped and waved to a couple of friends before sliding into the passenger's seat.

"How was the meeting tonight?"

"It was great. I'm starting to make some good friends. I think they actually like me. I mean *me*, as a person."

"You shouldn't be surprised. I liked you as a person from the first moment we met in—" she stopped.

"It's OK, Jenn. That seems like years ago." Katie paused and appeared deep in thought. "You know, before we went to see Granddad last week, you said he didn't believe in heaven?"

"That's right. Granddad is a good and honorable man, but he just—"

"Jenn, I've got something to confess."

"What did you do this time, Katie?"

"I was reading the Bible you got for me. The book of John, like you suggested, trying to picture those things John wrote to prove Jesus was the Son of God. That's when it hit me."

"Hit you? I hope it didn't hurt." She teased.

"The word *master* hit me. Granddad is a master at Karate. He said he learned from another master. So, when we went to Granddad's place on Friday, I left him a note, asking him to read about The Master in the book of John. Only, I think I lost the note at his house."

"Granddad is meticulous in every detail about his house. If the note is there, he'll find it."

"That's what I've been praying."

"Granddad really likes you, Katie. Maybe you'll have more influence than I have. I've certainly gotten nowhere with him on that subject."

They were approaching her apartment. Jennifer glanced at the opposite side of the street. It was only yesterday the police car left that spot. "It'll seem strange for a while not seeing someone over there watching our apartment. But since Trader left the country, well, we don't have to think about him anymore."

"No. But if it hadn't been for him capturing me, my life never would have been this good."

Jenn centered the little SUV on her parking space. "I'm not so sure about that. You're a remarkable young lady. You would've made your mark."

"Our Bible lesson tonight was about Joseph. I guess God really does make good things happen out of the bad things evil people do. My life was a little bit like Joseph's, except Potiphar's wife was Trader, in my case."

"What God did wasn't good only for Joseph." She pulled her key from the ignition. "Joseph saved his family and many others. Much like you saved Mel,

Kirsten, Lee, and me."

"I feel bad, though. I didn't even recognize that it was actually Him working to save all of us." Katie's voice quivered.

Physically strong, spiritually so tender. Who would have guessed? "But the important thing is you recognize it now. C'mon, let's go inside. Lee usually calls about this time."

"We wouldn't want to miss that call, would we, sweetheart?" Katie mimicked Lee's voice as they walked towards the door.

Jennifer unlocked the door, stepped in, and stopped. "That's strange. I thought I turned on the alarm when I left. I must have forgotten."

"Too many wedding plans on your mind,"

"That could very well be," Still something felt wrong. Her gun. It was in her bedroom.

The sound of a door and the shuffle of feet spun her around.

A large hand slapped over Katie's mouth. Another hand shoved a gun into the back of Katie's neck.

"Well, well, well. Half of my merchandise, right here in one place."

This wasn't possible.

"Trader—"

"Silence! If one of you screams, I'll kill the other one, or both of you, if need be. Old lady, you know the drill. Wrists together."

"Not this time." The words slipped out before she could control her emotions.

"Have it your way." Trader cocked the gun.

The loud click froze her body.

"OK!" She glared at him. "But you won't get away with this."

"I must disagree, old lady. Your watchdog left yesterday. Wrists. Now!"

He couldn't have her wrists. Not yet. Slowly she yielded them. There must be something she could try.

He kept the gun pointed at the base of Katie's neck while his free hand slipped the loop over her hands. He yanked downward, pulling her to the floor.

When Jennifer's knees hit the floor, Katie ducked under the handgun. She pushed Trader's forearm up. Her strong right arm drove an elbow well below Trader's belt.

Trader roared in pain and rage.

Katie landed on the floor.

He brought the butt of the handgun down on her head.

Katie lay still.

The red-hot energy of fury exploded inside Jennifer. It powered a vicious kick that landed where Katie's elbow had pounded.

Grunting, Trader doubled over. His head bent forward.

Jennifer's bound fists pounded down on the back of his neck. The blow drove him to the floor.

The gun fell from his hand. Trader reached for his gun.

She had to stop him.

Her powerful foot stomp hit him squarely in the face.

Trader's nose flattened. Blood splattered across the carpet and the wall.

Jennifer drew back her leg to kick again.

He grabbed the gun.

The report slammed into Jennifer's head like a fist.

She stopped. With her ears ringing, she focused on

Katie's head.

Please, God.

The gun pointed harmlessly towards the wall, where a hole appeared near the floor.

She turned to attack again.

Trader shoved the gun against Katie's head. "Stop! Now! Or she's dead, old lady!"

Heart racing, adrenaline pumping through her body, everything in her said action. Jennifer willed herself to stop. But what could she do now?

The answer came. With Katie unconscious, she had to take the brunt of Trader's anger. It was a calculated risk, but no other choice remained.

"You're really a tough old man. You let a bound, one-hundred-ten-pound girl nearly take you out. Maybe I should finish the job now."

Trader leaped at her and drew back his gun hand. His voice roared out something undistinguishable. Before he could deliver the blow to her face, he stopped and took a deep breath. "I don't deliver damaged goods. Lay down on the floor. Face down."

She had to keep his attention away from Katie. She didn't comply. "Do you think you can make me, you idiot? How do you like slashed tires?"

Trader's face contorted. He took another deep breath and exhaled slowly. "Sticks and stones. You know the rest. But a bullet to her head, that would seriously hurt her unless you lay down. Now! And keep your mouth shut, you…"

He couldn't intimidate her with his string of vile words. She'd heard them from him before.

Had the gunshot alerted one of her neighbors? The gunshot meant Trader must do quickly whatever he intended.

She prayed silently for rescue, for strength, for wisdom, and for Katie.

Jennifer lay face down on the floor. Her body pressed her bound hands beneath her, trapping them. She was as helpless as Katie and with the nauseating knot in her stomach, she was near vomiting.

"Keep quiet or the girl dies." Trader paused. "I saw your white wedding dress." His voice changed. It now sounded devoid of emotion, devoid of life. "You won't need it where you're going, not ever. In fact, you'll never wear white again."

She needed some new plan of action, but nothing emerged from her jumble of fragmented thoughts.

"There's a Gulfstream 650 waiting for you at the airport, old lady. You're no sixteen-year-old, exotic beauty. Twenty-six years old. I wouldn't pay two cents for you, but my fool of a client thinks you're worth a million dollars."

An involuntary grunt left her when Trader yanked her hair to pull her head up from the floor.

Then came the sucking sound of a sealed container opening. A sickening, sweet odor assaulted her, sending her nauseated stomach into spasms.

Then Trader pressed a box over her mouth and nose.

In order to breathe, she had to inhale. Couldn't hold her breath. Panic only deepened her breathing. The sweet smell added to her nausea. Her head buzzed and her vision faded…

****

Lee's men's meeting had ended early. He wanted to see Katie, and he needed to see Jennifer. The wedding, still two weeks away, couldn't come soon enough for him.

A block from Jennifer's place, a man ran down the sidewalk, away from the apartment.

He was tall and his gait looked familiar. Trader!

Lee's mind exploded into panic. He hit the accelerator. His car surged forward, and then screeched to a stop in front of the apartment building. He ran through the open door and into Jennifer's apartment.

Blood on the carpet. More blood splattered all over one wall. His chest pounded out his rising panic.

He moved into the kitchen. Someone left the knife drawer open.

As his gaze took in one ominous bit of evidence after another, his thoughts raced towards a destination he could not let them reach.

God, please help Jennifer. Help Katie...and me.

He needed the FBI. He hit the speed dial for Peterson and explained the situation At least, he thought he did. Perhaps he'd spoken incoherent rubbish to an answering machine. Either way, Peterson would figure it out.

Across the street, a van sat fifty yards away. It appeared to have one or more flat tires. Flat tires were encouraging, and if that was Trader's van, he couldn't have gotten away. But where was Jennifer? He needed to check the vehicle.

When he reached the back of the van, a noise sounded to his right. He spun towards it, ready to defend himself.

A voice came from some shrubbery along the sidewalk. "Lee, we're over here."

"Katie, are you all right?"

"Yes, I'm OK, but—"

"What about Jennifer?"

"She's asleep. Trader drugged her. She let him do it to save me, so I had to think of a way to save her."

"Where is she, Katie?"

"Here in the bushes. I hid her."

"You carried her?"

"Only from the van. I had to. I slashed his tires and he was really mad. He would have killed both of us, so I hid Jennifer, and Trader ran away when he saw the flat tires."

Jennifer lay in the grass between waist-high shrubs.

"She's breathing, Lee, but it's not normal. Something's wrong."

"Watch for Trader while I call for help." He dialed 911 on his cell. *Why had he called Peterson instead of 911? What was he thinking?*

The call-center operator answered with her well-rehearsed questions. At least now he knew what to tell them about Jennifer. He could be thankful for that much.

Katie stepped close. He curled an arm around her while he relayed information to the call center.

"I hear the sirens, Katie. You flag them down. I'm going to watch Jenn."

Her irregular breathing grew worse, but the operator said the ambulance was almost there.

A police car slid around the corner, siren wailing, red and blue lights flashing. It rolled down the street towards them.

He closed his cell and lifted Jennifer, carrying her in his arms to the edge of the street.

The lines in Katie's face revealed an agony nearly

as great as his own.

He kissed Jennifer's forehead, and then looked at Katie. "I can never thank you enough. You saved her from Trader. You're as amazing as Jennifer."

At his words, tears streamed down Katie's face. She stood beside him, one arm around his waist and her other hand lightly stroking Jennifer's head. "He was going to sell her, Lee. I don't think he would've intentionally hurt her. She'll be all right. She has to be."

Katie's head. She wasn't all right. "Is that a lump on your head?" He looked more closely. "There's blood, too."

"He hit me with his gun. It knocked me out for...I think only a few seconds. But real life isn't like the movies. People don't stay unconscious just because you hit them on the head. I faked it." She paused. "You should've seen what Jennifer did to Trader's face. I only caught a glimpse from the corner of one eye, but when she kicked him, she smashed his nose completely flat. Blood splattered all over the place. The blood in the apartment is all Trader's."

The first police car pulled to the curb.

An ambulance trailed closely behind it.

"When the ambulance gets here, I'm going to insist they check you out for a concussion."

"I'm OK. I'm not leaving Jennifer. Not now. Not ever."

"You're not going anywhere until I'm sure you have no serious injuries. I think there's a lot more about the war in Jennifer's apartment I haven't heard yet."

"Some of it you don't want to hear. What Trader said was awful. I don't see how a human being can become that evil."

The policeman jumped from his vehicle and approached them. "Are you Lee Brandt?"

"Yes, officer."

"Agent Peterson, FBI, said to tell you he's all over this. The guy called Trader, he won't get away this time. We have his description and we've sealed off the whole area. Is that his van?"

"Yeah. The apartment where this started is the one down the street. The one with the door standing open. But we've got two injured ladies here. My fiancée has been drugged and she's not breathing well. My daughter, Katie, was hit on the head. Can I ride in the ambulance with them?"

Katie's mouth dropped open.

"I'll talk to the EMTs. It's up to them."

The officer ran to the ambulance which had stopped behind the police car. The ambulance doors flew open. A man and a woman jumped out.

The officer returned with the two EMTs. The man checked Jennifer while the woman examined Katie's head wound and launched into a series of questions.

Lee watched as a male EMT checked Jennifer's vital signs. "How is she doing?"

"We need to get her stabilized. Since we don't know what's in her bloodstream, I can't say more at this point."

"May I ride to the hospital with you? She's my fiancée."

The man looked at Katie as if waiting for her to respond.

They were going to leave him here because of Katie. He had to remedy that.

"And she's my daughter."

"Mister, you don't look old enough to—never

mind. If you promise to sit by your daughter and not interfere, it's OK."

"Thanks, guys."

Katie put her hand in Lee's and leaned on his shoulder. "What you said to the driver, it wasn't—"

"You *are* my daughter. We've already committed to that. Just like the police and these EMTs, we do what's needed and let the paperwork catch up."

****

After the ambulance stopped in front of the wide emergency-room doors, two men unloaded Jennifer.

Doctors and nurses swarmed around the gurney when it passed through the doors.

Jennifer was in good hands, but the obvious concern of the medical staff gave him a sick feeling. He fought off the nausea. It wouldn't do to let Katie see him throwing up.

In a few moments, they took Katie into an examining room, and he waited alone.

An hour later, Katie emerged with an ER doctor.

"She doesn't have a concussion. But, as a precaution, watch for these symptoms." The doctor handed Lee a piece of paper. "And you need to sign some forms in the office."

A man in scrubs came down the hall.

"Are you Lee Brandt, Jennifer Akihara's fiancé?"

"Yes. How is Jennifer?"

"I'm Doctor Pruitt. The reason we haven't provided status earlier is it took some detective work to determine what drugs were used on her. There were things we couldn't risk doing until we knew—"

"Doctor, please just tell me her condition." His

voice and stomach shook.

"Jennifer is in intensive care. We think she inhaled chloroformyle, a fast-acting form of chloroform. Then someone injected her with one of the benzodiazepines. We thought she was stabilized, but she slipped into a coma. Unfortunately, Jennifer is a small person. For her, the amount was an overdose. In addition, her body reacted badly to the drug. We are—"

"What's her prognosis, doctor?" Any more delays and he would lose it.

The doctor's expression said he understood. "We've started her on a reversal agent to counteract the overdose of the sedative and administered something for the allergic reaction. We should know soon how effectively the treatment is working. The coma…we have to wait to see if she comes out of—"

"*If* she comes out of the coma? Are you saying she might not?"

"We can't be certain about that. But let's assume she will respond and soon wake up. Then we'll have to evaluate her further to see if there are any long-term effects from of the overdose. That's as accurate a picture as I can give you right now."

"When…" His voice broke. "When will you know more?"

Tears streaked down Katie's cheeks. "Jenn is going to make it through this, isn't she?"

"May I ask who you are, miss?"

"This is Katie, our daughter."

"Katie, it's not a certainty, but we're hopeful Jennifer will make it through this crisis. As I said, then we have to address the question of possible long-term impacts. I'll make sure someone gives you regular updates—immediately, if there are any changes. Right now, we just have to wait on Jennifer's body to respond." Doctor Pruitt motioned towards the elevator. "Mr. Brandt, if you go up to the ICU waiting area on the second floor, it will be easier to reach you with updates."

"Thanks, doctor."

"I guess we need to pray now." Katie's intense blue eyes displayed hope for the first time since he found her by the van.

"Yes, Katie, we need to pray."

****

An hour later, Lee and Katie still sat in the ICU waiting area. They had prayed for Jennifer, but Lee hadn't prayed for patience.

His floor-tapping foot refused to stop, and he sought an excuse to pace. "I'm going to get something to drink from the vending machine down the hall. Do you want anything?"

"Nothing for me, thanks."

When he turned to step through the door to the hallway, a tall figure filled the doorway. A tall man with a familiar face. "Peterson, what are you doing here?"

"I came to see how Jennifer's doing. I heard they released Katie."

"Trader injected Jennifer with something that knocked her out. She's in a coma and there might be complications. We won't know how this is going to turn out for a while." Lee's anger flashed like a bolt of lightning. "She'll never be safe until you get Trader. Why aren't—"

Doctor Pruitt stepped out of the door of the ICU.

Katie came to stand beside Lee, wrapping her arm around his waist.

"We have some good news." The doctor smiled.

The breath Lee had been holding blasted out of his lungs.

Katie's arm relaxed its constriction.

The doctor eyed Peterson suspiciously.

"This is Agent Peterson, FBI. He's working the case involving Jennifer."

Peterson flashed his badge.

Dr. Pruitt nodded. "Jennifer is responding well to the reversal agent. She's out of the coma. Our concern about the respiratory depression has been resolved. We gave her some motion tests and there seems to be no ataxia...no lack of coordination. If the remaining tests go well, we'll move her out of ICU. They're preparing room 204. Unless we uncover something unexpected, she'll be there in about thirty minutes. After that, we'll need to watch her for a few hours before we make any decisions about sending her home."

Sending her home? A few minutes ago it seemed that might never happen. "Thanks, doctor." Lee pulled Katie close, kissed her forehead, and brushed the tears from her cheeks.

Peterson shuffled his feet and cleared his throat. "I'll see you in a bit, probably in room 204. I need to make some phone calls."

Katie looked at the vending machines. "I am a little hungry."

"You were probably hungry when I asked, just too preoccupied to realize it."

"Probably. But you know what, Lee?"

"Did you learn that question from Jenn? No, I don't know anything."

Katie's eyebrows pinched together in a serious frown. "Peterson didn't tell us about Trader."

"He'll tell us in Jennifer's room. Let's hope it's good news."

"Yeah," Katie replied. "Four weeks ago, I didn't even know Trader existed. Now, I hope he doesn't."

"I know what you mean, Katie."

****

A nurse pushed Jennifer into the room.

When Jennifer saw Lee and Katie, she locked the brake on the wheelchair. It jerked to a stop, and she slid out onto her feet.

"Whoa, young lady. You're not supposed to be running around yet." The nurse tried to snag her arm.

Jennifer barely heard the nurse's admonition. The nurse meant well, but this wasn't a time for caution. Jennifer stepped into Lee and Katie's waiting arms.

Lee kissed her forehead.

She hugged him and then focused on Katie. "How's your head, young lady?"

"It's OK. No concussion, no headache, just a lump on my head."

"Thank God." She clenched her jaw. "I wanted to kill him when he hit you. I tried—"

"Knock, knock. May I come in?" A deep voice sounded from outside the door.

The nurse threw her hands up in the air. "I don't see why not. Bring the elephants, the lions, and the clowns. Strike up the band. Why listen to me when you can have a circus? Please, Jennifer, at least sit on the bed. If you fall, I could lose my job."

"Sorry, ma'am." Jennifer sat down.

The nurse left the room, and Peterson stepped in.

"Peterson, did you get that…that—"

"You can stop there, Jennifer. We can add our own expletives."

"And Peterson's got a couple of pretty good ones to add," Lee murmured.

"Trader's dead." Peterson pursed his lips and let them digest the news. "He left some blood along his trail, and the dogs sniffed him out." He focused on Jennifer. "What did you do to him?"

"You should have seen what Jennifer did to his nose." Katie became animated as she blurted out the story. "I didn't see all of the kick, because I was supposed to be unconscious on the floor. But blood sprayed all over the wall."

"Jenn, Katie saved your life. After Trader drugged you, she hid, and then she carried you from the van when Trader went back to get her," Lee said, putting a hand on Katie's shoulder.

Peterson looked from Jennifer to Katie. "It sounds like there's plenty of glory to go around. As I was saying, police dogs found Trader. He wouldn't surrender. There was a firefight. Of course, the SWAT team won, one to nothing."

"That's probably for the best." Jenn sighed. It was all finally over. "He'll have no more chances to—" She looked up, gave them a warm smile, and then reached out. "Katie, I can never thank…" She tugged on Katie, who sprawled across the bed.

"Easy, Jenn." Katie sat up. "The fight's over and we won. I can't believe how you taunted Trader, making him so mad he forgot about me."

"But you were unconscious."

"Only for a few seconds. I saw his nose. You

kicked it clear to kingdom come."

"More likely, to the other place," Peterson pointed a thumb downward. "Well, that's all the news I've got for tonight. When you're feeling better, I'll need statements from you and Katie. Probably from you, too, Lee. We wrapped up the forensics in your apartment, Jennifer. It's all yours again and it will be clean. The clean-up crew will be done before you get there. See you all later. Probably tomorrow." He turned to leave then stopped. "Lee, one of my men is staying on here until Jennifer is released. He can take you to get your car or wherever you need to go."

Lee, Katie, and Jennifer were silent for a few moments.

Jennifer let the implications of Peterson's news sink in. Their individual roles in the recent drama were now becoming visible to her, woven into the tapestry of a story only a good God could write.

"It's just like you told Katie," Lee said to her. "All things work together for good, even evil deeds performed by evil men who are only seeking to further the cause of evil."

"Will He always take bad, and then turn it into good?" Katie asked.

He reached for Katie's hand. "For those who trust Him, yes, He will. But at the end of this age, everything bad will be set right, either by God's justice or by His love and grace."

"There's so much evil." Katie frowned. "I don't understand how He can deal with it all."

"Me, either. But I believe Him when He says He will," Lee said.

Another nurse came in.

Lee met the woman's gaze. "What do you think

about that, ma'am, God turning evil to good?"

"Uh, I agree with the young lady. There's a whole lot of bad in this world. You see a lot of it in a hospital."

"Only an all-powerful, all-knowing God can deal with all of it. Have you heard these two young ladies' stories of what He just did in their lives?"

"Not really."

Lee gave her a nutshell version of the human-trafficking operation, including how Jennifer and Katie thwarted Trader's plans.

"You know, I heard part of that on the news. It gives one something to think about."

"*Someone* to think about, ma'am," Lee replied.

"Changing the subject. Jennifer, the doctor has decided you can go home soon. He'll be in to talk to you in a few minutes. Good luck, and"—she turned to Lee—"thanks for sharing your story."

"Thanks." Lee said, smiling.

The nurse left the room.

"Does he always do that?" Katie rolled her eyes.

"Get used to it. He used to take me out of my comfort zone all the time. But now he mostly puts me in it." She smiled warmly at Lee.

He bent down and kissed her, slowly, gently.

Jennifer smiled at Katie. "See what I mean?"

"Excuse me." A voice came from the doorway.

Jennifer sat up as a tall man in scrubs entered the room.

"How would you all like to go home?"

She gave him a courteous smile. "We would love that."

The doctor told her there would be no long-term impacts from her brush with death. With a few words, he ended her ordeal. But surely there had to be more. "So I'm good to go? Life as usual?"

"Good to go, yes." The doctor smiled. "Life as usual? After hearing about tonight's events, I rather doubt that. Newspaper reporters, TV stations—"

"Enough. I've been there before." She gave him the cutting-throat gesture.

The doctor cocked his head. "So I wasn't mistaken. The human-trafficking story, a terrorist plot last spring. That was you and this gentleman?"

She nodded.

He patted her hand, and then left.

"Jenn, you're not like a special agent, are you?" Katie eyed her with suspicion.

"Yeah, Katie. Jenn's a special agent...for God. She only works for NSA to make a living."

"Katie," Jennifer took her hand, "Didn't Lee tell you about the terrorists? You know, when Lee and I fell in love in a cave."

"He told me about the terrorists. But seriously, you fell in love in a cave? This story gets weirder every time I hear it."

"We'll de-weird it for you sometime," Lee said. "The story has a really nice ending, though. You'll see in about two weeks."

Jennifer took his hand, kissed it, and then looked up into his bright blue eyes. "In about two weeks, sweetheart, the story begins."

****

An hour later, Lee, Jennifer, and Katie, stepped inside her apartment.

Thoughts of Katie escaping from this apartment

and carrying Jennifer to the bushes played through Lee's mind. He sought words to tell her what was on his heart. "Without you, Katie, this would have probably been the saddest day of my life. Thanks for what you did."

Katie's gaze dropped to the floor and her cheeks flushed. She looked up again. "Thanks for treating me like your daughter tonight."

"Come here." He pulled Jennifer into the huddle and spent some time thanking God for the outcome of the evening.

Tears rolled down Katie's cheeks once more, but this time her eyes were bright and full of life as she went to her bedroom.

"Sweetheart, give me a few minutes to wash the hospital off. Then let's talk. We've got a wedding in two weeks and a pile of adoption papers."

"After everything you've been through, are you sure? It's really late."

"I just slept for three hours. I'm fine."

"And I'm not about to leave you alone in this apartment after what happened here. So, it's a date. Your couch in a few minutes."

****

Ten minutes later, Jennifer returned.

Lee's eyes were closed. He had been through a lot. She'd slept through most of it.

She sat down and leaned against him. Some date this had turned out to be. But she smiled as she thought how fortunate they were to be safe and to be together.

Eyes still closed, Lee slipped his arm around her.

"One more thing for our agenda, we need to plan the details of our Maui honeymoon, the one that starts in about two weeks."

She leaned against him. "I thought you were out for the night."

"Have I ever stood you up?"

"No, you've never done that. But, Lee, honeymoons, like all romantic things, just sort of unfold. You don't plan them, certainly not all the details." Why had she added the last part? It must be the drugs. Jennifer could feel the heat in her cheeks.

"I was talking about romantic activities."

"Uh, what kind of...romantic activities?"

"You know, a Haleakala sunrise, a Molikini snorkel cruise, a getaway to Lanai—those kinds of activities. For the rest, we'll just wing it unless you really want to plan—"

She smacked him on the head with a couch pillow.

31

Saturday, November 30, Maplewood Community Church

Jennifer slipped into her wedding gown, and then looked around the partition.

Her sisters, Jess and Julie, stood in front of a long mirror wearing their bridesmaids' dresses, working on their hair and makeup.

Katie glanced at her. "Are you ready for me to help, Jenn?"

"You finish getting ready first. Then I need you to look out front and tell me if things are going smoothly."

"OK, I'll be back in five minutes."

Katie returned a few minutes later.

"How are things going in the sanctuary?"

"They're right as rain. Or maybe as a thunderstorm."

What had she meant by that? Katie. She looked so grown up, so beautiful.

Jennifer reached for her soon-to-be daughter, but Katie jumped back.

"Careful, Jenn, you don't want my makeup rubbing off on your white dress."

"Katie, you look absolutely perfect."

"Thanks, but looks can be deceiving."

Thunderstorm, hmmm. "What are you up to,

young lady?"

"Well, somebody just put some carefully selected stormy weather symbols on the bottom of Lee's shoes with a white marker. When you two kneel for the prayer—"

"What somebody and what symbols?" Jennifer feigned a frown.

"The symbols for rain and thunderstorm, because we became a family in a rainstorm. You aren't mad, are you?"

"No. Lee's a big boy. He can take it."

"Yep. Now, tell me how to fasten the back of your dress."

The music had transitioned from praise and worship songs to a classical piece. The wedding was underway, and Jennifer would soon walk down the aisle. As she stood waiting for her cue, one of the women helping with the wedding slipped her a note. It read, "All set." Good. The surprise was ready.

The guests should all be seated now. Would Howie, Agent Peterson, and Captain Lewis be there? Mel and Kirsten said they would come. It would be a wonderful reunion for the girls. Hopefully, Jennifer could find a moment to talk with their parents about the speaking engagements. One was scheduled for mid-January.

Katie's head popped around the corner. "It's show time, Jenn."

Outside of the dressing room, Granddad waited for her, smiling and looking handsome in his tux.

Together they watched Katie walk arm-in-arm with Jim Williamson, Lee's friend.

"Jennifer, you found a real princess when you found Katie."

"Granddad, just don't ever call her princess, or you'll have to duck an eighty mile-per-hour rock aimed at your head."

"That is a good thing to know. Are there any other things I should know about Katie?"

"Don't call her Goldilocks either, or you'll see high heat—high and way inside."

"Thank you, Jennifer. Anything else?"

"Only that it's our turn, now. Granddad, thank you so much for taking a chance on Lee when he asked to court me."

"It wasn't a chance. It was a sure thing. I hear the ukulele playing. Shall we go give you to Lee, now?"

"Let's roll."

****

Lee had been standing at the front of the church for what seemed like an hour. Finally, there were signs of life at the rear of the sanctuary.

His breath caught when he saw Katie walking with a graceful bearing that far exceeded her fifteen years.

For one brief moment, the thought of what Trader meant to do with her stabbed his conscious mind. He forced it out and buried it in the graveyard of dead thoughts.

When Katie passed by and smiled, he nearly ran out to hug her. Instead, he mouthed, "I love you, Katie." Proud father? That was an understatement.

The music changed from classical to a soft, melodic ukulele melody. A pure, sweet, Hawaiian lady's voice sang "Aloha 'Oe."

Katie was staring at Lee like she was expecting

something to happen up front. She should be looking at Jennifer.

When she appeared, nothing existed but Jennifer. The dress took her beyond mere beauty, to what she was, God's masterpiece here in the flesh, his bride.

Lee's tongue was dry and sticky, while his palms became wet and slippery. Thoughts stacked on top of each other in a pile of confusion.

A voice in his mind spoke. The voice of logic.

This is Jennifer. Settle down, man.

A different voice responded.

Wow! Call her woman.

It sounded like Adam's voice, but it wasn't speaking Aramaic.

Granddad tried to hand her off to him, but he couldn't seem to respond.

Take her arm. That's what he was supposed to do.

Jennifer smiled at him. Her almond-shaped, brown eyes, like on the evening they first met, were so deep he feared he might drown in them. And they saw everything.

He looked away, feeling if he met her gaze his mind would turn inside out, exposed for everyone in the room to see. His heart had borrowed the racing cam from his Impala's 283 engine.

Pastor Nelson, standing next to them, raised his Bible to start the ceremony.

How could he continue in this state of mindlessness? He reached for the pastor's arm and spoke softly, but the church had grown silent as the audience stared at his strange behavior.

Jennifer was supposed to be the focus of attention, not him.

Unable to talk, he cleared his throat. "Pastor,

please give me a moment." He croaked out the words.

"Take all the time you need, son." Pastor Nelson gave him a knowing smile.

It didn't help. How could *he* know what this was like?

A murmur of whispers sounded throughout the room. They were talking about him. Did they think he was backing out at the altar?

The audience was still staring at him. And Jennifer wasn't Jennifer. She was so much more. He wasn't even in her class. Wasn't fit to be standing beside her. "Jenn, please tell me something. Tell me—"

"I'll tell you something, buster." She wasn't whispering. "You just went gaga-eyes. This time takes the cake. I almost bet Katie five dollars you wouldn't. I would've lost. I'm going to kill you when this is over."

People in the audience gasped.

"You'll kill me? That's good. It is you. The same Jenn."

"Of course, you silly man. Is that your problem? I can fix that." Jennifer lifted her veil, causing more audible gasps. She kissed him. Not just any kiss. It was last night's kiss, replicated in detail.

A twitching smile twisted his lips. *That's definitely Jenn.*

"OK, Pastor. It's time for me to marry Jennifer. Uh, rather for you to marry us. And would you please speed things up a bit?"

****

Jennifer looked at her maid of honor. She rolled her eyes at Katie and shook her head.

Katie shoved her fist halfway into her mouth to

mute the sound of her giggles, but they were visible through the spasmodic jerking of her shoulders. "I told you so." Katie mouthed.

When they came to the exchanging of vows, Lee seemed to regain his composure. All distractions ceased to exist as they expressed their hearts' desire to live as man and wife with God's blessing on their relationship.

Their kneeling prayer was interrupted by brief laughter. What was that about? Lee's shoes? Then the ceremony was over, except for the final kiss.

When Lee raised her veil, his eyes spoke the unspeakable to her. "I love you, Jenn. And thanks for throwing in the extra kiss. Is that the surprise?"

"No. Now kiss me, and then we'll see about the surprise."

Their discussion before the final kiss brought more murmurs from the audience.

Their first kiss, the one in the cave, *she* had initiated. But Lee's kiss was like the one on the Benson's front lawn seven months ago, but there was no embarrassment and no national television audience. After their lips parted they peered deeply into each other's eyes for the first time as man and wife.

Mr. and Mrs. Lee Brandt turned to face the wedding guests.

Pastor Nelson reached for one of the microphones. "Before I introduce this newly married couple, the bride has requested to speak to you." He handed Jennifer the microphone.

Lee looked at her with a questioning frown.

He would soon understand. She raised the mike. "God has richly blessed Lee and me over the past several months. But he blessed me with a personal relationship with Himself here in this church eight months ago. I responded to a message from Pastor Nelson about Jesus, the Way, the Truth and the Life, and I responded to a song that invited me into a relationship with God. My life changed forever. I know this is a wedding, but God is present at weddings. After all, He instituted them. So I want to give anyone here an opportunity to respond to the same invitation I was given. Listen to the words of this song. If your desire is to accept its message, come here and tell us. Someone will meet with you to answer any questions you have and to give you an opportunity to talk to God about your response."

A deep, rich, contralto voice began to sing. "Come now as the Spirit calls…"

The smiling man in the front row stood, gave Jennifer a hug, shook Lee's hand, and then walked straight to Katie.

"Granddad! Oh…oh my gosh! You found my note."

Jennifer moved the microphone close enough to pick up his words.

"Someone told me just as you learn karate from a master, I should learn about God's love from the Master by reading the book of John. So now I understand about Jesus, the Way, the Truth, and the Life. But I read the other Gospels, too. One thing that amazed me is what Matthew wrote. I think it is in the twentieth chapter. He wrote down Jesus' words— words that said workers hired at the very end of the day, in the eleventh hour, get the same wages as those who worked all day long. So here I come, in the eleventh hour of my life, to work in His vineyard."

Katie stepped from the platform and threw her

arms around his neck.

Jennifer covered the microphone with her hand and whispered to Katie. "I asked you to pray, and this is what God did."

Lee put his arm around Jennifer and drew her close. "So this was your secret surprise?"

"The secret was the song and the invitation. The surprise is what God did with it." Jennifer turned to the pastor who stood patiently, watching the events unfold. "Pastor Nelson, would you please introduce us and then answer any questions my granddad has? Lee and I have a plane to catch...to Maui."

Lee glanced at the pastor. "Amen to that, preacher."

Epilogue

January 17

From one side of the stage, Jennifer Brandt peered around the curtain and scanned the auditorium at Washington High School. It was filled to overflowing with parents and students.

She stepped back behind the curtain, where Kirsten, Katie, Mel, and Jennifer formed a circle, holding hands.

Kirsten led them in prayer.

"Let's go." Jennifer led the group onto the stage.

The three girls sat down in chairs as Jennifer stepped to the podium. She waited for the first picture to fill the screen above her.

The photo depicted a young girl, about eleven or twelve years old, shrinking in fear from a large man who placed restraints around her wrists. It painted the awful picture sufficiently without being too explicit.

Gasps spread across the auditorium. That was her cue.

"My name is Jennifer Brandt. The picture you're viewing is an actual photograph seized during a raid of a human trafficker's palatial residence. What it appears to be...it actually is. The picture speaks for itself and for the millions of young girls who have been forced into sexual slavery."

Clenched jaws showed on fathers' faces.

The wide-eyed horror on mothers' faces brought a knot to her stomach. Jennifer remembered the terror in Mel's eyes after being shocked with the stun gun. Her heart shifted to a higher gear.

The conviction in her heart would be heard in her voice. And the picture had done its intended work. The audience would listen to her words.

"There is an epidemic, no, a *pandemic* of child trafficking. Its dark, evil thread has become deeply woven into the fabric of our society. First came ethical quandary, then a loss of our moral compass, followed by the proliferation of pornography and the view that prostitution is a victimless crime, perhaps no crime at all.

"Now we have children being lured by predators into a life they would *never* voluntarily choose, while others are snatched literally from their own front yards.

"The average lifespan of a young girl sold into sexual slavery is less than four years. If she is properly marketed in the right location, she will make four to five million dollars for her owner before she dies. Sex trafficking is so profitable that arms and drug dealers are incorporating it into their highly organized operations.

"The average age of girls entering prostitution is thirteen, but it drops every year. Next year it will probably be twelve. For every eighteen year old, how many nine-, ten-, and eleven-year-old girls are required to produce that average? You can do the math. The numbers paint an incredibly evil, ugly, perverted picture.

"Behind me are Katie, Melanie, and Kirsten. Katie was lured to the street in front of her house by a girlfriend, where she was grabbed and pulled into an SUV by two men. Someone abducted Melanie while she walked home from school in plain view of other classmates. A van pulled alongside, and Mel was gone. Kirsten went shopping at a mall with her mother. She left her mother's side to visit the ladies' room. Before she could rejoin her mother, Kirsten disappeared.

"I accidentally discovered the traffickers who abducted these girls while working on the Olympic Peninsula. My husband and I went searching for the place where the girls were held and I was captured, too. The traffickers held the four of us, planning to smuggle us out of the country and to sell us who knows where? Southeast Asia? The Middle East?

"Can you imagine what it feels like when a young girl who is helpless and hopeless catches a glimpse of what's in store for her? Before I could find the traffickers' holding location, a sixteen-year-old girl hanged herself with her own shoestrings rather than let the traffickers sell her.

"Sell her, that's an understatement. Children are sold not once, but a dozen times a night for as long as they live." Jennifer paused to let the information sink in. "And every thirty seconds, somewhere in the world, another girl is victimized by traffickers. In the United States, every two minutes someone's daughter falls victim."

Many mothers' cheeks were wet. Others appeared in shock.

Jennifer continued, telling each parent what to look for to prevent their children from being lured into prostitution, what precautions to take to reduce the chance of a child being taken, how to attack the epidemic at its roots—laws with deadly teeth, a moral awakening in the nation, and a sustained public outcry.

Near the conclusion of her presentation, Jennifer asked the three girls to stand. She gestured towards them. "Beautiful, aren't they? That was their only crime. Look at them closely. Any one of them could be your daughter."

"In fact, though she doesn't know it yet, one of these girls just became my daughter earlier this morning."

Katie sprinted to her side and her arms circled Jennifer's neck.

Mel and Kirsten joined her.

In a few seconds, Lee walked onto the stage.

Once again they were a huddle of five.

Katie Brandt broke from the huddle and stepped to the microphone. "Mel, Kirsten, and I were facing oppression, the very worst kind. Sexual slavery. There have been many times throughout history when people were oppressed. The Bible describes one of those times. The passage says when the people were oppressed, they cried out to God. He heard them from heaven and because of his great compassion, He sent them deliverers to rescue them from their enemies. He heard our prayers. For Mel, Kirsten, and me, He also sent deliverers, Jennifer and Lee.

"When they came, they came on the Pineapple Express. The storm—the winds and waves it produced—nearly took their lives.

"But a moral storm, even more destructive than those winds and waves, threatens the life of our country. Who will cry out with me for a deliverer for other girls...and a deliverer for our nation?

"Just as my mom and dad helped rescue me from

evil, please consider that maybe you are the deliverer God wants to send. If you sense that He wants to use you, please answer His call."

How can I help fight human trafficking?

1. Give to worthy organizations that minister to victims.

See Child Trafficking and Labor on the World Vision web site: http://www.worldvision.org/

Give to the Salvation Army's Stop-It Program: http://www.usc.salvationarmy.org/stopit

2. Report any known or suspected incidences of trafficking.

If you know about someone who is being trafficked or sexually exploited, call the Nineline for immediate help: 1-800-999-9999 or the National Human Trafficking Hotline at 1-888-3737-888.